DARK HORIZON

BOOK 3 OF THE FRACTURED TIME TRILOGY

MICHAEL D'AMBROSIO

ISBN
978-1-958690-76-5 (Paperback)
978-1-958690-77-2 (eBook)
978-1-964982-24-3 (Hardcover)

TABLE OF CONTENTS

CHAPTER 1

REUNION

A tall, lizard-like alien Pendragon stood on the bridge of a spaceship. He stared at a monitor and waited impatiently for a response to his request. An Archaenian alien, the size of a mouse, appeared on the screen. Pendragon pressed a button on the monitor. "Well, Carthis, I hope you have news for me," he uttered.

The Archaenian looked uncomfortable. "We've made some progress, sir."

"Is the weapon ready?" Pendragon questioned him.

"Not yet," Carthis replied, his voice trembling in fear.

Pendragon pounded his clawed fist against the panel. "What do you mean 'not yet'?" he bellowed.

"The device will detonate as designed," Carthis explained, "but we can't control the reaction."

"What the hell good is that to me?" shouted Pendragon.

"I told you we've never created anything like this before," Carthis responded defensively.

"Figure it out fast or I'll start killing your offspring, one at a time," Pendragon threatened. "I promise you; it will be slow and it will be painful."

The Archaenian's eyes filled with fear. "Yes, Pendragon, I understand."

Pendragon turned off the monitor switch and stormed away.

— ✕ —

Billy and Penny exited the Greyhound bus station in Washington, D.C. Billy paced back and forth impatiently across the sidewalk as the cold wind blew briskly, sending chills down his spine. He glanced up at the gloomy, gray sky and grimaced.

"I can't understand why we couldn't wait another week," complained Penny. "It's not like Washington's on the other side of the world."

"I told you, Penny, something's not right in Firenghia," fretted Billy. "I can feel it."

"Here we go again - Billy and his gut feelings. When are you going to get over this?"

Billy grew irate and reminded her. "Those gut feelings saved your ass many a time. Maybe you should grow the hell up!"

"Look, Billy, I'm really messed up right now. My mother has only been dead a week and I'm hurting inside. I don't need this."

Billy looked away at the traffic and sighed. He turned back to her and hugged her. "I'm sorry. I know you were close to her but it's done. Nothing is going to bring her back."

Penny threw her arms up in the air in frustration. "You're always so insensitive, Billy!" Several people stared at them as they passed.

"What are you talking about? I'm always sensitive to you," Billy responded, baffled by her behavior.

"No matter how frightened I am or how much I need you to be there for me, you just march right on."

"What does that have to do with your mother?"

"She suffered so much for three months. I'll never forget it but I guess you have. You only worry about poor Billy!"

Penny's depressed attitude wore on Billy. He searched the traffic, hoping their ride would come soon. "Don't you have anything to say?" she nagged at him.

A black limo stopped and backed toward them. "Yeah. There's our ride."

Penny crossed her arms and grew red-faced. "That's your answer to every argument. Just move on to the next obstacle."

Billy felt defeated by her constant bickering. "I don't know what you want from me, Penny, but I'm tired of being your whipping boy. Everything I do is wrong in your eyes."

"Because it always has to be your way!" Billy bit his lip and became silent.

The limousine slowed to a stop in front of them. The tinted window slid down and Doc Smith's friendly face appeared from within. "Looking for a ride, my friends?"

"I'm so glad to see you. I thought you'd never get here!" exclaimed Billy.

"Sorry for the delay. D.C. traffic is a mess at this time of day," answered Doc. "Why didn't you fly down?"

Penny frowned at Billy, knowing she feared flying. "It's a long story," Billy replied.

Doc chuckled as he realized that Billy and Penny hadn't changed much since they last saw each other. "Aren't they all?"

The driver stepped out of the limo and opened the door for them. Penny entered first, followed by Billy. Doc smiled at Penny and asked, "How are you doing?"

"My mom passed away and I'm going through a tough time. I wasn't sure if I was ready to come down here."

"I was surprised to hear from you, Billy," said Doc earnestly. "I thought you forgot about us."

"No way. It's just that so many things happened when we got back. Things were finally getting back to normal but then Penny's mom became ill and it's been downhill ever since."

"I informed Xerxes that you felt it necessary to visit Seneca," Doc mentioned. "He said that, so long as you have the orb, it wouldn't be a problem."

Billy reached under his coat and pulled out the small transparent orb on a silver chain. "I put this little thing away and never expected to use it."

"Why not?" kidded Doc. "It doesn't bite."

"Everything we experienced before seemed like it was only a bad dream," Billy explained. "I've tried to forget as much as I could."

"Come now, Billy. There must be something you cherish from the old world."

"Strangely enough, I feel an urge to carry my sword with me on the street."

Penny complained, "I still have nightmares from those horrible Neanderthals, the giant spiders and that stupid lizard."

"I know how you feel," Doc sympathized. "Maggie took a while to get over them as well. She had many restless nights."

"How about you?" she inquired.

"I still have a hard time accepting the magic part and the theories behind the new technologies. It was very difficult for me to break away from the teachings of the old school. There's just no basis in my mind for a lot of this stuff."

"Sometimes I felt like I had a dual personality," explained Billy. "It's difficult when the one starts to interfere with the other."

"What kind of problems are you having with it?" asked Doc, curious.

"Sometimes I feel like a part of me is in the other world. I was really motivated when we were in danger. Then there are times when my new behavior affects me here. I sometimes become too outspoken at work. Everything seems unimportant and trivial, so I don't have the patience for stupid stuff after living on the edge for two months."

"How about you, Penny? Are you okay with what happened?"

"I don't know. Maybe I liked it too much. I think I'd like to go back to Firenghia and live with Seneca's tribe."

Doc was surprised by her response. "How come?"

"It's so much simpler than the everyday chaos of this world. I could be free there. Now that my mother's gone, I really think about it a lot."

"Well, that's good that you're facing it."

"I don't know about that."

"What do you really want out of life?" Doc queried her, concerned about her well-being.

"I want to lead a simple life where I can be free. I'd love to be like Seneca and be a free spirit."

"That's an interesting way of looking at it. Maggie feels that our experience in the other world has opened her eyes to things that she never considered before as well."

"How is Maggie doing?" Penny inquired. "She didn't come with you."

"She's taking care of the lunch arrangements for us. She really missed you both."

"I should have called her," said Penny apologetically. "I'm sorry."

"We understand. It was quite a traumatic experience for all of us."

"The toughest part was coming back to our world a day before everything happened," remarked Billy. "That makes it even harder to believe."

The limousine stopped in front of a black, wrought iron gate, which stood about twelve feet tall. An armed security guard approached them. The driver handed the guard a red badge with his picture on it. After scrutinizing it for several seconds, the guard looked in. "Hello, Dr. Smith. I didn't realize it was you in the back. Have a nice day."

The driver closed the window. The guard entered his booth and opened the gates. The limousine proceeded along a cement driveway.

Billy and Penny gazed in awe as they approached a massive, tan building at the end of the driveway. It was surrounded by Crepe Myrtles, which looked a bit naked at this time of the year. The black lettering on the upper part of the building immediately caught their eyes.

"Smith-Miller Research Center!" exclaimed Billy. "How did you get a facility like this named after you?"

"Why? Is there something wrong with it?" Doc asked playfully.

"No, but..."

"Well, Xerxes wanted no part of his name on the facility, so Joe and I decided 'why not'?"

"Congratulations, Doc, but how could you afford such a large facility?" Billy inquired.

"We have a lot of government sponsored projects. But then, there are a lot of private ventures we're involved in that are sponsored by very wealthy organizations."

"So, you have money coming in from all over," Billy teased.

"At least for now, we do. This facility has created an economic boon of sorts in a variety of fields, but we have to be careful. If we get careless, the economic results could be disastrous."

Penny became curious with his reference to 'fields' and inquired, "What kind of research are you doing here?"

"Well, Xerxes has given us more than enough new technology to keep us busy for one lifetime. We've got new fuel sources, communication and transportation. He's shown us how to recycle many of our byproducts; how to revitalize the lakes and oceans; cures for treating some of our diseases, and many other things."

"How long before we see this new technology in action?" inquired Billy.

"That's the hard part," confessed Doc. "We have to integrate the new processes and devices carefully to prevent upsetting the world's economies.

We've recruited some help from friends in London; otherwise, we'd never get these new advances implemented."

"Who do you know in London?" asked Penny.

"There's a foundation that goes by the acronym LISA- the London Institute for Scientific Advancement. They are very interested in helping us integrate new technology into our societies. It's really quite important to enlist responsible help because of how these new changes will affect companies, corporations and employment around the world. We really have to make these transitions carefully."

"Wow, what a responsibility! I guess you have your hands full," remarked Penny.

"Yes, and on top of that, we're in the process of installing weapons systems on twenty of the Council's spacecraft. That's our biggest priority right now."

"Why do they need weapons systems on their craft?" Billy asked. "Are they expecting a war or something?"

"No, nothing like that. Xerxes claims that there are space pirates in certain galaxies that prey upon their ships. They need defensive capabilities to protect them from these pirates."

The limousine stopped in front of a tinted glass wall with three revolving doors. The driver opened the doors for them. When Penny stepped onto the sidewalk, Maggie exited the glass door from the lobby and rushed to greet her. "Penny! How are you?"

"Maggie!" The two women hugged.

"Look at this place! It's amazing," Penny blurted excitedly as she looked up at the huge facility in awe.

"Yes, it is," said Maggie proudly. "There is so much more on the inside than what meets the eye, too."

"Let's go ladies. Lunch is waiting," interrupted Doc. He led them through the lobby and down a long, marble corridor. At the end were four stainless steel elevators, of which one took them to the third floor.

Billy couldn't help noticing the vast number of buttons on the panel indicating various floors. "Does this place really have all these floors?" asked Billy.

"Yes, it does, but only ten are above ground," boasted Doc. "The other seventeen are below ground."

"That's incredible!" exclaimed Billy. "What do you do on all those floors?"

"Each one is dedicated to its own field of research. The bottom level is the most impressive, though. That's the transport bay. There's a large duct that runs through the middle of the building so that our spacecraft can fly local as well. It's an outside access more or less; otherwise, the spacecraft come and go through the portals. We aren't anxious to advertise their existence yet."

"That's phenomenal!" Billy replied excitedly.

The elevator reached the third level without exhibiting any evidence of motion. The doors slid open with no sound whatsoever.

"Ronnie and Randy will be returning shortly with their sidekicks," Maggie informed them. "They were in London for a week."

"I guess John and Seamus had to report for guard duty," kidded Billy.

"The queen summoned them to meet with her to discuss their history," explained Doc.

"I'll bet that's going to be interesting," kidded Billy.

"Ronnie and Randy are still with John and Seamus?" asked Penny curiously.

"Yes, they are," replied Maggie enthusiastically.

"What did they do to get invited to London?" Billy asked.

"It seems that our friends at LISA informed the queen of the boys' background. I hear that she was quite interested in her ancestral history."

"I'd love to be a fly on the wall for that discussion."

"They'll be joining us shortly and you can ask them about it," Maggie mentioned.

Doc led them into a large conference room where the caterers laid out a beautiful buffet. A friendly, old woman removed the covers one by one and introduced with a Spanish accent what each entrée was.

Doc's pager beeped, attracting everyone's attention. "Ah, Ronnie and Randy have returned with their beaus," he announced. "They'll be here shortly."

"Did they fly back from England?" asked Billy.

"Oh, not at all," he answered proudly. "We've established a portal to link us directly to LISA. It saves a lot of time and money in addition to maintaining our security."

"How about Jarret? Did he recover from his injury?" inquired Penny.

"Jarret had his arm amputated when he returned. He was lucky they were able to develop an antitoxin for the poison. It saved his life."

"What's he doing, now?"

"He's working as a recruiter for the Marines. Colonel Jackson pulled some strings for him to stay active. Normally, they would discharge someone with a handicap like that."

The door swung open, startling them. Randy, Seamus, John and Ronnie entered the room. "Well, look what the cat dragged in," exclaimed Randy. "It's Billy and Penny!"

"Well, if it isn't my worst nightmare! Have you come back to torment me?" he asked excitedly.

"No, I have Seamus to torture these days. Right, honey?" she said playfully as she squeezed his arm.

"Oh, yes. And do you ever." Everyone laughed.

Seamus extended a hand to Billy. "It's good to see you two again. How are you?"

"Not bad at all now that we got the band back together. The question is 'how are you doing'?" Billy winked at Randy.

"Don't make me kick your ass so soon, Brock," she warned. Everyone laughed again. Randy grabbed Billy by the chin and kissed his lips, leaving him stunned.

"Wow! What was that for?"

Penny was shocked but ignored Randy's act. "Seamus doesn't give me quite the same battle that you did."

"Is that a complement?"

"No, just an acknowledgement. He is good at other things that would surprise you."

"You devil," teased Billy.

"Don't listen to her. She's insane," replied Seamus.

John hugged Billy and Penny. "It's good to see you both."

"Yeah, it's been too long," Billy said somberly.

"Things just aren't the same after what we went through," remarked Penny.

"How's the queen mum?" asked Billy playfully. Everyone looked at John and Seamus with amused expressions.

"She's doing very well," answered John. "We spent quite a bit of time exchanging history lessons."

"It seems that the queen had someone do a little investigating into the royal past and found several documents pertaining to John and his deeds," Seamus mentioned giddily.

"It was nothing special," replied John humbly.

"Anything you saw or learned from the Queen of England had to be special," remarked Penny.

John changed the subject and commented, "So you finally came back to see us, Billy."

"I didn't think we'd see you again. It's as if you dropped off the face of the earth," joked Ronnie. She hugged Billy and kissed his cheek.

"I always knew you cared for me." Ronnie groaned at him.

Randy hugged Penny and put her arm around her shoulder. "How are you making out with Senor Jackass?" she questioned her, curious.

Penny smiled for the first time. "It's funny you should ask." Everyone chuckled.

"Things aren't the same without you," John ribbed Billy.

"I see you and Seamus can still smile after spending six months with the Sisters of Sin."

"Don't start something you can't finish, Billy," warned Randy.

"Did I miss something here?" asked Penny defensively.

"It was a little joke when we were in the pub," replied Billy.

"Should I know about it?"

"No, it's not a big deal."

Randy elbowed Ronnie and whispered, "He's not kidding." Penny grew irritated with the puns and what they might have alluded to.

Billy quickly changed the topic. "John and Seamus, you look so different without the beards. They haven't taken anything else away from you, have they?"

John laughed and tarried back, "Not yet, but I see you haven't been as lucky." Everyone responded with "oohs" and "ahs". Randy and Ronnie then offered Penny condolences for her mom.

The group split up for lunch. The women sat at one end of the table while the men sat together at the other. After an hour of conversation, Xerxes entered the room. "Hello, my friends. It's good to see you again," he said cheerfully.

Billy and Penny approached Xerxes and shook hands. "How've you been, Xerxes?" asked Billy.

"Very well, thank you."

"Hey, I brought the orb with me. Can you help us get to Firenghia?"

"The orb is already programmed. I just have to activate it."

"We'd like to visit Seneca and Cassius for a few days," Penny commented to him. "Then we'll return and spend some time here."

"I have a feeling that something's wrong in Firenghia. I really need to check it out," explained Billy.

"Hand me the orb and I'll activate it," Xerxes instructed him.

Billy took the orb from around his neck and handed it to Xerxes. Xerxes studied it and took his portal control unit from under his long, white coat. He pushed several buttons, pointed the PCU at the orb and pressed two more buttons. The orb illuminated a soft blue glow and then changed to an eerie green.

"That should do it. When you close your hand around the orb, it will take you there. Do the same in Firenghia and it will bring you back here. It toggles your destination based on where you are."

"Boy, if I knew it was that easy, I might have used it sooner."

"Enjoy your trip."

"Thanks, Xerxes."

Penny was a little more upbeat now. "Thanks so much, Xerxes."

"Anytime, young lady."

"It's good to see everyone again. Unfortunately, we have to leave for a few days. We're going to Firenghia, to visit Seneca and her baby," announced Billy.

Ronnie couldn't resist the urge to torment him. "Does 'said' baby have anything to do with you, Billy?"

"You could say he has a vested interest in the situation," replied Penny.

"Hey Doc, can you store our luggage until we return?" requested Billy.

"Certainly. It'll be in my office. Is there anything you need from them before you leave?"

"As a matter of fact, there is. I'm glad you asked."

"Follow me. I'll take you there."

Billy followed Doc up to his office on the fourth floor. When they entered the room, Billy's luggage was already there. He anxiously opened his suitcase and poked through his belongings. He pulled out a brown leather sack with something the size of a large grapefruit inside. "This is my security blanket, Doc."

"Your what?"

"Remember the skull I took when we were in the cave?"

Doc's eyes widened with surprise. "You brought that thing back with you?"

"Of course. I didn't know if I'd ever need it again and they're hard to come by."

"Oh, Billy, I hope you know what you're doing."

"My sword and scabbard are in here. If anything happens to me and you come looking, bring it with you."

"When you return, I'll show you around," Doc offered. "Besides, I'm sure Sam McDermott wants to say hello."

Billy's eyes lit up with interest. "Sam's here, too?"

"He sure is. He works downstairs developing weapons and protective clothing."

"I'll have to see him when I get back. Tell him hello and I'd like to share one of his victory cigars with him when I get back."

"I sure will. I'll see him at dinner, tonight."

They returned to the conference room. Penny recognized the leather bag immediately. "I hope that isn't what I think it is."

"Yeah, it's my skull."

"What's it doing here?" she asked, disgusted. "It gives me the creeps."

"I thought I'd bring it for protection."

"From who? Me?" she exclaimed angrily.

"You never know."

Penny glared at Billy with a look as cold as steel. The others took notice but said nothing.

"See you all in a few days," announced Billy.

Penny waved and said, "Goodbye, everyone." Billy and Penny disappeared through the green portal.

"I don't think all is well in paradise with those two," Ronnie commented aloud.

"Penny was close to her mother. It's going to be tough on her for a while," replied Maggie.

Xerxes moved to the end of the table and sat with the others. Doc and Maggie had so much to speak with him about. "Do you have information on the space flights, Xerxes?" asked Doc.

"Are we going to Alpha-17?" asked Maggie excitedly.

"Yes, you are. You'll meet some new team members once you arrive there as well. They're returning with you to help out here with the implementation of certain technologies. Randy and Ronnie will be joining you on the trip as well."

"That's great! When do we leave?"

"Your flight will be departing later today. You need to be at the transport bay at 19:30."

The door opened and two men entered the conference room. The first man was tall with a dark complexion and jet-black hair. He had a handlebar mustache and long sideburns. He stood much taller than the other man at over six-feet tall. The second man was a bit stout with bushy auburn hair and a short beard. He was only about five-and-a-half-feet tall. Both men appeared to be in their late forties.

"Good evening, sir. I hope we aren't interrupting," The man greeted Xerxes.

"No, not at all. This is Doc Smith and his assistant/wife, Maggie. The two young ladies are Randy Timmins and Ronnie Vander Slice."

"Hello, everyone. I'm Nazir Mustafo, the commander of the *Excelsior*. This is Tur Farrish, commander of the *Starfire*. I understand the four of you will be joining him."

"We're really looking forward to this flight. No one on our planet has ever traveled beyond the moon," replied Doc.

"You're going to Alpha-17 with me, although I'm sure you already knew that. We'll meet with several scientists for starters. Then I'll have one of my men take you on a tour of the metropolis. I'm sure you'll find it unlike anything you've ever seen," explained Tur.

"What about the flight?" asked Maggie. "Is there anything we need to know? After all, this is new to us."

"No. I don't expect any problems, since we'll travel through a secure zone. If anything arises, the CS-11s will warn the crew."

"What's a CS-11?" asked Doc inquisitively.

"The CS-11 is a combat satellite. Several of them are strategically positioned in or near our space portals to protect our ships during entry and departure. They were made for us by the Dracorians a long time ago."

"But why do you need them?"

"Pirates and renegade aliens. We need to defend ourselves from their random attacks."

"I thought the Dracorians were the enemy."

"The Dracorians are an intelligent species and we dealt with them a very long time ago. They tend to change from time to time, and their last morphosis was rather unusual. They've assumed a very hostile form and we tend to steer clear of them these days."

"What do the CS-11s do?"

"They are armed with high density lasers, spotting lasers and infrared scanners. The infrareds are a bit primitive but still quite effective."

"How often do these pirates come around?"

"Don't worry about them. I'm sure you won't see any of them on this trip."

"For the gentlemen traveling with me, we can leave anytime," Mustafo announced. "My communications officer has informed me that everything is ready, so we can move up our takeoff time if you like."

"That's fine with us," replied John. "We can meet you in an hour at the transport bay." The two men departed the room with a sense of urgency.

"Gee, where's the fire?" quipped Ronnie. "They sure left in a hurry."

"They must check in with the Council prior to departure for any last-minute instructions or changes," explained Xerxes.

"We need to get going, too," Maggie reminded Doc. "It's getting late and we've got to pack a few things."

"Yes, Dear. I'm ready when you are." The Smiths left the briefing room and went their way.

"This is fantastic!" exclaimed Seamus. "We're actually going into space to another part of the universe by ship."

"Yes, you are. And it will only take two days to get there and back using our technology," explained Xerxes.

"Are we going to meet people like us?" asked Ronnie.

"Oh, yes. The people on Alpha-17 are your closest relatives. Your trip will take about five days to complete."

"I never thought this would happen in my lifetime," remarked Randy.

Xerxes checked his pager and frowned. "I'll leave you now. I must take care of a few things." Everyone thanked Xerxes and he left the room.

"You two boys better behave out there," warned Randy. "I'd love to go with you too, but Xerxes asked us to accompany the doc and Maggie."

"Don't worry. It's only target shooting. Besides, John and I have a little wager over who can shoot better," said Seamus confidently.

"Xerxes tells me you both did fine in the simulators." Randy remarked.

"Simulators aren't real," said Seamus modestly. "This test will be the real thing. Hopefully the new system will operate as it should. I'd hate to get all the way out there and it fails to fire properly."

"You'll do fine," Randy assured him. "I'll pull Ronnie off of John and we'll let the two of you get ready."

"See you soon, Honey."

Randy tugged on Ronnie's arm and teased, "Come on, girl. They have to get ready."

Ronnie waved to the men. "Good luck, fellas."

CHAPTER 2

CLOSE CALLS

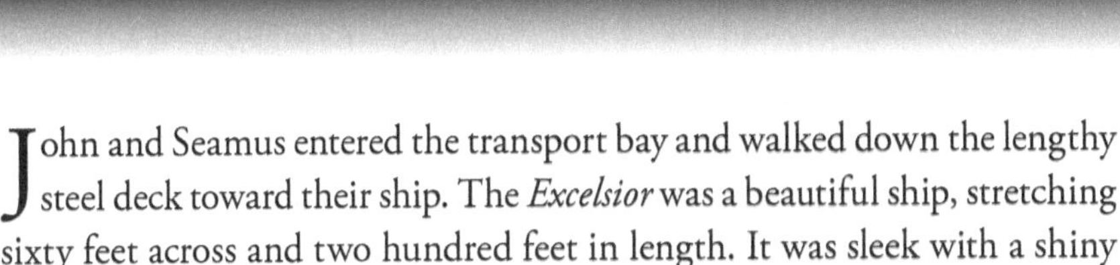

John and Seamus entered the transport bay and walked down the lengthy steel deck toward their ship. The *Excelsior* was a beautiful ship, stretching sixty feet across and two hundred feet in length. It was sleek with a shiny black surface. The name was painted proudly on the sides and tail with a crown of stars above it.

Xerxes emerged from an open hatch on the side of the craft and surprised the two men. "I didn't know you were going with us, Xerxes," John commented, surprised.

"Change of plans. I decided that I'd like to see how this new weapons system performs for myself."

"Forgive me for saying so, but you seem very concerned about the new weapons systems. Are you sure we're only talking space pirates here?"

"I wouldn't be going along if I thought I was placing myself in danger."

John gave Seamus a suspicious glance. He shrugged his shoulders in reply. Xerxes sensed their distrust. "I understand your unease but space is a big place. There are many alien races out there and humans who stretch capitalism beyond legal bounds."

"I'm just surprised that the weapons systems became a priority so quickly."

"Come on, gentlemen. Let's get on board and prepare for departure. I want you to enjoy your first trip into space."

"How many other crew members do we have aboard with us?" inquired Seamus.

"Besides us, there are Commander Mustafo, Varta, and Tera. You'll meet them later, during the flight." John and Seamus took their seats in the cargo area.

The bay was empty except for three crates, which had been secured to the floor with lightweight cord. Twelve seats were added for passenger travel on the *Excelsior* when Earth was included in the Council's travel plans. There were four digital monitors on the front wall.

Commander Mustafo's voice rang from the speakers in the ceiling, "Take your seats, gentleman. We're departing now." Moments later, the ship was in motion. It raced through the portal toward an asteroid field in the seventh sector.

Commander Mustafo piloted the spacecraft past several large pieces of debris. He frowned as the ship passed near a section of wreckage with the name *Aurora-32* on it. John noticed the wreckage as well from the monitors in the lower bay. He decided to visit the flight deck and inquire as to the ship's fate.

When he reached the second level, he noticed a female officer, whom he assumed to be Tera, at the communication/navigation station. "Can I help you?" she asked, callously.

"I'm looking for Commander Mustafo."

"Next level up. Knock before you enter."

"Thank you, ma'am."

John ascended the metal stairs. When he reached the door labeled 'Flight Deck', he paused before knocking. He felt like a guest and was apprehensive about taking liberties on the ship. Finally, he rapped lightly and leaned through the doorway. "Excuse me, sir."

"Ah, Mr. Murdoch. Come in," Mustafo replied pleasantly.

John entered and stood between Mustafo and Varta as they scanned the monitors. He gazed at the controls and lighted panels surrounding them and marveled at the complexity of the controls.

"What can I do for you, sir?"

"Do you know anything about the wreck we just passed?"

"That's the remains of one of our transports from Borealis-3. It was attacked a short while back."

"By whom, space pirates?"

"No, just some hostile aliens. Nothing to worry about, though."

"Were there any survivors?"

"Negative. They barely had enough time to issue a distress signal; otherwise, we might not have known about the incident at all."

Xerxes entered the cabin behind John. "Ah, you've come up for a little tour."

"I sense that there's more to the story than you're telling me, Xerxes. What's going on out here?"

"Whatever do you mean?"

"You never mentioned anything about ships being destroyed. We're all friends here. You have to trust us if there's something going on."

Xerxes sat down and sighed. "I hoped that things would be settled by now with the pirates but unfortunately they aren't."

"You're quite evasive in answering our questions. What's to stop us from being attacked by the same assailants that the *Aurora-32* encountered? Who are these combatants?"

"They're just renegades."

"I'm not stupid. My whole life revolved around warfare and survival. I think you should have mentioned that this little problem of yours has resulted in ships being destroyed before we made the trip."

"Would it have made a difference?"

"Probably not, but you still should have told us. So, what's the real story out here?" John persisted.

"Let's go downstairs and I'll explain." Xerxes and John returned to the cargo hold, where they joined Seamus.

"I didn't want to alarm you or your friends," Xerxes said apologetically.

"About what?" asked John.

Xerxes hesitated as the female officer from the comm/nav station entered the bay with an irritated expression and caught their attention.

She wore a teal uniform with a black belt around her slender waist. Her pitch-black hair was wrapped in a tight bun on top of her head. "I can tell you exactly what's going on," she announced sarcastically.

"And who are you?" inquired John.

"My name is Tera. I'm the communications officer and the ship's navigator. I'm responsible for receiving and disseminating information to our people."

"Enough, Tera!" shouted Xerxes. "I'll tell them what they need to know. Return to your station, immediately."

"No! I think I'll stay and make sure you tell them everything."

"Xerxes, what's the meaning of this?" bellowed John.

Xerxes glanced at each of them and then stared at the floor in shame. "We're involved in an intergalactic war and it's not going too well."

"Why didn't you mention that before?"

"We've ignored your world for centuries because of your barbaric ways. Your people were never happy with peace. Your friends call you warriors. That carries more dignity in your world than a peacemaker."

"That's not entirely true. We were the King's personal guards, assigned to royal responsibilities. We guarded royal family members and high-ranking officials. Our special training was to protect, not to kill."

"Regardless, it's difficult for us to accept the fact that we need your help."

"And how do you expect us to help you?"

"Surely you and your people should be able to devise a way for us to win this war before it erodes into a catastrophe. We hoped that, with our technology, you could relate some of your strategies and weapons to our situation. Warriors like you are survivors."

"That's just marvelous! We've never even been in space before and you think we're going to help you win a galactic war."

"Think of it this way. If we lose, it's only a matter of time before your planet is drawn into the fray. One way or another, you'll be involved."

"I think we need to talk to Dr. Smith about this. He's better suited to make a decision on this."

Xerxes glared at Tera then turned his attention back to John and Seamus. "Let's concentrate on our mission. We can't do anything until we get back to the research center. Hopefully now you'll understand why I want to make sure these weapons work as your people have advertised. I need to know that we can protect ourselves."

"He's right, John," replied Seamus. "We can prove the weapons system is reliable and that we can operate them effectively as well. When we return, we'll hash out the blame."

"John, I need to know that the simulators are providing adequate training, not just for the two of you, but for the others who are going through them now."

"But Xerxes, shooting asteroids is a lot easier than shooting spaceships and projectiles. There's no comparison."

"What other alternatives do we have? I'm counting on your reflexes to make the necessary adjustments to the speed of an alien ship should it become necessary."

"Do we even know if these weapons will work against an alien vessel?"

"The information and metal samples we gave your people should have been sufficient for developing the appropriate weapons."

"For all our sakes, I hope you're right."

"We'll be hitting the second gate shortly. Then it'll be about seven hours to the asteroid field by your time."

Xerxes excused himself from the cabin and followed Tera back to her station. She ignored his presence and scanned several screens on the comm/nav panel. "Don't you ever countermand my authority like that again!" he chastised her.

"If you expect their help, I strongly suggest that you build some trust with them. You've already damaged your credibility."

"That's my responsibility. You worry about yours. Speaking of which, what news have we gotten on the war?"

"It's not going well. The alien forces have gathered new allies against us. Our efforts to court any of the potentials from the Gandoran Nebula have failed. Everyone is afraid to get involved. They're hoping the war will remain contained in our part of the universe."

"I was afraid of this."

"Do you think the Earthers will let you move the Council to their planet?"

"I don't know. I'm sure they'll realize that, if they do, it will draw them into the conflict almost immediately."

"Yes, but they are no strangers to conflict."

"And that's why I loathe them."

"Why? Because they'll fight for their freedom at all costs!"

"Yes, maybe that's why. We never had to fight before. In the past, we hired mercenary races to fight our battles. Now we're on our own and we're dependent on the Earthers for our freedom."

"You should have thought about that before. You should have blocked Jasper's plans. Now look at the mess we're in."

"You're right, Tera. I'm so sorry that I didn't stand up to him. We made a terrible mistake and it could cost us everything we have."

"It's going to be a lot harder to accept your mistake when we're drawn into battle, so I suggest you get used to dealing with the Earthers truthfully."

"Perhaps you're right. They are our only hope."

Xerxes returned to the cabin. Mustafo and Varta were busy at the controls. "How close are we to the field, Mustafo?" asked Xerxes.

Mustafo checked one of the monitors located on the upper panel in front of him. "Not far. If you look at this monitor, you'll see the field ahead of us." Xerxes left the cabin and returned to the cargo bay.

John and Seamus sat quietly and watched the passing stars on the screens. Xerxes approached them, attempting to sound upbeat. "We're approaching the first asteroid field. It's time to man the cannons, gentlemen," he announced. "Tera will instruct you as to the targets you'll aim for. We'll keep a tally of hits and misses for the sake of measuring the accuracy of the weapons versus the accuracy of the gunners."

John and Seamus each climbed up a six-rung ladder into their respective turrets. The turret was a ball of metal with three-dimensional monitors mounted on the curved walls. There was a cushioned seat for the gunner as well as a helmet with fiber-optic cables attached in the rear. Two joystick handles stuck out from the arm rests. Each one had four buttons mounted vertically on the front of the handle.

John strapped himself in and placed the helmet on. He was amazed when he saw the asteroids through the visor. He felt as though he could reach out and touch them. He never dreamed that someday he might fly across the sky let alone travel through galaxies just to use asteroids for target practice. Seamus strapped himself in and placed the helmet on his head. He was uncomfortable with the new high-tech weaponry.

Tera manually fed the coordinates of various asteroids into their headsets. The data streamed across the top of the visor. Tera spoke to them through the headset, "Are you ready to begin the exercise?"

"Affirmative," replied John.

"Ready," answered Seamus.

John's visor magnified the asteroid field until it seemed close up. A red X appeared on one of the asteroids. A small window positioned in the upper right corner of the visor showed a numerical value that changed for several seconds and stopped at 174.3. He recalled that, when the software is installed, the computer could determine the power required to vaporize an object. For now, he operated the turret until a gold X overlapped the red X and the phrase "target lock" flashed. He pressed the small knob with a particular amount of pressure and a pulse of energy destroyed the asteroid.

"Good shot, John," Tera said. "A little too much pressure on the trigger but it was acceptable."

"Thanks, Tera."

Soon another red X appeared and he repeated the process. He could feel his reflexes grow faster as each X appeared. In the back of his mind, though, he knew this didn't compare with targeting a fast-moving projectile.

Seamus looked at the indications on his visor and tried to refresh his memory. He recalled the exercises in the simulator and how the firing system operated. He recited to himself, "A laser is directed at the target and feeds back the density, speed and distance."

"Are you awake, Seamus?" John kidded.

"Yeah, I'm wondering what we're doing up here."

"Your mission is to test the firing capability and accuracy of the new cannons. The software will be added later and tested in simulation," Tera reminded him.

"Yeah, yeah. I remember." The numbers streamed onto Seamus' visor. The lessons quickly came back to him and he initiated his firing sequence. The red X appeared and followed an asteroid. Seamus efficiently guided the gold X over it and fired. The asteroid exploded into dust and debris.

"Nice shot, Seamus," said Tera.

"This is too easy. It's not going to help us against moving objects," complained Seamus.

"Patience, Seamus. You'll get your chance, soon enough."

"You sound like a veteran, Tera," he commented. "Seen much action?"

"More than I care to talk about," she replied humbly.

The trial was tiresome for John and Seamus as they waited for their target data. Tera needed time as she learned to feed the coordinates into the tracking system, which in turn loaded the information into the weapons system.

The *Excelsior* passed the asteroid field and reached open space. Four hours later, they reached a denser field with larger targets to pick from and greater distances. The men fired for over two hours until the power unit dropped below fifty percent.

"How long can we fire the cannons before they require charging?" inquired Seamus.

"It depends on the power level that you fire at. You're using minimal power right now, which allows you to fire for long intervals. As you increase pressure on the trigger, the power level increases proportionately and the available time for firing decreases significantly. That's why accuracy is so important."

"That's an interesting point," replied John.

"When the software is operational," she continued, "the computer will set the power level automatically. You'll only need to point and squeeze, giving you maximum efficiency."

When John and Seamus finished their live fire training, they climbed down from the turrets, looking drained. Xerxes met them as they reached the floor. "Not bad. You boys looked like seasoned pros."

Tera passed them and climbed up the ladder to the turret. "What do you think you're doing, Tera?" Xerxes asked curiously.

"I expect to be able to handle the cannons as well as anyone else on my ship," replied Tera. "I've watched the simulator screens and there's no comparison to the real thing."

John sensed that Xerxes and Tera had a little more than a working relationship. Her arrogance toward Xerxes was more than evident and he seemed to tolerate her insubordination as a minor annoyance judging by the look on his face.

Tera methodically destroyed one asteroid after another without the use of target data, which she previously supplied to the men. After every ten shots, she chose targets that were smaller and further away. The men were astonished by her accuracy. When the power bank dropped to thirty percent, she shut down the turret and climbed down.

"I don't mind saying, Ms. Tera, that you have an uncanny knack for that firing system," complimented John. Tera smiled in appreciation and removed the headset. She hung it on a rack and quietly returned to her workstation.

"She doesn't say much, does she?" Seamus commented.

"She's a very unusual woman," explained Xerxes. "What you see on the outside is nothing like what's inside. Everyone who has worked with her will tell you one of two things: 'don't get in her way' and 'don't get on her bad side'."

"I'll remember that," responded Seamus, grinning sheepishly.

"On that note, let's go home. Our mission was quite satisfactory."

"I thought we had another day of live-fire," Seamus questioned him, disappointed.

"I don't think we need it. The results were conclusive." Xerxes used his comm-link to contact Commander Mustafo. "Commander, take us back to the research center. Our work here is done."

"From what I saw up here, it was quite successful," Mustafo remarked.

"I think this is going to make a big difference in dealing with our problem," Xerxes said confidently. He disappeared into a small cubicle on the middle deck and rested. Tera remained at her station. John and Seamus settled comfortably in their seats and napped.

The *Excelsior* closed in on the first portal and shuddered. Mustafo's voice rang from the intercom and shattered the silence, "Everyone, please fasten your harnesses. We're approaching the first gate."

A second voice blared from the intercom, "Xerxes, please contact Varta immediately." Xerxes awoke abruptly and retrieved the comm-link from his pocket. Two beeps preceded a response. "Xerxes, is that you?"

"Yes, Varta, what's going on?"

"There are three enemy ships closing on us. We'll barely make the gate."

"Proceed at full speed," Xerxes instructed Varta. Have Tera notify the Council that we have company. Never mind, I'll tell her myself." He paced back and forth nervously before using the comm-link to contact Tera. He pressed three digits and waited.

Tera sat at her station and watched the approaching blips on her screen. She reached down and took the comm-link from her belt. "Yes, Xerxes."

"Contact the Council and have them close the gate behind us as soon as we're clear. It's going to be a close one."

"Right away."

The ship rocked violently and a thundering roar shattered the silence. Xerxes returned to the cargo bay as the ship shuddered. He stumbled and fell down the last few steps.

"What the hell is going on?" screamed John.

Xerxes got up and calmly fixed his robe. "We're being pursued by alien cruisers. We should reach the gate in time, though."

John watched the giant portal on the monitor in awe. It was a beautiful gold mass of clouds sprinkled with sparkling lights around its perimeter. Their brief moment of complacency was interrupted by another loud boom, which rocked the ship again.

Xerxes yelled into the page, "Varta! Mustafo! Get me a damage report!"

The ship raced through the portal and suffered no further disturbances. The portal quickly closed behind them. "The gate closed successfully, Xerxes. There is no further pursuit by the intruders," announced Tera over the page.

"Thanks, Tera. Next time use the comm-link," Xerxes replied cynically.

John sensed the sarcasm in Xerxes' voice. He was deeply concerned about their situation and Xerxes' reluctance to reveal any more details than necessary about it.

Xerxes comm-link beeped. "Go ahead," he replied somberly.

"Xerxes, we've suffered irreparable damage. We'll never make it back to the research center."

"How severe?"

"Half of the coolers are shot. We only have thirty percent of core power. The aft stabilizers are damaged as well, so we have limited steering."

"Get us to the Council's headquarters," Xerxes ordered.

"We have no braking ability."

"Prognosis?"

"A rough landing. After that, it'll be the scrapyard for this ship."

"Understood. Thanks, Varta." Xerxes dialed Tera.

"What is it?" she reluctantly answered.

"We're landing at the Council's base."

"I'll arrange it."

"Thanks."

Tera latched the comm-link on her belt and resumed her duties.

"We're headed to the Council's headquarters," announced Xerxes. "Tera will arrange for the Council to set the protective force field at low power to cushion our approach. She performed this technique successfully on a previous mission in another craft with battle damage."

"In another ship with battle damage! So, this isn't new," challenged John sarcastically.

"No, it isn't."

In her first battle experience, Tera was scared to death, but these attacks became a regular event for her. This time, she was better prepared to handle the situation. A face appeared on her monitor. It was an elderly, gray-haired man. "Why are you coming here, Tera?"

"A social call," she replied cynically.

"Cut the sarcasm if you want our help."

"Oh, so you'll actually help this time," she commented.

"I will speak to Xerxes about your disrespect."

"Save it. We're coming in hot."

"You did that last time."

"Yeah, and we got our asses shot off that time, too, if you remember."

"What do you want from us?"

"Low power force field."

"Done. Is that it?"

"Yeah," she replied coldly, annoyed by the Council's disrespect toward them. The monitor went blank. "Those arrogant bastards. I hope they get theirs," she uttered.

— ⧗ —

"Why didn't your scanners pick them up? What about the CS-11s?" questioned John. "Those ships were pretty close to the portal, weren't they?"

"Good question," Xerxes responded. "We'll discuss it with Mustafo and Varta when we land."

"How many spacecraft are being fitted with the new weapons systems?" John continued to interrogate.

"We've provided your people with four of our latest spaceships with designs for weaponry from other races sympathetic to our cause," Xerxes informed him. "Eventually, all thirty-one will be armed."

"How long before the first four are ready?"

"The *Excelsior* was ready until now, but we'll have three more by next week. The *Starfire* hasn't been tested for 'weapons ready' yet. We're doing a trial run to Mordor's Quadrant in two days with the *Specter* and the *Exeter*."

"Aren't any of our people suspicious about why your ships need weaponry?"

"Not yet. We've promoted the idea that we're investigating unknown and possibly hostile areas, thus we need protection."

"Do you expect any hostilities for the others along the way to Alpha-17?" questioned Seamus, concerned.

"No. That's a secure area."

"Tell me about the mission to Alpha-17?" asked John curiously.

"It's strictly a science mission for your people on the *Starfire*. You were invited on this trip so I could ascertain your feelings and your friends' attitudes regarding a battle of this magnitude. I need to know if we can count on you."

"I can't make that decision for the others, but as far as I'm concerned, I'll do what I can to help you. I would, however, like to know more about the enemy and the politics of this war. No secrets."

"Then we'll discuss it together with Dr. Smith when he returns from Alpha-17. I'll explain everything then."

— X —

Doc and Maggie showed up at the transport bay and gazed at the *Starfire* docked at the end of the flight deck. They marveled at the ship's beauty. "This is clearly an engineering masterpiece," remarked Doc.

Ronnie and Randy stood nearby and conversed with Tur Farrish. Tur noticed the astonishment on Doc's face. "I see this is your first look at our spacecraft," he mentioned.

"Yes, and it's absolutely stunning," remarked Ronnie.

"Tomorrow, the *Specter* and the *Exeter* will arrive. They are special models. I'm sure you'll appreciate them when you see them."

"I don't know what to say."

"Say that you have enough room. There are twenty-seven more ships to come after those two. We're looking forward to basing them here."

"What? You're basing them all here?" questioned Doc, shocked by the news.

"Yes, is something wrong with that?"

"No, it's just that Xerxes didn't mention anything to me about all those ships coming so soon."

"Perhaps he hasn't had a chance. I heard that the Council is moving its headquarters here as well."

Doc looked at Maggie with a concerned expressed. "But why would they move the Council and all their craft here? Why are we arming all of the ships if they're only worried about space pirates?" asked Doc.

"Tur, what else do you know about the situation?" Maggie queried.

"Not much. I did hear that they're having difficulties with some of the alien races honoring their alliances."

"Come on, everyone. Let's get the show on the road," Ronnie urged them.

Tur laughed at her exuberance. "Yes, commander, right away," he teased.

Ronnie blushed. "I'm sorry. It's just that we're so excited."

"I understand. Where's your friend, Randy?"

"She's already on board."

"Then we'd better get a move on," he suggested. They boarded the ship and found Randy in the gun turret.

"What are you doing up there? We haven't even left port yet," chided Ronnie.

"I'm getting comfortable," Randy replied excitedly. "This is going to be my position someday."

"Sorry, Randy. The sensors haven't been installed yet, only the hardware," Tur informed her.

"Do the cannons work at all?" Ronnie inquired.

"Yes, but it's like shooting blind. You have no system operation; just a gun and turret."

"It looks easy enough to operate," she remarked.

"Yes, but it's even better when you have coordinates and computer enhanced assistance."

"Hey, I'm a barbarian at heart. I do my own targeting."

"Perhaps someday you'll give us a demonstration," Tur mentioned. "In the meantime, take your seats. I'll keep you posted along the way of any points of interest."

They thanked him and strapped themselves into their seats for takeoff. Doc took a notebook and a pencil from his brief case and wrote some notes down. Maggie took her digital camcorder from its case and checked the batteries.

Randy took notice of Ronnie's plastic black pants and red velvet blouse. "Hey, Ronnie, what are you dressed for, a job interview with a pimp?" she taunted.

"No, I want to make a good impression on our new friends. Besides, at least I don't look like a farm girl from East Jebip."

Randy looked down at her black jeans and green plaid flannel shirt. She straightened the pant legs and admired her natural-colored snake skin boots. "You don't like my clothes?"

"I didn't say that. I just wondered what you're expecting things to be like on Alpha-17."

"Well, since I don't know, I want to be prepared," Randy responded defensively.

"Oh, you look prepared okay. If they have farms, you'll fit right in."

"I'm sure our new friends will be quite intelligent and very reserved in our presence. Besides, we are considered the barbarians of the race. I suggest we try to prove otherwise," suggested Doc. The girls agreed and reserved further comment for another time.

— X —

Things were quiet and the sights outside mesmerized everyone. Shooting stars were prominent and the colorful planets they passed along the way were stunning in color. Tur's voice sounded from the intercom, "We're approaching Alpha-17. It'll be coming up on the left shortly."

Everyone in the cargo bay watched the screens anxiously as the ship drew closer to the green planet.

Tur tried unsuccessfully to make contact with Alpha-17. "What do you think, Hassim? Have you ever had this problem before?"

"I find this very unusual."

"Turn on the forward scanners," requested Tur. "I have a bad feeling about this."

They watched intently as the screen zoomed in on the surface of Alpha-17. The pictures that appeared stunned the men. Everything on the surface was a smoldering mass.

"What the hell!" exclaimed Hassim.

"They lied to us!" cried Tur. "They said this couldn't happen!"

"Who is responsible for this?" Hassim asked, saddened by the destruction.

"I don't know but I'm sure going to find out. Take the ship down. I'll inform the others."

Tur entered the cargo bay with a concerned look on his face. "What is it, Tur?" asked Doc.

"It appears that much of Alpha-17 has been destroyed. We scanned several locations on the surface and everything is in ruins."

"What can we do?" asked Doc, fearing what they were drawn into.

"We're going to land and investigate," Tur answered somberly. "I suspect only one of the alien races, the Andorans, would go through the trouble to come out here and attack a civilian planet."

"But why would they do this?" questioned Doc.

"When we return to your research center, I will get some answers. They assured me that this couldn't happen."

The *Starfire* landed amid smoking debris. Buildings everywhere were destroyed.

"Search the area for possible survivors," ordered Tur. "Limit your range to shouting distance and stay in pairs. I'm issuing hand pulsers to each of you. They're set for stun. If necessary, slide the lever on top to the forward position. That will create enough blast to seriously hurt or kill an attacker."

After receiving their weapons, everyone split up in different directions. Ronnie and Randy went north, Doc and Maggie went east. Tur and Hassim went south, and the two remaining crewmen went west.

Ronnie and Randy poked around the rubble but found nothing. They climbed to the top of a collapsed building and hoped to cover more territory. After looking further, they conceded there were no survivors in their area.

Tur and Hassim searched through a badly damaged living complex but found nothing. Tur grew increasingly irate. His family lived where he now stood. There was no way anyone would have survived an assault of this magnitude. After inspecting the ruined complex, he and Hassim searched the area behind it. When that turned up no results, they reluctantly returned to the *Starfire*.

Ronnie and Randy searched through the remains of several razed buildings. Ronnie found a narrow opening into an underground shopping center. "Hey, Randy, check this out." She slid down into the lower level. The only daylight was from above, making it difficult to see anything.

Randy slid through the opening and took out a small flashlight from her pants pocket. "You're still just a country bumpkin," joked Ronnie.

Randy pointed the light and searched the area. "Yeah, but I bet I'd last on the streets a lot longer than you."

"In those clothes, who'd want to come near you?"

Randy shined the light on several corpses in a small room. Their bodies had large holes burned through the chest and stomach areas. The girls became nauseous.

"I've seen enough. Let's get out of here," said Ronnie, disgusted.

"Me, too. This is rough."

— **X** —

Doc and Maggie searched through some debris and found a hinged plate. Doc strained to lift the plate but had no luck. A child's cry startled them. Doc pushed a broken section of wall aside and found another hinged plate just like the first one. He strained to lift the second plate and this time was successful. When the plate was fully opened, he discovered a handful of youngsters struggling to see in the light.

"Did the monsters go away?" asked a frightened little girl.

"Yes, they have. Come out of there where I can see you."

Four boys and the girl climbed out of the hold and stood before them. They huddled around Doc and Maggie, while sobbing. "What monsters are you talking about?" asked Doc.

"Can you tell us what happened?" Maggie inquired in a soothing voice.

The children were horrified by the destruction around them and grew more hysterical. "We saw a large black cloud form in the sky," explained one little boy. He told them that it started yesterday evening and grew throughout the night. This morning they saw a giant spaceship come out of the cloud. Then a whole bunch of smaller ships came out of the big ship. When they landed, green monsters came out and took everyone onto the ships. "Then they started shooting at the buildings and things exploded," said a young girl. "A man told us to get in here and he locked us in."

"Come with us," instructed Doc. "We'll get you out of here."

When they returned to the *Starfire*, a strange sound buzzed through the air.

"Everyone, get on the ship," ordered Tur.

"But the others aren't back yet!" replied Doc.

"Get on board - NOW!"

They hustled onto the ship as Ronnie and Randy appeared nearby. The girls raced to the hatch and leaped through just as it closed. Ronnie looked at the children's frightened faces, then at Doc and Maggie. "Damn, that was close," she remarked.

Ronnie and Randy immediately went to the flight deck. "What the hell is happening out there?" Ronnie demanded to know.

"Not now," answered Tur as he piloted the ship away from the planet's surface.

"We still have two on the ground," Hassim reminded him.

"We'll try to get them on the fly," Tur responded. "We can't defend ourselves so we'll have to move quickly."

"How did you know we were in trouble when you heard the noise?" asked Ronnie.

"When I heard the recorded SOS message from the *Aurora-32*, that sound filled the background. It's some sort of beacon or transmitter."

"But why the cloud?" questioned Ronnie. "I don't understand."

"Go to the hatch and wait for my order. When I tell you, open the hatch and get them in here as fast as possible." The girls reluctantly obeyed.

Down in the cargo bay, the children anxiously watched the monitors with Doc and Maggie. Across the horizon, a large black cloud formed. "That's the cloud that the monsters came from!" shouted the oldest boy.

"Good Lord!" exclaimed Maggie.

Doc left her and hurried to the flight deck. "Tur, one of the boys says that the alien ships came out of that cloud," he announced.

Tur eyed the monitor. The spaceship hovered over the ruined city. His voice came over the intercom, "Ronnie, we're getting close. Please man the hatch and I'll instruct you when to open it."

As the *Starfire* hovered westward, tiny bright lights shot from the cloud on the horizon. Tur's voice came over the page, "Forget it, Ronnie! We're getting out of here now."

Doc and Maggie strapped the children into their seats. They, too, sat and watched the tiny lights growing larger on the monitor. "We're being attacked, aren't we?" asked Maggie nervously.

"It looks that way," answered Doc.

"Come on, Randy, let's man the guns," Ronnie ordered her.

"But they don't work."

"Yes, they do. Only the targeting system is inoperative."

Ronnie informed Tur of their intentions and climbed into the turret. Tur guided the ship away from Alpha-17 as fast as he could. Once they cleared the atmosphere, their speed picked up. Unfortunately, the alien ships still closed on them.

Tur addressed everyone on the page, "We'll be very close to the portal before they catch us. The CS-11's will cover us from there."

"Yeah, if there's any left," Randy commented over the intercom.

"So far, our friends haven't called a very good game, have they?" Ronnie commented cynically over the intercom.

"We'll teach them a lesson," Randy stated confidently. "They'll learn to appreciate us Earth women before this is over."

The approaching lights awed Ronnie. "Look at them all!"

"That's okay. There's more for us to shoot at," Randy responded cynically.

The girls attempted to pick off some of the approaching fighters from long range. After a number of attempts, Ronnie hit one. A small red burst of light spread to a second one. "Well, how about that, two for one," Ronnie said proudly.

"I'm just warming up. Don't get cocky," warned Randy.

The alien fighters drew perilously close as the *Starfire* neared the portal. Tur entered the code for the CS-11s to ignore the *Starfire*.

"No response, Hassim."

"I'll bet they already destroyed the CS-11s." The two men glanced sullenly at each other.

Randy picked off three fighters and Ronnie struck another one.

"How are you girls making out?" Tur asked, not expecting much from them.

"We took care of six of the rodents," Ronnie announced proudly. "There's still at least fourteen; make that thirteen left."

"We can't let the fighters through the portal, girls. If I circle around, can you give us a fighting chance?"

"Just watch us," answered Randy enthusiastically. "The closer they get, the deader they are."

"Ditto," added Ronnie.

"All right girls. It's up to you whether or not we're going home."

"You just fly this thing," Ronnie instructed him, "and we'll take care of the problem children."

The *Starfire* banked into a wide turn and did a loop. Unfortunately, the alien craft were now close enough to fire at them. The *Starfire* was rocked by cannon fire.

The girls repeatedly fired at the aliens and struck several of the fighters. The number of attackers dwindled gradually. The *Starfire* shook violently as a shot from one of the remaining seven fighters hit the rear section. "We've lost two engines and about a quarter of our speed," announced Tur frantically over the page.

"Just keep us moving," instructed Randy. "We're down to five. Damn, I mean four. Ronnie got another one. I've got to focus."

Another hit sent the *Starfire* into a slow spiral. Another engine failed and several of the controls malfunctioned.

"Tur, shut down all the lighting on board and try to level us off," requested Randy.

"What for?"

"Just do it fast!"

Tur shut down all internal and external lighting. The remaining four alien craft did a loop and came in slowly for the kill.

"This is it. Winner takes all. Can you hang?" taunted Randy.

"Best three out of four," challenged Ronnie.

"On my mark."

They waited until they had high percentage shots at the fighters. "Fire!" shouted Randy.

Two short bursts of fire from each cannon took out the remaining four attackers.

Tur and Hassim saw the monitor go clear and breathed a sigh of relief. "Nice work girls, but we aren't out of this yet," said Tur uneasily.

"How bad are we hit?" asked Randy.

"We're going to limp through the portal and flop into the dock, so make sure everyone's strapped into their seats."

"Where are the rest of the fighters?" asked Ronnie disappointedly.

"They went down to the surface again."

"Damn! We could have handled them," complained Randy.

"Yeah, but I'm glad you didn't have to," Tur replied.

"You girls are the best! I don't care what anyone says," kidded Hassim.

"Neither do we," said Ronnie proudly.

Tur and Hassim maneuvered the *Starfire* toward the portal. They passed wreckage from the CS-11 satellites. "There's your answer, Tur," said Hassim. "They destroyed every one of them."

"The Council will have to reprogram the coordinates of the portals to change their locations; otherwise, the aliens might be targeting them as we speak," Tur responded. "I think we surprised them by having the cannons on board. Next time, they'll be expecting them."

"The girls did quite a job back there," Hassim commented.

"I'm amazed. They've had no simulator training at all, yet they fired quite well without any targeting assistance."

"It must be an Earth trait – they're perfect fighting machines."

"Or it could be an Earth woman thing, too," kidded Tur.

"If that's true, remind me not to date any of them." The two men enjoyed the humor until they passed through the portal.

CHAPTER 3

RETURN TO FIRENGHIA

When Billy and Penny exited the portal, Ruger's castle was the first thing they saw. It stood out against the bright blue sky and the green fields, spoiling the natural beauty of the land. The black edifice sat high on a plateau and a spring-fed moat surrounded the castle making it all the more ominous. Strangely, enough, the drawbridge was up.

Billy sat on a nearby rock and stared at the castle for several minutes. The sight rekindled horrible memories from the past. Penny waited impatiently next to him also sensing that something was wrong. Faint noises could be heard over the wind's shrill whistle.

"Maybe Seneca's people moved into the castle," suggested Penny.

"I don't think it's the Firenghi inside the castle. Why don't you head to Firenghia and find Seneca? I'll check out the castle and see what's going on."

"That's a stupid idea, Billy."

"There's no point in the two of us getting caught in there. At least you can warn them about the castle."

"You know, Billy, I'm not going to argue with you so do what you want. I'll see you later."

Billy approached the castle, wary of anything suspicious. When he reached the moat, he recognized the log floating in the middle of the murky water. He recalled that fateful night when he pursued Pantheos into the castle. There were large snakes crawling in the water. Billy wondered how many of them were real and how many were part of Ruger's ill-fated magic show. He took a running start and jumped onto the log, followed by three quick steps and another leap toward solid ground. His left foot landed short and splashed in the ooze. Quickly, he planted his right foot on solid ground and stepped out of the water.

Billy hurried into the tunnel to the left of the drawbridge and hoped that none of Ruger's creatures remained inside. He looked back and saw six Dracor marching toward the castle. A loud clanking filled the air as chains scraped against the stone wall. The drawbridge descended as if on cue.

Billy trembled at the sight of the Dracor. He patted the leather bag on his belt for security. At the portal on the mountain, he used the skull successfully against the Dracor, so he knew he had some protection against them. After some deliberation, he ducked under the drawbridge and waited patiently. The sound of metal clapped against the thick wood and echoed through the tunnel as the Dracor passed over the drawbridge.

Billy's eyes adjusted to the darkness inside the tunnel. He hadn't used any of the skills and traits he inherited from Seneca since he returned home so they were degraded since his last excursion to Firenghia. He remembered Brutus, the saber-toothed tiger that saved his life on several occasions. It would have been nice to have the big cat with him now, even if only for companionship. The tiger's presence always gave him courage in situations like this.

Billy found the stairs that led to the main chamber. They were covered with cobwebs as thick as a baby's blanket in some places. Routinely, he swatted them from his face and hair. At times, he worried if the spiders that made them were poisonous.

— X —

Penny paused in a densely wooded area and pondered. In this land she was free: no cars, jobs, or responsibilities. Life was so simple here. She wondered if she could take her alter-shape and race the distance to Seneca's village. The sounds of snapping branches and crashing tree trunks alarmed her. She ducked behind the trees and watched warily for the source of the sounds.

Without warning, a hand covered her mouth and she was pulled down from behind. Her assailant quickly dragged her into a small cave and released her. When she looked up, she was surprised to see Rena, Seneca's cousin. Rena placed a finger to her lips, indicating silence.

The two women watched from the cave as six Dracor marched by, knocking down anything that stood in their way. "What's going on?" whispered Penny.

"Those robots came out of the castle seven nights ago. They've killed some of our people and sent the rest into hiding. Some were captured and taken into the castle."

"What about Seneca and Cassius? Are they okay?"

"Cassius led some of our people into the mountains."

"How about Seneca?"

"She was taken to the castle as a prisoner."

"How about the baby? Has Seneca given birth?"

"Yes. We have the baby in the cave. Seneca named him Will after Billy." Penny followed Rena to an open area in the rear of the cave.

A blonde-haired girl about six years old held Will. Penny instinctively reached for him but the young girl turned away defensively. Rena soothed her by patting her head gently. "It's okay Maya. Let her hold the baby. She's a friend." Young Maya reluctantly handed the baby to Penny.

"He's so cute," remarked Penny. "He even looks like Billy."

"What can we do, Penny?"

"Let's go back to the portal and wait for Billy."

"We'll follow you, but we must be careful of the robots. They are constantly patrolling the area."

"It's not far from here." Penny led Rena and the children to the portal. They were careful to stay hidden in the trees. When they reached the rocks near the portal, Penny directed them behind a large boulder. "We'll wait a little while for Billy to come back."

"Where did he go?" inquired Rena, concerned.

"Into the castle, like a nitwit," grumbled Penny.

"What was he thinking? It's dangerous in there."

"Sometimes Billy isn't the smartest person in the world. After a while you get used to his antics."

"Maybe he'll rescue Seneca."

"And maybe he'll get his fool self killed."

— X —

Billy ascended the steps to the landing at the top. The door was open just about the width of his body so he peered through. The walls were caked with thick layers of red and white meat-like substances that pulsed. The chamber looked a lot smaller than before and the pink glow made it all the more frightening.

Billy was horrified at what had become of the chamber. He feared that he was about to enter an alien creature's lair. As he inspected the lair, he recognized the shapes of people in the mass. He entered the room and examined the walls more closely. When he touched the strange matter, his finger tingled like a small electric current had passed from his hand. He pulled away and watched in awe. The substance quivered and shook.

Billy stared in horror at the figures buried inside the organic mass. Hysteria swept through him as he recognized Seneca, her face barely visible through the gelatinous substance. He immediately tried to use telepathy to communicate with her. She was alive but she was too weak to acknowledge him. He searched the room for something to cut her free, but found nothing. Then he remembered the skull and how it reacted to forces against it. He held the skull close to her and waited but nothing happened. He grew impatient and held his free hand close to the mass.

Then the tingle started again and the skull's eyes took on a blue tint. The fleshy substance quivered and peeled back from Seneca's face. Billy heard a vague sound like static electricity passing between the skull and the mass around Seneca. His heart raced as the process quickened. The substance slowly peeled away from Seneca's face and shoulders. After several minutes, Billy was able to pull Seneca free and lay her on the ground. He resumed the process of obliterating the mass, and the small buzz increased to a loud crackle.

Soon, the entire mass was reduced to a small luminous creature and the floor was littered with the bodies of seven other Firenghians. Tentacles emerged from underneath the creature and a high-pitched screech filled the room. Billy felt a stinging sensation inside his brain. He dropped the skull and placed his hands against his head. The small creature quickly retreated to a corner of the room and retracted its tentacles. The sensation stopped as quickly as it started.

Billy turned his attention to Seneca. She opened her eyes and strained to touch his face with her hand. He lifted her up and hugged her. "It's all right, Seneca. I'm here." He picked up the skull with his free hand and threw it at the alien creature. The skull embedded itself in the gelatinous creature's back and settled inside of it. Billy felt the stinging sensation return inside his head. "My head is killing me!"

Seneca pulled him toward her and whispered. "She's asking for mercy."

Billy was confused. How could a creature like this ask for mercy? He stared at the pink mass and wondered what Seneca meant. Seneca struggled to sit up. She was too weak to move or to use her telepathy. "Do you want me to retrieve the skull from that mess?" he asked.

"Yes. She won't hurt you."

Billy was uncomfortable with the idea of reaching inside the creature's body to retrieve the skull. Then he remembered that the skull would prevent it from doing any harm to him. He peered around the room at the bodies that lay lifeless on the floor. It was too late for them, but what about Seneca? He wondered if she would survive the ordeal.

Billy stuck his hand into the gooey mass and grasped the skull. He was surprised how easily he was able to reach through the mass and retrieve it. The warm ooze that dripped from his hand onto the floor repulsed him. He watched in amazement as the drops of gel scurried across the black stone floor to the host body. The creature slid across the floor until it reached Seneca's feet.

Billy poised with the skull to defend Seneca, but she gently touched his wrist. "No, Billy. She'll help me now." He was more confused than ever over what was happening. He watched and waited.

The creature reached for Seneca's legs with two tentacles. For a moment, the tentacles glowed and quivered. When the glowing ceased, the creature withdrew them. Seneca gained some of her strength back. "Thank you for saving me," said Seneca weakly.

"I don't understand. What's happening here?" he asked.

"She is the Dracor matriarch. With the skull in her, the others would die. She wouldn't be able to morph or nourish them in this state."

"Is that a bad thing? I thought we hated the Dracor."

"They are fighting a battle on their world for the survival of their race."

"With who?" asked Billy.

"Another alien race. By sparing her, we've earned her loyalty. She owes us her life and the lives of the other Dracor."

"So now what?" asked Billy curiously.

"She's going to transform into another shape. The Dracor change like shape-shifters do, except that their shapes can only mimic their hosts. She will mimic qualities of my body to transform into one of us."

Billy held Seneca in his arms, while the creature grew into a giant larva. "I don't like this, Seneca. Let's get out of here."

"No, Billy. Not yet."

"What did that thing do to you?"

"I don't know. Maybe it's my life force, I have no idea."

"Are you going to be okay?"

"Now I will. My body has begun to heal."

After an hour had passed, the white larva quivered. Billy and Seneca watched in awe as the larva peeled away and a woman emerged from the jelly like substance. The wet residue dried from her pale skin and blond hair. She lay naked on the floor, shivering. When she opened her eyes, a smile came across her face.

Billy was shocked by the appearance of such a lovely woman from something so horrible who, in many ways, resembled Seneca. The woman stood before him and struggled for several seconds to speak. Finally, words flowed from her mouth. "Thank you for sparing me."

"For what?" challenged Billy. "So you can kill more of my friends."

"I'm sorry for what I've done to your friends. When we discovered the portal to your world, we thought we could escape our enemies."

"But why did they attack our people? We could have helped you."

"We watched the cloaked one for a period of time from the portal. He was evil and we assumed that all of you were evil. Besides, you killed some of our people too."

Billy took off his long sleeve shirt and offered it to her for warmth. "Put this on. You're trembling."

"Thank you for your concern," she said, grateful for his understanding. The shirt was just long enough to provide her with sufficient coverage for modesty.

"While I was inside her, we communicated," explained Seneca.

"The Dracor assumed the shapes of certain creatures to hide from their attackers. Before doing so, they designed the robot shell for their protection."

Billy was both impressed and mortified by the story. He thought of all the Firenghi and Sarcassons that died at the hands of the Dracor. "Okay, so where do we go from here?" he asked.

"I will take you through the portal and show you what's happening to my people," the woman explained.

"Do you have a name?" asked Billy.

"Ginea," she replied humbly.

"Why are your people being attacked?"

"Pendragon has united a number of alien races to strike at the inhabitants of this quadrant."

"But why would he do that?"

"The people of this quadrant assassinated several of the alien leaders and soon after that, Pendragon's offspring. They believe it was a conspiracy by all of us who live in this quadrant."

"Who is Pendragon?" Billy questioned her.

"He is the leader of one of the fiercest alien races, you'll ever encounter – the Andorans. Our robots were designed to fight them off, but their weapons have proved too much for our armor. In my former shape, my people could not develop new armor. We were constantly fighting for our lives."

"But if someone really wanted to assassinate them, then perhaps you could turn them over to Pendragon."

"I don't think you want to us to do that."

"Why not?" asked Billy, baffled by her remark.

"Because they were humans."

"What?" exclaimed Billy. "That's impossible!"

"No, it's the truth. It wasn't our business to interfere, but Pendragon's attack against us made it our business."

"Why would humans do this? There must have been something to provoke them."

"It seems that the Andoran race is plagued with a disease that they can't overcome. They hoped that by improving their bloodline, they could cure the disease or have the intelligence to overcome it. Pendragon mated with a human woman, a witch, from a distant colony, to create a more stable bloodline. The humans were afraid that a smarter bloodline would threaten them. They like to think they are the smartest race in the universe."

"I'll bet that Diomedes was Pendragon's mate," remarked Billy.

"This could have other implications as well," warned Seneca.

Billy thought for a moment and realized something terrible. "Pendragon will really be upset if he knows that it was me and Penny who killed his mate!"

"It is our understanding that Pendragon and his mate had an ability to communicate over long distances. If you killed his mate, I'm sure he knows it was you," said Ginea somberly.

Billy wore a pained expression on his face. "Let's get this over with. I'm getting jittery already."

Billy helped Seneca to her feet. She was wobbly at first, but her balance and strength soon increased to a point where she could walk slowly. Once she stood without support, they followed Ginea into the portal. When they emerged on the other side, they were in one of a series of caves.

Ginea guided them through the dark and damp cave toward an eerie light. Drops of moisture fell from the roof of the cave, giving Billy a chilled sensation. Occasionally, the sounds of small, flying creatures could be heard rustling about in the darkness. Ginea sensed Billy's uneasiness at the sounds. She assured him that they were safe.

They exited the cave and Billy's first impression of the Dracor world was a gloomy one. The landscape was barren and rocky. The sky was filled with plumes of smoke, and alien spaceships hovered across the battlefield. They fired random shots at the retreating Dracor. A green, reptilian creature jumped on the back of a Dracor robot about twenty yards from Billy. It pounded relentlessly on the glass cover that protected the tiny creature.

"That's the only weak spot in the design of the armor," Ginea admitted.

"That's horrible," Seneca replied. "Isn't there anything you can do?"

"No. I must survive for the others to survive."

"I'll be right back," Billy whispered and rushed from the shelter of the cave toward the combatants. He picked up the Dracor's weapon and attempted to fire a shot at the Andoran. It wasn't equipped with a trigger like he expected. "Squeeze it!" shouted Ginea. "The weapon works off of pressure."

Billy frantically clutched the gun in various places, hoping it would fire. When he squeezed the barrel, the gun fired a weak pulse at the Andoran and knocked it down. The creature got up and marched toward him.

"Squeeze harder, Billy!" shouted Ginea. Billy squeezed the barrel as hard as he could. The gun generated a bright pulse that burned a huge hole through the creature's midsection. He and the injured Dracor retreated toward the cave.

Another Andoran perched over the corpse of its comrade and let loose a blood-curdling scream. Billy was terrified of the creature and froze while the others fled into the cave. The Andoran spotted Billy near the cave's entrance. Its eyes grew wide as if it recognized him. It stood seven feet tall, with two ridges from its head down to the end of its short tail. Its eyes bulged big, with a green glow. The Andoran was amazingly mobile, while hunched on two powerful legs. Its arms were human-like and ended with three finger-shaped appendages on each hand. In four quick strides, it drew close enough to Billy to study him.

"I know you!" screamed the Andoran.

"Oh shit!" Billy blurted.

"Who are you? Tell me!"

Chills went down Billy's spine as he wondered whether or not he should respond. He already made eye contact with the creature and knew he had to say something. "I'm no one important." Billy rushed into the cave and disappeared through the portal before the Andoran could catch him.

When they returned to the chamber, Billy uttered, "It looks like the Dracor world is in a lot of trouble."

"It looks like you're in bigger trouble than we are," replied Ginea. "He recognized you."

"Thanks a lot, Ginea."

"Now you understand our plight."

"Yeah, I do," Billy admitted.

"I want to bring the surviving Dracor here, inside the castle," she explained. "They'll morph with me and take a human shape. It takes a few days and, as you saw, it's a messy process. I'd prefer we did this in privacy. We'll close the drawbridge during the transformation."

"Then what?"

"I don't know. Maybe your people can think of something by then."

"Do you know who the humans were that caused this?"

"I've heard them referred to as the Council."

Billy was stunned. "Not the Council of Guardians!"

"That's all I know of the matter."

"Seneca, this means Xerxes lied to us. Why would he do that?"

"Don't get ahead of yourself, Billy. Let's find out what happened first."

"Ginea, we're going to leave you now. We'll come back later when you've restored your people. In the meantime, I've got to get some answers."

"Please don't forget us. We're on the verge of extinction."

"I won't. Do you want the portal closed? I can do that."

"No. The remaining Dracor would be cut off and slaughtered. We'll be careful to keep it concealed."

"Well, good luck, Ginea."

"You, too. I think you're going to need it."

Billy put an arm around Seneca's waist and helped her out of the chamber. She still had some difficulty maintaining her balance, but she continued to improve. After much effort, Billy and Seneca left the castle and set out for the portal.

When they reached the trees at the bottom of the plateau, Seneca paused.

"Are you okay?" asked Billy, concerned for her.

Seneca put her arms around Billy's shoulders and pulled him toward her. They kissed passionately. "I'm so glad to see you, Billy. I dreamed of you every night."

"I missed you, too, Seneca. Things have really been tough since we last met."

"I could feel your pain and Penny's as well, despite the distance."

"I sensed that something was wrong here," Billy revealed. "That's how I knew to come back."

"It's good that you did. I don't think I would have survived much longer." They continued toward Seneca's village.

"How is the baby?" inquired Billy.

Seneca smiled slyly. "Have you seen Will?"

"No, not yet. I'm sorry I missed his birth."

"He came a bit early. I guess he was in a hurry, just like his father."

"We'll make up for lost time."

"There's always going to be something that will interfere with our lives. We'll never make up lost time."

"Come on, Seneca. You've got to believe that we can. Even if things are bad, our love and friendship will keep us going."

"What are we going to do now?" she inquired.

"We'll return to the portal first to see if Penny's there. She was supposed to go to Firenghia and find you. I stayed because I saw the drawbridge up."

"What really made you come back?"

Billy stopped and took Seneca's hands in his. He kissed her again. "I missed you, Seneca. Besides, I wanted to see how you and the baby were doing."

"I named him Will Saris. I hope you approve."

"Of course, I do. Where is he now?"

"With Rena. She left with the baby and some of the children to escape the Dracor patrols."

"We'll find them. Maybe, Penny already has."

They walked again along the tree line at the edge of a vast field. "You and Penny are struggling with your relationship," commented Seneca.

"Yeah, we are. I don't know how much more I can put up with her."

"Be patient with her."

"But Seneca, everything I do is wrong in her eyes."

"Maybe that's not the reason. Maybe she needs to feel important to you."

"She is important to me."

"Then you must show her. I feel that she's going through a difficult time."

"Her mother just passed away," Billy informed her.

"Then you must support her like a father."

"I'll keep trying."

"I'm glad you came back, and not a moment too soon, I might add."

"I still don't understand why Ginea helped you."

"Because she needed me to have you remove the skull. It would have prevented her from morphing the other Dracor into a different shape. Even worse, she would not be able to nourish herself nor the others in their current shape. If she tried, the skull would deplete her of her own nutrients. In a short time, the Dracor would cease to exist. So, not only did you spare her, you spared her race."

"And now we're friends?"

"Yes, we are. I think we can count on them as loyal allies, especially after you saved the Dracor soldier back there."

"Well, now you have new neighbors in the castle," he joked.

Penny heard their voices and rushed from behind the boulder. "Billy! Seneca! You're back." Rena followed Penny, carrying Will in her arms.

Penny and Seneca embraced. "Hello, sister. It's been a while," said Seneca.

"Yes, it has," replied Penny tearfully.

"I know you're hurting. I'll help you find peace."

"I hope so. I'm going crazy like this."

Billy felt bad for Penny and realized that maybe he wasn't there for her emotionally.

Rena offered the baby to Billy. He was speechless as he took the baby from her and hugged him affectionately. "I don't know what to say. This is my son!" he exclaimed.

Seneca smiled proudly. "Isn't he adorable?"

"Congratulations on a lovely baby," Penny said cheerfully as her mood improved. "Are you okay? You don't look well."

"I'm better now, thanks to Billy," stated Seneca.

"Shall we go on to Firenghia?" suggested Billy.

"Yes. We'll send word to Cassius that it's safe to return. He'll be glad to see you."

"Is anybody going to tell me what happened?" asked Penny anxiously.

"Perhaps you can relate the story to her, Seneca. I'm still not sure what happened back there."

"Very well, then. Come with me to the village and I'll tell you everything."

Seneca sent two of the young girls into the mountains to find Cassius and give him the news of Billy's return and the new truce with the Dracor. They continued their trek to Firenghia. Billy carried the baby until feeding time.

When they finally reached Firenghia, the area was desolate. Most of the houses had been destroyed and the beautiful trees were toppled. "I guess we'll have to rebuild and start over again," said Seneca dejectedly. Billy felt sympathy for Seneca and her people.

The evening air was cool and damp outside. A light breeze made soothing sounds against the patched, thatched roof. Billy sat quietly in the corner of the room with Will in his arms. He found it hard to believe that this was his own flesh and blood. He witnessed neither Seneca's term nor the birth of Will, which created a feeling of guilt within him. Inside, he still felt confused about the whole relationship.

Seneca entered the room. "This is hard for you, isn't it?" she asked humbly.

"Yes, it is. My world is so different. There you had nine months to think about the baby's birth. You saw your partner through the whole pregnancy."

"I'm sorry. I didn't think it would be this complicated for you."

Billy smiled at Seneca. "You're beautiful, Seneca. Will is beautiful, too."

Seneca kissed Billy on the cheek. "I missed you and Penny so much. I didn't know how to contact you. I just wanted to hear your voices again."

"Well, we're taking care of that problem. Xerxes is supposed to relocate a portal near your home."

"What do you think about Ginea's situation?" she asked him, concerned by Ginea's revelation.

"I need to meet with Xerxes and find out what actually happened. I hope the story isn't true but, if it is, it changes everything."

Penny joined them and they sat together for most of the evening. They discussed how their lives had changed since they met. As the daylight faded, Billy stood up and kissed Seneca. "It's time for me to go. I'll be back."

"Come back soon, Billy," pleaded Seneca.

"I will." Billy left the girls.

A roar of laughter filled the street as Cassius and Xanther approached him, accompanied by Tybis. Cassius looked like the masculine specimen that Billy first met, with his long brown hair tossed across his brawny shoulders. Billy was impressed with his muscle-bound features. He wished that someday he might have a physique like that.

Cassius seemed fully recovered from his torture and captivity in Ruger's Castle. Xanther was tall like Seneca but with long, beautiful, blond hair. She held onto Cassius' arm tightly as they approached Billy. She made no bones about it that Cassius was her mate.

"It's good to see you again, my friend!" shouted Cassius and he man-hugged Billy. "How does it feel to be a father?"

"I'm still getting used to it. You look great Cassius. Xanther, you look stunning as usual."

"Thank you, Billy," she replied modestly. "That's so nice of you to say so."

Xanther and Cassius each placed an arm on Billy's shoulder. "So, Billy, you saved us again," Cassius commented proudly. "Thanks so much for rescuing Seneca and taking care of the Dracor. How did you do it?"

"It wasn't quite what you'd expect. Once I freed Seneca, she took over from there. Besides, the skull did the hard part."

"So, the Dracor are our friends, I mean neighbors now."

"I think you'll see them in a different way, from now on."

"What do you mean?"

"They won't look like jelly fish or ride around in high tech armor anymore."

"No? Then what will they be?"

"Like us. Can you believe that?"

"That's a relief. They were unstoppable in their robot form."

"Not for the Andorans. They beat the crap out of the Dracor."

"The Andorans?"

"Yeah, they're invading the Dracor world as we speak."

"Will they come here?"

"I hope not. At least not until we can defend against them."

"I knew you'd find some way to stop the Dracor assault. You are so lucky to have your technology for protection."

"It's not like the old days with spears and swords," said Billy disappointedly.

"And magic, too," added Xanther.

"Yeah, and magic, too. What a pain in the ass that was," Billy complained.

"How long are you staying?" asked Cassius.

"Not very long, I'm afraid. I found out some disturbing news from the Dracor so I need to go back and meet with Xerxes."

"Will you have time later on? Xanther would like for you and Penny to join us for dinner."

"That would be great. I'll get back to you as soon as I resolve this new business."

"We must leave you now so we can rebuild our home," Cassius uttered regretfully.

"I understand."

"We'll see you in a few days," said Xanther and they left him.

Billy found Penny sitting under a shady tree. She enjoyed herself in the cool breeze. "Are you ready to go back?" he asked.

"Would it bother you if I stayed for a little while?"

"Why? Is something wrong?"

"No, it's just that I feel so alive here. I'm at peace in this world."

"If that's what you really want to do."

"It is. I think it would do me good to spend some time here with Seneca, Rena and the baby."

"Penny, I can tell something is bothering you. You've learned to cloak your thoughts from me quite well. What's wrong?"

"Billy, I don't know how to say this. I've been thinking about it for a while and I don't want to go back. I feel like I belong here. Would you consider staying here?"

"I can't, Penny. Maybe in the future, but not now."

"Then I think we should part ways. I think it's what's best for both of us." Billy was speechless and couldn't believe what he just heard.

Penny sensed his disappointment. "Billy, we're still friends. Maybe later things will be different."

Billy felt betrayed and would never come to terms with her decision. "Then so be it," he said somberly and left.

Something still didn't feel right in his gut. He couldn't stop thinking about Pendragon as he entered the portal and returned to the research center.

Seneca invited Penny to walk with her while Rena tended to Will. The two women left the village in the evening and went into the hills. They hiked in the dark until they found a peaceful clearing. "Seneca, let's sit for a bit. There's something I want to talk to you about."

"What is it, Penny?"

"It's Billy. No, I mean me. I feel like I belong here. I want to stay here and be a Firenghi like you and Rena. Since we met and I became like you, I've developed and matured in a lot of ways. I feel like I'm in control of my life for once and I don't need anyone."

"And that includes Billy?"

"Well, yes. I'm not dependent on him anymore. I want to be free to experience my alter-shape without fear. Billy doesn't want to embrace his alter-shape like I do."

"What do you want to do?"

"I'd like to stay here, at least for a while. I'll always want Billy when he's around, but when he's not, I want to live."

"Does he know that you feel this way?"

"Well, yes. I just told him that I was staying."

"How do you think he'll handle it?"

"I don't know. Sadly, I really don't care," she remarked callously.

"It's wise to express your feelings now than to hurt him later. You are welcome to stay with me as a Firenghi and as my sister. You do realize that later Billy may not be there for you?"

"Yes, I do. So long as I have my freedom here, I'm not worried about it."

"So long as you've weighed the consequences of you decision, you will be fine."

"Thanks for listening and understanding."

CHAPTER 4

CHAOS

Goliathan stood before Xerxes in a flowing white robe, displaying a look of arrogance across his face. "Why did you bring them here, Xerxes?"

"Because we couldn't make it back to the research center," responded Xerxes with an attitude. "The *Excelsior* is too badly damaged."

"You know we forbid anyone other than the Council to come here. Take those people back to base. I don't want them here."

"Excuse me, Goliathan, but do you have any idea what is happening out there? The CS-11s are gone. We're vulnerable at the portals now."

"It's nothing that the Earthers can't handle."

Xerxes became enraged. "That's exactly the attitude that created this mess!"

"You should remember whom you're speaking to. I am head of the Council and you are a subordinate member," Goliathan replied smugly.

"Once upon a time, that was something to be proud of. Now, I don't care. I'm disappointed in you and the Council. Instead of being the guardians for these people, you're playing them like pawns. You and the others are content to lavish in your private colony and play God."

"Remember, Xerxes, I made you what you are – a member of the Council."

"I'm sure you'll never let me forget it either!" Xerxes stormed from the room and returned to the *Excelsior*.

— ✗ —

The Englishmen and Mustafo's crew waited anxiously for his response. "Come on, everyone. We're taking a portal back to Earth," Xerxes announced reluctantly. "The ship is done."

"That's it?" asked Tera impatiently.

'Not now, Tera."

"Did you talk to the Council?"

"It's a long story. Right now we need to get back to Earth and make preparations."

"What kind of preparations?" asked John.

"I don't know. We need to figure out what's going on with the alien races and how we're going to deal with them."

Xerxes pointed the PCU at the wall and pressed several buttons. A blue ball of light formed in front of them. It continued to grow until it formed the swirling mist that they were accustomed to. He led them through to the other side.

— ✗ —

Tur did his best to control the *Starfire* but the ship vibrated violently and bounced off the outer edges of the portal. The fields didn't react very well each time the ship strayed from the center of the portal and made contact. When the *Starfire* cleared the portal, it skidded across one of the decks inside the transport bay and drifted into the wall with a bang. The damage to the bay wall was minimal but the ship was a fiery disaster. Fire crews raced out and sprayed the fuselage down with foam to contain the fire and prevent any further damage.

When Tur and Hassim emerged from the crippled spacecraft, Tur immediately noticed that the *Excelsior* was missing. "Wasn't the *Excelsior* due back by now?"

"Yes, she was," replied Hassim.

"We'd better get upstairs and see what's going on."

Tur instructed Doc, Maggie, Ronnie and Randy to bring the children with them. He had no idea what to do with them or who to leave them with.

— X —

Xerxes pager beeped and displayed a message. He frowned as he read it.

"What is it, Xerxes?" inquired John worriedly.

"The *Starfire* is badly damaged and crashed into the transport bay wall upon landing. No apparent injuries."

"So, ours isn't an isolated incident," remarked Seamus. "Apparently, no one is safe out here."

"Does anybody know how far the alien forces have come or where they are positioned?" asked John.

"Let's see what happened to the *Starfire* first before we jump to conclusions."

"It's a little late to jump to conclusions!" shouted Mustafo angrily. "Why weren't we warned about the alien advances?"

"I know how you feel. I was there, too," Xerxes reminded him. "The Council made the decision that the aliens weren't a threat in this quadrant."

The door opened and Tur led his group into the room. Ronnie and Randy entered last behind the children. John and Seamus were relieved to see them safe.

"Are you girls alright?" asked Seamus anxiously.

"Absolutely," replied Ronnie. "Randy and I shot up the alien air force. What a rush!"

"Whose children are these? Why are they here?" inquired Xerxes.

"These are the only survivors from Alpha-17," answered Tur sarcastically. "My sister lived on Alpha-17. It's a secure sector. This could never happen, according to the Council. What else did the Council guarantee us?"

Xerxes looked shocked. "Tell me what happened on Alpha-17!"

Tur related the story while everyone in the room listened intently. John and Seamus felt somewhat embarrassed by the success that Ronnie and Randy had with the cannons.

"All that simulator training and we shoot up a bunch of rocks. The two of you go out there with no training at all and go right into real combat," complained John.

"Aren't you happy for us, John?" asked Ronnie.

"Yeah, but…"

Tur added, "It's a good thing they shot as well as they did because the weapons system power bank was down to ten percent. They had about twelve shots left and the system would have shut down."

"Look everyone; we have a big problem here," Xerxes admitted. "Our defenses, the CS-11s, are destroyed. Going into and out of the portals is going to be dangerous from now on. The alien forces have found a way to reach this part of the universe. Let's put our heads together and figure out what we're going to do about it."

The door opened and Billy entered. The conversation stopped as he stood in front of them. "Sorry to interrupt the meeting, everyone, but we have some big problems."

"Welcome to the club," Xerxes replied cynically. "What have you encountered?"

"The Dracor planet has been invaded by Andorans," Billy announced.

"How do you know this?"

"I was there. I met the matriarch of the Dracor in Ruger's castle. She took me through a portal that Ruger left open. I witnessed the Dracor and the Andorans fighting."

"What does that have to do with us?" questioned Xerxes, curious.

"Ginea the Dracor matriarch told me how the war started."

"She doesn't know anything about the war!" shouted Xerxes, frustrated.

"I beg to differ. The Council attempted to assassinate the alien leaders and failed. The Council then killed the offspring of the Andoran leader, Pendragon."

"I was told by the Council that they were a threat," responded Xerxes. "They were mutated and bred to kill."

"No, Xerxes. The Andoran race is dying. They are trying to breed a generation that can either cure their disease or become immune to it."

"That can't be!" Xerxes exclaimed. "That's not what Jasper said."

"Pendragon's mate was Diomedes, the same Diomedes that we killed. Pendragon knows that it was Penny and I who killed her. So, not only does he want revenge on the humans who assassinated some of their leaders and offspring, he wants me and Penny, too."

"Do you believe all this propaganda, Billy?" an embarrassed Xerxes asked defensively.

"Yes, I do. Pendragon has united several of the alien races and they will not stop until they destroy all of us."

"When we heard the message from the *Aurora-32*, we heard a loud humming sound," explained Tur. "We heard that same sound when a large black cloud grew in the distance on Alpha-17. The alien fighters appeared from within the cloud in large numbers. What is the black cloud and what is the humming sound that precedes it?"

Xerxes paced the floor and thought about Tur's observation. "It seems that the aliens have generated their own wormhole technology. It sounds primitive compared to ours but it obviously works."

"How do you know it's primitive?" asked Ronnie.

"It's like comparing a beam of light to a pipe. Which would you prefer to travel in?"

"But why a black cloud?"

"The cloud is caused by elements from another atmosphere combining with the oxygen in our environment."

"What do we have available for defense?" inquired Billy.

"The *Excelsior* and the *Starfire* are scrap, which leaves us the *Exeter* and the *Specter*. They aren't ready for weapons testing yet. What we can do is transfer the weapons systems from the *Excelsior* and the *Starfire* to the *Luna C* and *Trav ST*, as your people have aptly named them. By next week, the *Specter* and the *Exeter* should be ready."

"We need to find out where the enemy is positioned. We'll need numbers and capability before we confront them," John informed Xerxes.

"So how do you suggest we find that out?" Xerxes countered cynically.

"We should send one of our ships out there to scout the area around the portal," suggested Randy. "It's risky but we can't do anything unless we know where they are."

"I can arrange to have the *Specter* ready to go by tomorrow. Do any of you want to volunteer for this mission?"

Commander Mustafo immediately raised his hand. "I'll go. I want those bastards."

"As do I," added Tur.

"I want some more of those bad boys," Ronnie declared anxiously.

"I think John and Seamus should stay here and help establish a battle plan," suggested Xerxes.

"Is one ship going to be enough?" asked Seamus.

"It has to be," Xerxes replied somberly.

"That's not much of a defense against a swarm of fighters."

"There's not much choice, Seamus. We have to do this," replied Ronnie.

Neither Seamus nor John was happy with the arrangement. "Doc, I'd like you to put together a team to figure out a way to block their wormhole," requested Xerxes. "Hopefully you'll have an idea how it works before the information comes in from the *Specter*. Perhaps, we can develop a strategy to push the Andoran forces back from Dracor. We have to start the battle somewhere, so it might as well be there."

"It will take time for us to change our sphere of thinking to a galactic level, but we'll do our best," promised John.

"I'll return to the Dracor world and see what else I can find out," volunteered Billy. "Perhaps, I can find out more about the aliens. I can talk to Ginea, too. Maybe the remaining Dracor can help provide us with intelligence as well."

"Anything you learn could at least help us buy some time until we get a plan together. Maybe we can gather enough of the Dracor forces to join us in battle."

"I don't think there's much left of their forces to fight," Billy mentioned pessimistically.

"Then, it's all we can do at this point. I'll arrange for the *Specter* to be ready for flight by morning. For now, I think we can all use some rest. It's getting late and we have a lot to accomplish tomorrow."

Billy accompanied Doc to his office, where he gathered both his and Penny's luggage. "I can give you a room on the fifth floor. You can store your things there," offered Doc.

"Thanks. I'd appreciate that."

"I'm sure you're a bit nervous about this Pendragon character," Doc commented.

"I met the green bastard already," confessed Billy. "He's scary as hell and he recognized me."

As they approached the elevator, Doc briefed Billy on everything that happened to the *Excelsior* and the *Starfire*. They took the luggage to Billy's room on the fifth floor and dropped everything in the middle of the floor. Billy requested a visit with Sam before he departed.

Doc picked up the telephone located on the wall, punched in four numbers and paged him. "Sam McDermott, please dial 4331. Sam McDermott, please dial 4331."

"His lab?" questioned Billy, surprised. "Is this the same Sam McDermott I used to know?"

"Oh, believe me, he hasn't changed. He just has better resources to apply his skills to."

The phone rang, sending an echo down the hall. Doc answered, "Hi, Sam. It's Doc Smith. Where are you?" He listened briefly before answering. "Good. I have a visitor here who wants to see you. I believe he's an old friend of yours." Doc hung up the phone and said, "He's in the lab. Let's go." They entered the elevator at the end of the hall.

"What's he working on?" inquired Billy

"He's designing new weapons and protective gear. Some of Xerxes people from Iteria-5 are assisting him. They trade ideas, materials and concepts to develop new and useful equipment and gear."

"Good old Sam. Quite a crowd pleaser."

"Yes, he's a very unique individual."

They exited the elevator on level four and followed a long stretch of hallway. The last door on the left was marked "MATERIAL TESTING AND DEVELOPMENT-AUTHORIZED PERSONNEL ONLY."

"Well, Billy, here it is." Doc slid his card through the slot on the reader and the door silently slid open. They entered the room and found Sam sitting on a stool, working a set of robotic arms inside a tank.

Sam was surprised to see Billy. "Well, hello, stranger. What brings you to my netherworld?" He pulled his arms out of the artificial limbs.

"Sam, how the heck are you?" greeted Billy.

"I'm great. I wondered if I'd ever see you again." Sam stood up and shook Billy's hand.

"I know. It's been too long."

"So, what brings you back here?" Sam asked, curious.

"There's trouble in Firenghia," Billy replied. "And what's going on here," he asked, scanning Sam's lab.

"This is a little side project that's been bothering me for a while," explained Sam. "I got this gadget that looks like a watch from one of those furry creatures in the old world. I've been trying to figure out what it does and how it works."

Billy looked through the glass at the device and recognized it immediately. "Hey, Doc, isn't that one of those transmitter devices that you had me get rid of?"

Doc looked through the glass at the object. "Yes, it is," he said in a concerned tone.

"Where did you get that from, Sam?" inquired Billy.

"I took it off one of Ruger's minions the night we attacked his army and entered the castle."

"What have you found out about it?" asked Doc.

"Well, the inside has a strange ore in it. It's radioactive but in a different way than we've ever seen. Something on it reacts with oxygen and creates a black vapor. Between that and the radiation, it seemed safer to put it inside a vacuum tank."

"You said it gave off a black vapor?"

"Yeah, it was really funky."

"What about the radiation?"

"Well, it seems to pulse irregularly and the field is made up of some form of energy. It seems to be pretty strong, but I haven't figured out what it is. It's not like any radioactive material on this planet. I've been running tests on it and I have all the notes."

"That's great!" exclaimed Billy. "We need to get Xerxes' metallurgist on this right away. It could be the clue we're looking for." Sam offered to contact her and summon her immediately. Billy explained that it could be critical and directly related to the alien attacks on the other planets. "So how are you doing, Sam?" asked Billy.

"I'm fine. I'm a little lonely down here so it's good to see an old friend."

"Perhaps I can find you a friend to keep you out of trouble," Billy kidded.

"This lab stuff is good but it isn't like the old days. Those battles with the minions were something."

Doc ended their conversation, saying "Billy and I will leave now and contact you later."

"Sorry, Billy. Duty calls. Catch me next time for a drink."

"Will do, Sam. Take care, Buddy." Billy followed Doc out of the lab and down the corridor.

"The material in that device could be the same element used in their portal system. We might be able to disable it if we know how it works," suggested Doc.

"But what if it's a transmitter or a beacon? They may be using it to target us next."

"That's a good point. Let's see what the metallurgist comes up with, and then we'll decide what to do with it. What time will you leave tomorrow?"

"Probably around noon," replied Billy. "That will put me in Firenghia around daybreak."

— X —

Penny and Seneca changed into their alter-shapes. They dashed about the countryside playfully. Penny felt free and wild, forgetting all her troubles and grief. She was proud of her alter-shape as a snow leopard and craved every opportunity to transform. She felt as if this was her destiny - to roam freely without boundaries or limits. They rushed around the ancient oak trees before stopping near a ledge to examine the beautiful valley below.

Seneca noticed a large black cloud forming over the mountain. She and Penny changed back into their human forms and studied the cloud. "That can't be anything good, Penny."

"I know what you mean. Perhaps we should get back and warn the others."

The two changed again into their alter-shapes and hurried back to the village. Seneca found Cassius in his cottage, sitting peacefully with his mate Xanther. "Cassius, there's trouble in the mountains!"

Xanther was irritated at first by the intrusion but one look from Seneca told her that this was a serious matter. "Dear sister, whatever do you mean?" Cassius asked.

"There's a large black cloud forming over the mountain."

"So what? It's a cloud."

"No! There's something really frightening about this cloud. I think we need to evacuate and hide until we know what's happening."

Seneca hurried out of the cottage. "What did he say?" asked Penny.

"I instructed him to evacuate and hide. Follow me." Seneca spotted Rena a short distance away. She sat with baby Will on her lap as the other children played. "Rena, take the children back to the cave until we come for you," ordered Seneca.

Rena was surprised by her sense of urgency. "What's wrong?"

"Something evil's happening over the mountains."

Cassius and Xanther joined them. "When will this misery end? One problem leads into another," complained Cassius.

"I don't know if it ever will, my brother. We have been cursed since Ruger's sins were cast upon us."

"I want to stay with you and Cassius," said Penny adamantly.

"Are you sure?" questioned Seneca. "This could be your last chance to leave."

"Remember, Penny's our only link to Billy if we need help," Cassius reminded her.

"Don't worry, he'll be back tomorrow," Penny assured them.

Cassius cursed under his breath, arousing Seneca's concern. "What is it, Cassius?"

"Look at all those lights shooting from the cloud. There are hundreds of them, like tiny fireflies."

"Everyone, take cover, quickly!" ordered Seneca.

Smoke rose across the plains and from the mountains. When the red and yellow lights drew closer, they descended on Firenghia. "Those lights; they're spaceships. We're being attacked!" cried Penny.

"We're going into the mountains, now," ordered Cassius.

The alien spaceships were like flies, landing all around them. Before Penny and her friends could reach the safety of the trees, they were cut off by one of the ships. The hatch opened and dozens of Andorans emerged, carrying weapons. They wore thick leather vests over their lizard-like bodies and helmets to match. They quickly surrounded them.

One of the Andorans approached Cassius and studied him. "What do you want from us?" questioned Cassius. "We've done you no harm."

"And for that, you'll live. We're taking you prisoner."

"Where are we going?" Penny demanded to know.

"You'll never see this place again. Now, get on the ship!"

"They're Andorans," remarked Seneca. "They're the ones who invaded the Dracor world."

"How do you know this?" asked Cassius in surprise.

"Ginea showed us what was left of her world. She's the Dracor matriarch inside Ruger's castle."

The nearest Andoran had a keen sense of hearing and approached them. "What do you think you know of Andorans? After all, you conspired to wipe us out!"

"We knew nothing of the matter," replied Cassius. "For years, an evil wizard and his demons have hunted us down. We couldn't have been involved in this plot."

"This wizard, his name was Ruger?" questioned the Andoran.

"Yes, why?"

"You shouldn't have told him that, Cassius," said Penny nervously.

"What do you know of his demon mate?" the Andoran inquired further.

"She was the evil Diomedes," replied Seneca. "She and Ruger were both slain in the castle. We had nothing to do with hunting your people down."

Penny placed her hand across her forehead and uttered, "Oh, boy. You really shouldn't have told him that, Seneca."

"Why not?"

"If you only knew where this is going."

The alien removed his helmet and approached the three of them. "Who killed Diomedes?"

"Oh, shit!" stammered Penny. "You must be Pendragon."

"One of you will tell me who killed her or you'll all die. You have until the time we return to Andor to reveal who did it."

"But we don't know!" exclaimed Cassius. Pendragon punched Cassius in the face and knocked him to the ground. Cassius got up slowly, somewhat dazed and bloody.

"Get on the ship now or you'll die here," ordered the Andoran. Reluctantly, they boarded the ship with many other Firenghian captives.

— X —

Billy promptly returned to Firenghia and knew something bad had already happened when he saw the rising smoke over the plains and the mountains. Everywhere he searched, he found no traces of its inhabitants- neither survivors, nor corpses. He spotted the large black cloud on the horizon and watched in horror as hundreds of tiny lights disappeared into the cloud. *The Andorans must have taken them prisoner!* he thought.

Billy hurried to Ruger's castle in hopes of finding the Dracor. Perhaps they could help him find the Firenghi. He raced across the fields as fast as his legs would carry him. Inside, he felt an urge tear at him. Part of him wanted to change into his alter-shape and run but he suppressed it. As he ascended the wooded hill near the castle, he could see the drawbridge was down. *Ginea was supposed to close the drawbridge during the Dracor morphing. Something must have happened in the castle as well,* he surmised.

Billy stumbled across some rocks and fell to the ground. Frustration mounted inside and he became angry. "I'm getting fed up with all these friggin' aliens," he grumbled to himself. "They're really starting to get under my skin now."

Billy's insides cramped and his body quivered. He shed his clothes and feared what was happening to him. "Oh, no!" he cried. "Not now."

After several agonizing moments, he transformed into his alter shape, a fierce wolverine. His clothes quickly shredded and fell uselessly onto the damp, clay ground. As much as he tried to deny his alter-shape, it was a part of him, whether he liked it or not. He wondered if it could someday be a good thing when he learned to control it.

Billy raced up to the plateau in his alter-shape to the log in the moat. He crept across the drawbridge and entered the castle. Once he reached the courtyard, he changed back to his human form. He scanned the area and recollected some of the horrible memories he had in the castle. To his left was the large opening where Tybis' friend fell, only to be devoured by Ruger's creatures.

The remains of several corpses were scattered across the courtyard. The smell of their rotting flesh still clogged the air. Billy gagged with nausea as he passed the mutilated bodies of slain Firenghi and Sarcasson warriors. Then he reached the stables where the Dracor slaughtered so many of Tybis' warriors.

Billy cringed as he recalled how many people died in the castle. He felt as though the ghosts still haunted the grounds. As much as he dreaded going into those rooms, he needed to put on some clothes.

The castle was very chilly and a cold draft blew through the courtyard. Billy trembled as he thought of the souls of the departed biding their time in the castle. He searched several of the rooms until he found a blanket and some rope. He made himself a robe to cover his naked body.

Billy hurried down a long corridor and reached the steps leading up to the main chamber. He raced up the steps, breathing heavily, until he reached the door. When he pushed open the door, he expected to see the Dracor morphing into humans. Instead, there was no one. The floor was covered with slime and gel, indicating that the Dracor had completed their transformation.

Panic took over as he paced the floor and fretted over what to do next. There was no one left to help him now. He considered that Xerxes had no knowledge of the Andoran events and Seneca wasn't here to explain what happened to them. His last hope was that Ginea had some information that he could use. Now she was gone, too, and things appeared hopeless. *If the Andorans took everyone prisoner, then where did they take them to? How am I ever going to find them?* he fretted.

Questions overwhelmed his mind and the reality that he might never see anyone again pushed him to the brink of insanity. Billy leaned against the wall and tears rolled down his cheeks. This looked like a battle he couldn't win. He dropped to the floor on one knee and prayed that there was a way out of the nightmare.

A soft voice, barely audible, called to him, "Billy, come here." Billy scratched his head and wondered if his mind was playing games. He heard the voice again whisper across the chamber.

"Billy, come here. I need you." Billy trembled and wondered if he had gone mad. He stood up and approached the source of the sound.

"Who is it? Don't play with me!" he shouted.

"Billy, help me. I'm here." He approached a door that was slightly ajar. His heart raced as he opened the door.

Inside the room was a wooden table turned upside down. Billy inspected it closer and saw that the table covered someone or something.

He approached the table and lifted it up onto one end. In the dim light, he could make out the slender figure of Ginea. "Thank you, Billy," she said appreciatively.

Surprised to see her, Billy helped her to her feet and asked, "Where is everyone?"

"The Andorans came in great numbers and took everyone prisoner. My people pushed me into the room and put the table over me so I wouldn't be found."

"It looks like they've taken everyone, including Seneca. I told you we should have closed the portal."

"They didn't come through the portal. They came from across the horizon. We heard the loud hum and a huge, black cloud formed in the sky. The Andoran ships descended from the cloud like a plague of locusts. They were everywhere."

"I can't believe the attack happened so fast."

"What can we do, Billy?"

"I'm going back through the portal to Dracor. I want to see what's happening in your world. I need more information about these Andorans."

"That's insane!"

"Right now, we have nothing to go on, nor can we hunt them down."

"Then I'll go with you."

"No, it's too dangerous, Ginea. Stay here."

"It's no safer here than it is there."

Billy realized that she was right. "Then let's go." He escorted Ginea through the portal back to Dracor. They emerged from the dark cave that camouflaged their arrival and scanned the area. There wasn't much left of the Dracor civilization. The Andorans destroyed everything that represented the Dracor culture. Andoran corpses and broken robots littered the plains. Plumes of black smoke tainted the blue sky.

Billy and Ginea perched over the ledge and looked down at a passing Andoran patrol. "Stay here," whispered Billy.

"What are you going to do?"

"I have no idea." Billy crept down to the bottom of the hill and picked up a weapon from a Dracor corpse. He turned to go back but his path was blocked by an Andoran officer. The alien was decked with thick black leather and metal chest armor, a leather helmet with studs and a plume of feathers. *Now I'm really screwed*, thought Billy.

"Don't move or I'll kill you," warned the Andoran.

"Where did you come from?" asked Billy.

"It doesn't matter. I suggest you put the weapon down now."

"I can't do that. Why are you destroying these people?"

"Is that what you call it – destroying?"

"What else would you call it?"

"How about vanquishing an enemy?"

"What does it prove by 'vanquishing' helpless races?"

"I'm surprised you would ask such a question. The real question is 'why wouldn't I'?"

"We've done nothing to harm you, nor have the Dracor."

"Oh, come on now. Do you expect me to believe that none of you had anything to do with the assassinations and the murder of Pendragon's offspring?"

"Yes, that's right! We've never even heard of your race before."

"Why should I believe you? "I should kill you now, where you stand."

"You have nothing to lose. Why not tell me what happened?"

"Why do you care?"

"Because, if someone did take out your leaders, they deserve to be punished."

The Andoran rubbed his chin with a scaly hand. Then he related, "The ambassadors from the Council arrived at several of our worlds carrying a disease, developed to wipe out all of the Andoran races."

"Why would they do such a thing?"

"Our leader, Pendragon, had sired offspring through a human woman of magic. She believed that the new breed would be immune to a disease that was already killing our people."

Billy felt a little more at ease now that the Andoran would talk with him. "Why would this woman do such a thing?" Billy asked. "She must have gotten something in return."

"I'm sure she did. That was between her and Pendragon."

"Perhaps Pendragon planned to invade several worlds on her behalf before the assassinations ever happened."

"Why would he do that?" asked the Andoran.

"I know personally that Diomedes was insane with desire for power. She would do anything, including bearing offspring to an alien race."

"You know of Diomedes?"

"Yes, I do. She wasn't a very nice person either."

"So, let's say you're right, human. How would the Council find out about this?"

"Perhaps one of your people knew what she was up to and what kind of war would ensue. He may have warned the Council. The humans aligned by the Council never had to fight before, so, perhaps they were defending themselves."

"Do you condone what was done?"

"No, I don't. My race wasn't aligned with the Council. We didn't even know of their existence until Diomedes' meddling pulled us into her world. We didn't even know other human races existed besides our own."

"So, you claim to be ignorant of these events?"

"Yes, I do, but perhaps we can do something to stop all this death and destruction. What would it take to restore peace between the races?"

"I believe a lot of things would have to happen before peace can occur."

"What about a sign of good faith?"

"What do you propose?"

"I have a gun. If I wanted to, I could kill you, right?"

"And my men would swarm down on you in seconds."

"And we both wind up dead. Do you have this disease?"

"Every one of us has it."

"What if you come back with me and meet some of my people? They are experts in science. Perhaps they could help cure the disease that plagues your people."

"Do they have that capability?"

"They might. It could take some time, but…"

"You don't have much time. Your world has been targeted already and will be attacked soon."

"How do you know where I'm from?" questioned Billy uneasily.

"We studied your species on Earth and prepared our attacks accordingly."

Billy got a chill as he thought about aliens scoping out his world. "But how did your people find Earth so easily?"

"It's simple. Pendragon supplied Diomedes with a number of tracking devices. She gave them to her accomplice, a man of magic like her, who dispersed them. One of them must have been taken to your world. We were able to construct a path right to it."

Billy remembered the transmitter that Sam was working on. "How much time do we have?"

"About two days on this world."

"Well, if you'll trust me and come back with me, maybe we can make some progress."

"Perhaps it would be a good first step to restore peace. Nothing would make me happier than to cure my people."

Billy extended a hand to the Andoran and said, "My name is Billy."

The Andoran extended his clawed hand and touched Billy's. "I am Ramador, the vice-commander of the Andoran military. You're Billy, huh?"

"That's me."

"I seem to recall that Diomedes was killed by two humans. One of them was named Billy."

"Yes, I'm afraid to say, that was me. It was in self-defense, though. She and Ruger were evil people and were trying to kill everyone."

"I have three children on Andor. Each is stricken with the disease and it seems to accelerate with each generation."

"If you let the scientists have a blood sample, they may be able to come up with a cure. We'll have to hurry if time is short."

"A cure for this disease would be fantastic. But how can I trust your people?"

"If there's a chance they can cure your children, isn't it worth trying. I swear to protect you if you go back with me."

Ramador considered the options. "Let's go before my men become suspicious. I don't want to put them at risk."

Billy led Ramador into the cave. Ginea was aghast when she saw them. "What are you doing, Billy?"

"Trust me, Ginea. I know what I'm doing. This is Ramador. He's going back with me to my world."

"For what?"

"For peace. If we can help the Andorans, perhaps we can end the fighting." Ginea was frightened of the Andoran and reluctant to speak.

Billy and Ramador followed her through the portal. When they entered the castle, Ramador was amazed. "Our travel device isn't as efficient as this, nor is it as comfortable."

"Believe it or not, Ramador, this portal technology is what started all the trouble."

"I don't doubt it."

When they crossed the courtyard, Ramador surveyed the corpses, which littered the grounds. "I see my people have been here already. They are very proficient at war."

"Yes, they are, but is it worth it?" Billy queried.

"We can't be stopped. No one has the ability to wage war like the Andorans. That is why the other alien races were anxious to join our cause."

"But, Ramador, that's the very reason that the Council refused to acknowledge our existence on Earth. Our world has been plagued with wars since our history began. They fear our capabilities."

"So, your world could prove to be a worthy adversary?"

"I hope we don't have to find out." Then Billy asked, "What happens to the prisoners? Where are they taken?"

"They are taken to mining colonies where they are put to work as slaves."

"What do they mine?"

"There is an ore that we use to power our transportation equipment."

"Is it the same kind of ore that is used in the beacons?"

"Yes, it is. Why?"

"Because it emits rays of energy that will eventually kill anyone exposed to it for long periods of time. We call it radioactivity."

"That would explain why the prisoners don't live very long."

"Are you or your people exposed to the ore?"

"Some are. Many of us travel frequently so we aren't around the lode."

"I wondered if that had anything to do with your illness."

"I never thought of that."

When they reached Firenghia, Billy asked, "Would the two of you mind waiting here for a few moments? I need to change into my clothes."

"If I must," complained Ginea. She and Ramador stared coldly at each other.

Billy disappeared into the forest. He returned shortly, after wearing his torn and tattered clothes, his sword and leather sack.

"You carry a sword. You must be a warrior," Ramador commented.

"It comes in handy for self-defense."

"Why would you wear those tattered rags instead of the robe?"

"It's a blanket and I was getting a rash from it," Billy complained. While Ramador laughed, Ginea stared at the two of them in disbelief.

"I think you are both mentally debilitated."

"I don't expect you to understand, Ginea," Billy replied.

"Why not?"

"Because you're a woman."

Ramador laughed harder and responded, "I'm starting to like you, Billy."

"It's complicated and I think I understand some things here that you aren't aware of. That's all I'm saying," he said compassionately.

"Lucky for you, Billy," warned Ginea. "You don't know what I'm capable of."

"And I don't want to know either," Billy commented, frustrated with her defensive attitude toward him.

Billy pointed the orb on his silver chain at the side of a boulder and opened the portal back to the research center. Ramador and Ginea were quite curious how Billy could make a portal with a tiny object like the orb. Billy noted the looks on their faces. "Don't ask me how it works. I only follow the instructions."

CHAPTER 5

BREAKTHROUGH

When they passed through the portal and arrived in the transportation bay, a group of soldiers immediately surrounded them at gunpoint.

"Against the wall with your hands up!" ordered the sergeant.

"This is procedure until they identify who we are," explained Billy. Ramador and Ginea looked uncomfortable but they complied.

"Dr. Smith and Xerxes are expecting us," announced Billy. "Can you notify him that Billy Brock has returned from Dracor with two guests?"

As the sergeant dialed a cell phone, he instructed them, "You may put your hands down but stay by the wall."

"Thank you, Sergeant."

"You can relax now," Billy informed Ginea and Ramador. They put down their arms and watched the soldiers. The sergeant spoke into the cell phone. "Yes, Dr. Smith. Mr. Brock has returned from Dracor with two guests." He listened intently and replied, "Yes, sir. I'll send them up." The sergeant stowed his phone in his pants pocket. He motioned for his men to lower their weapons.

"Dr. Smith has requested that you and your guests go to the third floor. He will meet you there."

Billy led Ramador and Ginea to an elevator and took them to the third floor. The elevator stopped and the doors slid open. "We're going to meet Dr. Smith. He'll know who can help with the Andoran disease," explained Billy.

When they entered Doc's office, he was on the telephone. Doc held up his finger for a minute of patience and jotted down some numbers on a notepad. When he finished, he hung the phone up and looked in awe at Billy's companions. "Billy, who are they?"

Billy was amused by Doc's surprise at seeing an Andoran in his office. "This is Ramador. He's Vice-Commander of the Andoran military force and we need your help."

"Now is a bad time, Billy."

"But Doc, it's really urgent!"

"I guess no time is good these days."

"Why? Has something happened?" Billy asked, concerned about their situation.

"Yes. We were attacked earlier by alien fighters," Doc revealed. "The Air Force repelled the attack and took out a large number of the attacking fighters."

Billy looked at Ramador somberly. "So, it has already started."

"I didn't expect them to attack so soon," replied Ramador. "If your forces were able to repel the first attack, then we may have some time. My people will want to regroup and think this out. They've never been defeated before in an initial attack. I'm impressed."

"What's going on here?" asked Doc.

"The Andorans are afflicted with a disease that's slowly killing their people," explained Billy.

"Let me guess. You want us to find a cure for them."

"If we can find a cure, we can restore peace," suggested Billy.

"What makes you think we can find a cure, Billy? I don't even know what's wrong with them."

"We have to try, Doc. It's not our mess, but we're the middle of it."

"I'll see what I can do." Doc made a phone call and explained the situation to someone at the other end. When he hung up, he announced, "We're going to the bio-lab. They'll have lots of questions for our guest and I have lots of questions for you."

"I think we may have some answers as well," Billy responded.

"Good. Now who is your other friend?"

"This is Ginea. She's the matriarch of the Dracor."

"She looks to be a child."

"Come on, Doc. Nothing is what it seems anymore. Firenghia was raided earlier. Everyone was taken prisoner by the Andorans, including Penny."

"I'm confused. Isn't our visitor an Andoran?"

"Yes, I am," Ramador answered. "Billy has brought some things to my attention that I wasn't aware of. My people do not know I've come here."

"If I may ask, why have you come here?"

"I am looking for something to take back to my people as a gesture of good faith. I would like to see peace prevail as much as you do, but Pendragon, my leader, is stubborn and may pose a problem."

Billy interrupted, "The transmitter that Sam was working on is the beacon that allowed the Andorans to direct their portal to Earth."

"Well, I'll be "

"The prisoners are placed in mining colonies to mine the ore that's used in the transmitter," Billy explained. "It's radioactive and people tend to die while mining it."

"How can we stop it?" questioned Doc.

"Ramador is our only hope and we are his only hope. Can we help him?"

"We'll see what the bio-lab techs can do. Follow me."

Doc guided them to the elevator. The doors opened and he directed them inside. "After you, Ramador," said Billy politely.

Ramador nodded in appreciation of the respect. He entered, followed by Billy, Ginea and Doc. "You really didn't know of races other than those on Earth?" asked Ramador.

Doc pressed a button for the seventh floor and the doors closed. "No, we didn't. It's kind of embarrassing when we see how far everyone else came without us," explained Doc.

"That may not be a bad thing. If your people are innocent as Billy claims, we should stop our attack."

They entered the Bio-lab office and sat down. The lab tech arrived and gazed in amazement. "Holy cow! This is an Andoran?"

"Yes, he is," replied Billy. "This is Ramador. He'll answer your questions."

"Well, Ramador, come on back and we'll see what we can do for you."

"You can trust them. They're good people, Ramador. They won't hurt you," Billy assured him. Ramador proceeded to the lab area with the tech.

Doc took the opportunity to fill Billy in on the details of the attack. "We surprised them this time. They weren't expecting resistance from us."

"Did we have many casualties?"

"We lost three fighters. They lost close to seventy. As soon as the black cloud formed on the horizon, jets were scrambled from all over the east coast. We stopped this attack, but who knows what will happen the next time?"

"That's why we have to help Ramador. He can stop this carnage."

"Goliathan from the Council of Guardians contacted us about moving the Council's headquarters here on Earth."

"I don't know if that's a good idea. What does Xerxes say about it?"

"He doesn't know, yet. He's overseeing the weapons system installations."

"I think we should call him up here. The Council has a lot of explaining to do."

"I'll get him now."

The technician came to the door. "Doc Smith, can you come back for a moment?" Doc glanced at Billy with hopeful eyes and followed the tech.

Ginea held Billy's arm and reminded him, "I know how you feel. We've both lost close friends."

"I'm going to look for them," Billy stated firmly. "I won't stop until I've found them."

"I will help in any way I can. My people were taken as well."

Doc returned to the waiting room and sat down across from Billy and Ginea. "The lab techs took blood samples and are waiting for Dr. Watts to analyze them. He's back there now."

"Will that take long?"

"It could be a few hours, depending on the complexity of the disease. We're lucky to have the best equipment here. This will save us days of waiting for results."

"That's encouraging. What does Ramador think?"

"He actually cracked a smile when the lab tech mentioned their success rate for identifying and curing new infections and viruses. We're still a long way from a solution, but at least we have a start."

"I'd like to speak with Ramador as soon as possible," Billy requested.

They're running other tests on him. He'll be a little while."

"When is the *Specter* leaving?"

"It's gone. They pulled out three hours ago, right after the attack."

"What else do we have left for transportation?"

"The *Exeter* and the *Luna C*. The *Luna C* is ready now. The weapons system from the *Starfire* was swapped over so it was completed and deemed ready for action ahead of the *Exeter*."

"Can you get me a crew? I'm going after Seneca and Penny."

"Let's talk about this before we jump to conclusions. Do you even know where to look? It's a big universe."

"I'll ask Ramador for help."

"You're assuming an awful lot, aren't you?" suggested Doc.

"I don't have any choice, do I? My son might have been taken prisoner as well."

Doc was shocked by Billy's statement. "Did you say 'your son'?"

"Yes, I did. I'm the father of Seneca's child. That's how I got the strange traits and the mind reading abilities."

"And she gave you the ability to change shape as well?"

"Yeah, and now I'm sure you think I'm a freak!"

"Billy, I don't care. Now I understand your concern. I'll do what I can to help."

"Thanks, Doc. I'm sorry if I sound testy."

"Why don't you take Ginea back to your room? We can't do anything until they finish the tests on Ramador. Order some food from the cafeteria. I'm sure the two of you haven't eaten in a while."

"I haven't even thought about food over the last few days. I think we'll do that."

"You should try and rest."

"You'll let me know when I can speak with Ramador?"

"Of course, I will," Doc assured him. Billy invited Ginea to join him. She nodded in appreciation and followed Billy to his room.

Doc hurried down to the transport bay to speak with Xerxes. The bay was crowded with four spaceships in the docking area. The *Starfire* had just been towed out for scrap, opening up another berth at the dock.

Xerxes stepped out of the *Exeter's* hatch and greeted Doc. "I hope you have some good news for me. Things aren't looking too good, lately."

"Perhaps, but you'll have to validate that."

Xerxes immediately picked up on the seriousness of Doc's tone. "What is it?"

"We have Ramador here," Doc informed him. "Do you know of him?"

Xerxes eyes widened. "Not the Andoran vice-commander?"

"Yes, that Ramador."

"Why? How? Do you know what kind of danger he could put us in?"

"Relax, Xerxes. We're trying to solve a medical problem. Ramador has agreed to let us do testing on him."

"And then what?"

"If we can find a cure for them, it becomes a first step toward peace. Apparently, he and Billy had some interesting discussions regarding Diomedes and her fate."

"What else do we know?"

"Their portal is powered by ore, the same ore in the transmitter that Sam has been working on in the weapons lab. Unfortunately, that also acts as a trace beacon. That's how they found us."

Xerxes looked concerned. "Is that all?"

"No. The Firenghi, Dracor, Seneca and Penny have been captured. Ramador says they were taken to a mining colony."

"That's unfortunate."

"Do you know anything about those mining colonies?" asked Doc.

"I know where they are located but I've never been there."

"Good because Billy is going on the *Luna C* tomorrow with a crew to find them."

"That's insane!" exclaimed Xerxes. "How will they get there?"

"That's up to them. You give him directions and he'll find them."

"What about the Andorans? What if they attack again?"

"Since we know that the ore can give off enough energy to power a portal system, we only need to find a way to nullify it and the portal will be blocked shut."

"How can we do that?" questioned Xerxes.

"I'm hoping Ramador can tell us something more about it."

"So, what do we do now?"

"I'd like you to come with me and speak with Ramador. Having him for an ally could be the break we needed."

"I assume Billy pulled off this coup."

"Yeah, he did. Here's another item of interest. Did you know that the Council has requested permission to relocate here at the facility?"

"No, I didn't. I knew they were considering it, but I haven't been privy to their plans."

"Do you feel like you're being left out of the loop on some things, Xerxes?"

"Yes, I do. I'll be honest with you; there are a lot of things they did that I wasn't aware of. There were also some unpleasant things that were done before I became a member of the Council. I can't change that."

"Then what should we do?"

"Tell them 'no'. They are putting your people at risk and we don't quite know what they are up to. Personally, I don't trust them."

"I quite agree, but I wanted your opinion."

They proceeded to the Bio-lab.

— X —

Ramador sat patiently on the table as Dr. Watts reviewed all the data that the technician collected on him. Ramador was impressed by the technology that humans had at their disposal. "Dr. Watts, what was the purpose of putting me in that big white tube?" Ramador asked, curious.

"Would you like to see, big fellow?" The doctor invited him to come closer. Ramador leaned over the doctor's shoulder and looked at the films. Dr. Watts inserted a disk into his computer. "You had an MRI, a magnetic resonance imaging. This MRI gives us a layout of your whole body. Since we weren't looking for anything in particular, it gives us an approximate picture of your entire body."

"Will that tell you about the disease?"

"It could contribute information about the disease or how much of your body is affected by it. The blood samples were much more interesting. I won't bore you with details, but I'd like to treat you with a common serum we use. I believe your blood is close enough to ours that it may work."

"What if it doesn't work?"

"Well, then we'll have to look at some other possibilities. I believe you and your people are affected by a bacterium that, if left untreated, creates the problems you are experiencing today."

"What do you have to do to treat me?"

"I will give you an injection and we'll test your blood again tomorrow. Keep in mind that I'm treating you for something that looks simple. Normally, it takes a lot more research and testing to treat a disease, particularly in a species that we know nothing about."

"I understand. I realize that time is not something we have a lot of as well."

"If this works, then everything is simple. If not, it'll take time." Dr. Watts gave Ramador an injection of RF-34, an anti-bacterial serum. Ramador cringed briefly but relaxed afterward.

"Now, I'll return you to your friends and tomorrow we'll test your blood again to see if the bacterium is affected."

"Thank you for all your help," said Ramador, grateful.

"Let's wait until you're cured before you thank me."

"Fair enough."

Dr. Watts led Ramador into the waiting room and paged Doc to return. "Doc and Billy will be back shortly. If you need anything, I'll be in here."

"Thank you, Dr. Watts." Dr. Watts smiled and returned to the lab.

— **Ⅹ** —

Commander Mustafo wasn't taking any chances of getting caught in an ambush. He went to maximum power as they approached the portal. The *Specter* shot through at full speed.

Mustafo requested over the page, "Would Ronnie and Randy do the honors and man the cannons? I'm sure the enemy is nearby."

"Of course, we will. Just find us some targets," replied Randy zealously.

"Be careful what you wish for," warned Tur. "You might get more than you bargained for." Tur heard the girls chuckle over the intercom. He shook his head in disbelief. The *Specter* cruised away from the portal and took its position without incident.

Commander Mustafo kept a watchful eye on the scanners and looked for anything that resembled alien ships. Suddenly, a gigantic ship appeared from behind an asteroid. Mustafo immediately recognized it and was stunned. "Tur, look at this!"

"What is it, Commander?" Then a second behemoth ship appeared.

"It looks like…. It's a battle star! Make that two. They just came out of the asteroid field."

"I don't think we're going to outrun their weapons. We're already in range of their guns," fretted Tur.

"I have an idea. Let's approach them slowly. Shut down all lighting."

Tur immediately toggled several switches. He announced over the page, "The lighting systems are shutting down."

"Radio the Council to keep the portal open until we give the order. After that, we'll maintain radio silence," instructed Mustafo. Tur promptly complied.

Mustafo communicated with the girls through the headsets. "Ronnie. Randy. We have a change of plans. Do not fire the cannons. I repeat, do not fire the cannons. Look for a vent shaft or a thermal exhaust port on each of those ships. Then I want you to use the automatic guidance system and find me coordinates for those shafts."

"What are you thinking?" Ronnie asked, curious.

"We're going to fire torpedoes into those shafts and run like hell."

"Commander, look! There are two more!" exclaimed Tur. "Those aren't ships. Those are whole friggin' cities."

"They want the portal!" shouted Mustafo. "They want the Council!"

"Will our torpedoes be enough to knock them out?"

"I'm told by the Earthers that nuclear warheads are very capable of destroying a spaceship of considerable size. In this case, we only have to destroy their power generation. The resulting reaction will do the rest," explained Mustafo.

Ronnie and Randy scoured the images, looking for the ports. The ships were giant, silver balls with numerous components mounted on the surface. One of the ships could easily hold a hundred craft the size of the *Specter*. As they drew closer, the girls saw the gun turrets and the hatch covers on the monitors. It was an eerie sight, watching the giant ships drift by.

Ronnie noticed a glowing region underneath one of the ships. She pressed the targeting sensors and streams of information crossed her visor. "Commander, we've found what looks like a thermal exhaust vent on the bottom of each ship," she reported. "Sensors report excessively high temperatures at the ports. I don't see any protective grating in front of the vents."

"Excellent. Do you have coordinates?"

"I'm sending them now," she said and then added, "What if we target the first and third ships? The explosions could potentially take out the second and fourth."

Mustafo grinned at Tur. Tur nodded in approval of the idea. "I like it," Mustafo replied to her. "We're going to hit and run."

"They're ignoring us," said Tur. "They're going straight for the portal."

"Contact the Council and tell them to shut the portal. As soon as it's closed, we'll fire." Mustafo waited patiently as the portal closed. He pressed the codes, thus arming four of the torpedoes. He programmed each one by aligning an X on the monitor over a target and pressing an 'enter' key.

"Commander, how many torpedoes do we have on board?" inquired Ronnie.

"Eight. That's all they had time to load. The ship's capacity is sixteen." Mustafo dialed in 'pairs' on the control panel. He waited until they had just the right angle and pressed the 'fire' button twice. Four sparkling lights shot from the *Specter* and headed on their predetermined courses. "Full power, Tur! Let's get the hell out of here."

Ronnie and Randy had excellent views of the torpedoes from the turrets. Each pair of streaking energy bursts disappeared inside the ports of the first and third battle star.

The first battle star glowed briefly and exploded into a brief but fiery blast of energy. The explosion quickly engulfed the second ship. The third battle star exploded just like the first one and became a huge flaming mass. The fourth ship was thrust away from the explosions but its surface erupted in a series of tiny explosions.

The girls were terrified when they witnessed the shock wave spreading toward them. "Oh, shit! This can't be good," cried Ronnie.

Before Mustafo and Tur could respond, the *Specter* was slammed forward and spun wildly out of control. The panels in the flight deck overheated and sparked. The main power failed, followed shortly by the backup power. Sections of the passengers' cabin broke apart and the main engines broke away in pieces. The ship became still and dark like a tomb.

— X —

Penny huddled in the corner of the cargo hold with Seneca. *There has to be something we can do about this,* she thought. *What would Billy do?*

Pendragon perched at the top of the stairs and talked with another Andoran officer. He grew irritated as the conversation progressed. "What do you mean 'they must have been ready for us'?" he shouted.

"How else could they have handled our forces so easily?" replied the officer.

"Perhaps our forces are getting soft. I'll have to do something about that."

"But Pendragon, look at our string of victories. We've accomplished so much in a short time."

"That's all the more reason we shouldn't have failed. Why are these humans any different than the rest?"

"Perhaps the difference is why the Council has shunned that particular group over the ages."

"How do you know that?"

"Our sources have discovered that just recently by intercepting the Council's communications. They've asked for asylum on Earth. In the last transmission, received just minutes ago, the Earthers rejected the Council's request."

"They have backbone."

"Or they know the Council's not to be trusted."

"Very possible. I expect the Earthers will want to negotiate at some point. When they do, we'll be ready."

"Is that wise, sir, to cross a formidable enemy?"

"Are you afraid, Lucien?"

"No, sir. Just wary."

"How long before we rendezvous with the battle star?"

"Very soon, sir. We're passing through the last portal."

"Have we received any news from the other battle stars? I'm anxious to hear that they control both sides of the portal and that the members of the Council are at our mercy."

"Not yet, sir."

"Let me know when word comes in."

"Yes, sir."

Pendragon descended the stairs and approached Penny. She hid behind some of the prisoners, but his eyes followed her. When he reached her, he grabbed her by the hair and pulled her to a standing position. "Where are you from? I know you're not one of these people."

"Why do you care?" Penny challenged.

"If you and your friend Billy were smart enough to outwit Diomedes, perhaps you are Earthers. You seem to be the only people with backbone and the will to fight."

"Oh, you'll get fight all right!"

"Well, if I do, you'll never know. You'll be slaving in the mines on Orpheus, the farthest mining colony from any civilized world. Billy will never find you, even if his people succeed."

"You won't win this battle, Pendragon."

"Enough, wench! Sit down and shut up." Pendragon threw her to the ground.

Seneca stood up in her defense and demanded, "You treat us with respect or we'll..."

Pendragon grabbed her by the throat and hurled her against the bulkhead. "You'll what?" Seneca slumped to the floor, unconscious.

Lucien shouted down the stairs to Pendragon, "Sir, we have news. I think you'd better come up here quickly."

"Ah, Lucien. Give me the good news of sweet victory."

"Sir, we are docking on the battle star *Ciphones*."

"What else?" Pendragon replied with little interest.

"Sir, the other battle stars did not return. The last contact *Ciphones* had with them was a distress call. Their monitors showed a series of explosions and three of the battle stars are nonexistent. The fourth appears to be listing aimlessly without power."

Pendragon became enraged. "What! What in this cold-ass universe could cause our battle stars to explode like that?"

"I don't know, sir."

"Where's Ramador? Have they found him yet?"

"No, sir. They're still scouting the Dracorian planet. That's where he was last seen."

"When we dock, you'll take over the transfer of the prisoners. I'll find out what's going on," Pendragon instructed Lucien, while growing more agitated.

Penny cradled Seneca in her arms. Seneca stirred and regained consciousness. "Are you okay?" asked Penny.

"No. What's going on?"

"Pendragon's in a rage. Their plans backfired and my people are making headway against him. He was upset about three of his battle stars exploding and a fourth being disabled. Apparently, Lucien is the pilot and he's in charge of us now."

"Thank you for helping me," Seneca uttered weakly. "I thought I could overpower him. I can't believe how incredibly strong he is."

"We'll have to be smarter than these creatures. Maybe they're not as smart as they are strong."

Seneca appreciated Penny's optimism and nuzzled against her shoulder.

— X —

Doc returned to the lab and found Ramador waiting anxiously. "Did they tell you anything, Ramador?"

"Yes. Dr. Watts gave me an injection. He said that if this works, it will be easy to cure me."

Dr. Watts opened the door and entered the room. "This may be easier than we thought."

"What do you think?" asked Doc anxiously.

"It appears to be a simple bacterium that's causing the problem. I gave him a shot of RF-34. We'll test his blood again tomorrow."

"You gave him RF-34! But he's an Andoran."

"Yes, but his blood chemistry is similar to ours."

"But he's a lizard, I mean a reptile!"

"No, he isn't. Only his outer skin is reptilian. He has all the organs of a human."

"But the tail?"

"It's for balance because of his size. What can I tell you? Maybe it will fall off someday. Other than that, he's similar to us in a lot of ways."

"Well, I'll be…"

"Bring him back tomorrow and we'll find out if the serum works."

"If this works, how can we distribute the serum to your people?" Doc asked Ramador.

"I don't know. Perhaps I'll go back and talk to my men first. I'll need their support to convince Pendragon that we have the cure. What better proof than to see my unit healthy."

"That makes sense. Let's get you something to eat and a place to rest now. First thing tomorrow, we'll get a sample and see where we stand."

"Dr. Smith?"

"Yes, Ramador."

"Thank you very much."

"We're not there yet. If you don't mind, I'd like to ask you some questions?"

"Of course."

"Is there a way to block the Andoran portal?"

"I don't know much about the theory of how it works. I can tell you about some of the components."

"I would be grateful. We don't want to destroy your system, only protect ourselves from another attack."

"The ore that is mined by the prisoners was carved into a great number of rings with a thickness about my height. These rings have properties that vary when they are placed in different proximities of each other. When the rings are placed next to each other, they stick together. These rings are made in such a way that they form a huge ring from the smaller rings. A field of some sort is formed in the middle of the giant ring."

"How big is this ring?"

"It's big enough to send battle stars and an army of fighters through at one time."

"What is this battle star you speak of?"

"It's a very big spaceship that carries many small ships, supplies, equipment and weapons. It's like a mobile fortress."

"And the Andorans build these battle stars?"

"No. There are two distant alien races that build them for us. They are very smart, technically speaking."

"That's interesting," Doc mumbled to himself.

"The ring is only part of the system. There are four large lasers that are fueled by a melted mixture of the ore and a chemical. Somehow, these lasers project the field toward a destination. The sample of ore you have acts as a receiver for the portal. The projected field is sensitive and will only come so close to the surface of your planet because of the makeup of your atmosphere."

"Do you think we could enter your portal with our fighters to deter them?"

"I don't know if that's a good idea. It's very uncomfortable for Andorans to pass through this portal already. The Vax army attempted to pass through it when we began the war. They died a horrible death because their bodies weren't able to survive the fields."

"I see. Well, this has been very helpful. As I said, we only want to act in a defensive posture. I think that's the best way to start a move for peace."

"I quite agree. The Andorans are very proud of their fighting ability and the other human races aren't known for their courage. I'm sure my people are already having a hard time accepting defeat from your fighters."

"Hopefully, they won't take it personal." Doc guided Ramador up to his room and offered, "I'll order you some food from our cafeteria. It's probably not a good idea to take you into the cafeteria after the attack. There's no telling how the others would react to an Andoran in their cafeteria."

"I understand."

Doc picked up the phone and called in an order of food for delivery to the room. "How long has this 'problem' affected your people?" inquired Doc.

"Right after the Council took Pendragon's offspring from Andor. After several cycles, many of my people gradually lost their sanity. Then we learned that by staying awake, we could stop the disease from progressing. Why do you ask?"

"I'm trying to establish a timeline for how this 'poisoning' might have happened."

A man with a tray of food knocked at the door. Doc opened the door and remarked, "That was quick."

"We try, sir."

Doc signed the slip and took the tray from the man. He set it on a round table in the middle of the room. "Dig in Ramador." Doc closed the door and sat with him.

"What is this food?"

"Steak and lobster. I assume you eat meat."

"Yes, I do." Ramador cautiously tasted each item on the plate. "Not bad. Not bad at all!"

"I'm glad you like it." Doc and Ramador finished their meal and discussed Andoran politics.

— —

Billy asked, "Do you want to use the bathroom to freshen up?"

Ginea looked at him curiously. "What does that mean?"

Billy grinned sheepishly at her. "Sorry, I forgot you're new to this. I'll show you." He took her by the hand and led her into the bathroom. "This is the bathroom. You probably want to use the shower." Billy started the water in the shower. "You take off your clothes and stand under the water. There's soap to wash your skin," he explained.

"Will you shower with me, Billy?"

"No. I, uh. I'll take mine later," Billy stammered, red with embarrassment.

Ginea took off the shirt that Billy gave her earlier. Billy blushed again as he glanced at her perfect body and turned away. Ginea noticed and looked pleased. "Sorry, Ginea. I didn't mean to stare."

"I don't understand. What are you sorry for?"

"Never mind. Relax and enjoy your shower." Ginea smiled at him and stepped into the shower.

Billy anxiously left the bathroom. He rummaged through Penny's clothes and tried to find something comfortable for Ginea to wear. After pondering for several moments, he selected a black pair of jeans, a red sweater and undergarments.

Ginea was delighted with her first hot shower experience. When she exited the bathroom nude, Billy handed her some clothes to try on. "I hope these fit. You're nearly the same size as Penny."

Ginea gladly accepted the clothes from Billy. He directed her back to the bathroom to dress. When she returned, Billy was amazed at how beautiful she was. "How do I look?" asked Ginea.

"Absolutely stunning! I don't think Penny will mind if you borrow them for a little while."

"Who is Penny? Is she your mate?"

"Well, not exactly. She was going to be but I think that relationship is over."

Ginea sensed Billy's sadness. "Perhaps she will change her mind."

"No, I don't think so. She's a very confused woman and I don't think she'll ever know what she really wants."

"I'm sorry to hear that. So, what do we do now?"

"Do you know anything about the Dracor inventions like their weaponry, protective equipment and such?"

"Yes, I do. I designed most of it."

"You what?"

"I designed most of the things we use."

"But you seem so young to know all that?"

"Are you surprised?"

"I just never thought…"

"My age is probably equivalent to about twelve of your lifetimes. Remember, when I morphed, I developed a new body."

"That's unbelievable!"

"Your world is quite different than ours. There are some incredible genetic differences between humans and Dracor."

"I'll bet. Everything has changed for me since this mess started, even on my world."

"You seem to have adjusted well."

"Not really. Hey, we're going to visit a friend of mine. His name is Sam and he's working on some things that you might be able to help him with."

"Like what?"

"New lightweight body armor and a few special projects that I'm not familiar with."

"I'm sure I can be of some assistance."

"I'm going to leave you with Sam for a little while. Just remember the room number in case you get lost."

"Will we be sleeping together?"

"I'm not… I don't know. We'll see what happens when we get back." Billy felt awkward as he realized the innocence of her question. He hoped that she was as naïve as she seemed and that he didn't sound like a blundering fool.

Billy escorted Ginea down to Sam's lab. When they reached the smooth shiny door, he pressed the button on the speakerphone and joked, "Pizza for Sam McDermott!"

The door slid open and Sam stood there, grinning at them. "I see you brought something, I mean someone special, for dinner."

"Behave, Sam," chided Billy playfully. Ginea didn't understand the humor in Sam's remark.

"I ordered food for us. It'll be here soon," replied Sam.

"This is Ginea and she is going to educate you on Dracorian technology."

Sam was surprised. "This young lady knows about Dracorian technology?"

"Yes, she does."

"Hello, dear. I'm Sam." Sam extended his hand to her.

"Hello, Sam. I'm Ginea," she replied and shook his hand.

"It's a pleasure to have you in my humble domain. Forgive my surprise, but you seem so young."

She cast Billy a coy glance. "I seem to hear that a lot."

"Well, come on in." Sam pressed a button on the wall and a table descended from the ceiling, moored by several black cords. He pressed another button and four chairs emerged from the wall and slid in front of the table. Billy was amazed at the conveniences of the research center.

The three of them got acquainted. Then the doorbell sounded and Sam left them for a moment. "Are you hungry?" asked Billy.

"I think so," answered Ginea. "I'm still getting used to the physiology of the human body."

Sam returned and set three pizzas on the table. "I was only kidding about the pizza, Sam," remarked Billy.

"That's okay. I wasn't."

Sam went to the other room for a moment and returned with a cold six-pack of XXX beer.

"Are you old enough to drink?" kidded Sam.

She looked at him peculiarly and asked, "Why wouldn't I be?"

Sam popped the top on a can and said, "Try this and you'll see." He and Billy opened their cans and held them up for a toast. "Let's toast to the loveliest woman I ever met – Ginea," said Sam.

"I'll drink to that," replied Billy.

Ginea blushed over the compliment. "How about to one of the bravest and handsomest males I've ever met – Billy," she suggested.

Sam poked Billy's arm and teased, "Billy, you devil."

"It's not like that, Sam. She's a good person."

"Can you tell me about some of your adventures?" she asked.

"My dear, we have some of the best stories you'll ever hear," replied Sam.

"Well. I'm waiting."

They talked for hours. Ginea enjoyed hearing the story about how Billy and Sam stood up to Ruger and his minions in the city.

The phone rang and interrupted their discussion. Sam answered it. He covered the phone and said, "Billy, it's Xerxes. He'd like to speak with you."

"Thanks, Sam."

Billy finished talking and hung up the phone. He returned to the table, looking somber. "Sorry, I have to leave. There are a few very important issues I have to resolve with Xerxes."

"Is everything okay?" asked Sam.

"I don't know. I wanted a ship for tomorrow morning to search for Seneca and Penny."

"How are you going to pull that off?"

"We have an Andoran here, who I think will help me find them."

"So, what's the problem?"

"No crew available. Xerxes has another idea but he didn't say what it was."

"I'll take care of Ginea for you, while you're gone."

"I'm sure you will. Don't keep her up too late."

"I won't. Talk to you later."

"I'll see you later, Ginea. Don't fry old Sam's brain with too much of the new stuff."

"I'll try not to. Goodbye, Billy."

Billy left them and headed for Xerxes' quarters. He pushed the buzzer on the page box outside of his quarters. The door slid open and Xerxes greeted him. "Come on in, Billy. We have a lot to talk about."

"What about Seneca and Penny? I thought we agreed that the *Luna C* was going after them and I was going with it. What happened?"

"The Council has informed me that there was a gigantic explosion outside the portal in quadrant three. The area is littered with debris from not just one, but at least three Andoran battle stars. There is a fourth one drifting about without power."

"What does that tell us?"

"Your friends were on the *Specter*. The *Specter* was in the area at the time of the explosions. The Council hasn't been able to contact them, nor have they found any wreckage to indicate that the *Specter* was destroyed. The shock wave from an explosion that large could have disabled the ship and left her crippled."

"Oh, no!" moaned Billy. "They could be dying!"

"The *Luna C* is going to search for the *Specter* and for survivors on the battle star. I recommend you and Ramador go with the search party. If the RF-34 works and we rescue the Andorans, it might simplify things for us in terms of making peace with them."

"Have you talked to Ramador about this? Remember he left his men on Dracor. They're surely looking for him."

"No, but I'm hoping that Ramador can show us where the prisoners will be held. Then and only then, will we send our ships to rescue them. You know that the Andorans are not going to let you fly in there without an invitation."

"Maybe they won't believe that we'd really go that far just to get our people back."

"You'll have your hands full when they respond to your presence. Your life and those of the crew that accompany you will be at great risk. That's why I ask you to understand why we can't send the *Luna C* blindly to find your friends."

"Have you talked to Doc and Ramador about a rescue operation?"

"Not yet. I just got the information about the battle stars from the Council. I thought you'd be interested since your two lady friends were on board."

"I'll meet with Doc and discuss our options."

"Very well, Billy. In the meantime, I suggest you get some sleep. It's getting late."

Billy looked at his watch and frowned. "I lost track of time." He realized what he said and chuckled. "That's funny - losing track of time."

Xerxes grinned at him and kidded, "You're demented, Billy."

"I know. I'll see you in the morning."

Xerxes pondered Billy's remark about 'losing track of time'. He passed it off as unimportant and replied, "Good night, Billy."

Billy walked down the hall to his room. When he entered, he was disappointed to find it empty. Loneliness took its toll on him. He hoped that Ginea would be there for company. After contemplating all the issues at hand, he took a hot shower and laid down on the couch with a blanket over him. Tears rolled down his cheeks as he wondered what to do about Penny and Seneca. He worried if Ronnie and Randy were still alive. Things just kept getting worse. Everything overwhelmed him. Even if he rescued Penny and the Firenghians, he still had to endure the pain that his relationship with Penny was over. He had to face it; Penny wasn't interested in him or his world any more. He cried himself to sleep.

The next morning, Billy stirred. He looked at the digital clock on the table next to the bed. Billy felt a weight on his chest. He was surprised to see Ginea sleeping next to the bed with her head on his chest. It felt good to have someone near him. He wondered if it meant anything or if Ginea was lonely like him. After all, she had no other Dracor left to share her life with. Her people sacrificed their freedom to save her life.

Billy pushed Ginea's long, blond hair back from her eyes. She wriggled her nose and opened her eyes. "Good morning, Billy."

"Good morning, Ginea. Why didn't you sleep on the bed? It's much more comfortable."

"Did I displease you? I'm sorry if I did."

"No, not at all. It's a lot more comfortable on the bed, that's all."

Billy wondered what it would be like if he and Ginea had a relationship. It would be tough to find common ground, though. Ginea surprised him and commented, "You could just ask me, Billy. I won't be upset."

Billy was taken aback by her response. "What do you mean, Ginea?"

"I know what you're thinking. I'm not sure how, but I can read your thoughts."

Here we go again. Just like before, he thought.

"Are you mad about this?"

"No. I'm still not used to some of this stuff yet." Billy sat up and pulled Ginea onto the bed. She sat next to him and gazed at him. He placed his arm around her and pulled her close to him. "I forgot that you morphed from Seneca. Her species has some unusual traits."

"I'm not unaccustomed to picking up unusual traits."

"You might be unaccustomed to these traits. You have the ability to communicate telepathically, particularly with others who have this ability."

"That sounds really good."

"No, not always. You'll have to learn to shield your thoughts at times; otherwise, you may reveal unwise intentions to your enemies."

"How will I learn this?"

"It should come naturally. Just be aware of it since you don't always know who has this ability. It's best to learn to be a reader first. That way you can identify someone with that trait."

"You said 'traits'. There are more?"

"Yes, there are. Your senses will become very keen. You'll notice things you never imagined before. There is one thing that will happen but I don't know if this is the time to get into it."

"The alter-shape. What is it?"

"You read my mind again."

"Yes, I want to know what the alter-shape is."

"Well, at some point you'll change into this alter-shape. I don't know what turns it off or on but the first time it happens, it's really scary. When we have time, I'll tell you about my first experience."

"I would like that."

"We must meet with Xerxes and Dr. Smith. If you need to use the bathroom for anything, now is the time. I'll call them and see what's going on."

"Should I be doing something?" she asked.

Billy remembered that she hadn't been in human form before. He opened Penny's suitcase and took out a hairbrush, a new toothbrush and toothpaste.

"I'm going to give you a lesson in hygiene. It's very important." Billy instructed Ginea on good hygiene and offered to help her at any time. She stood up and placed the blanket on the bed. She wore only panties and a bra.

Billy was awestruck by her shapely figure in Penny's undergarments. The panties looked fine but the bra was undersized, particularly since Ginea was a bit bustier than Penny. Fortunately, the telephone rang, and Billy quickly answered it. "Hello." It was Doc calling. "Yes, we'll meet you in fifteen minutes."

Ginea exited the bathroom. She approached Billy from behind and put her arms around his waist and blew down his neck. Billy shivered as he felt a tingle. "The conference room? Right. We'll be there." Billy hung up the phone.

"Are you all right, Billy? You're worried."

"Yes, I am. We're meeting in the conference room shortly. I have to use the bathroom, so make yourself at home." Billy turned on the TV and put VH1 on. "Here's some music to enhance your knowledge of human culture." Billy closed the bathroom door.

Ginea opened Penny's suitcase and inspected the clothes. She pulled out a white blouse and black denim shorts. The clothes looked to be about her size so she put them on. The blouse was a little tight, but she didn't mind. She liked how it accented her shape. This was the first time she ever transformed into something that was beautiful. She enjoyed being human.

Ginea stood in front of the mirror and tried different things with her hair. After experimenting, she settled for a ponytail. She used one of Penny's ribbons to tie her hair back. Billy came out of the bathroom, took one look at Ginea and his jaw dropped. "Ginea, you look fantastic!"

"Thank you, Billy. Are we ready to go?"

"I believe we are. I can't believe how nice you look. I like your hair like that."

"Behave yourself, Billy. I know what you're thinking."

"I'm sorry. I didn't mean it. I'll try to cloak my thoughts next time."

"No harm. I'm actually flattered that you find me so attractive."

"I'm really sorry. I shouldn't. I won't…"

Ginea teased, "Perhaps another time."

"Yes, I agree. Let's get going."

— ⏳ —

Doc entered the lab and saw Ramador standing by the door.

"Good morning, Ramador. Did you sleep well, last night?"

"Yes, I did, Dr. Smith."

"Please, call me Doc."

"That was the first time in ages that I slept without the shakes, chills and cramping."

"Well, here comes Dr. Watts. Let's find out if we're really close to a cure."

Dr. Watts entered and greeted them. "Good morning, everyone. How are you doing, Ramador?"

"Very well, Dr. Watts."

"Come on back and we'll take a blood sample." They eagerly followed him.

Ramador sat nervously, as the doctor took the blood sample from his huge arm. Doc put a hand on his shoulder for comfort.

"Well, gentlemen, give me a few moments and I'll be back with the results." Dr. Watts disappeared into the rear of the lab, leaving Doc and Ramador alone in the office.

"If this works, Ramador, have you thought about how we'll break the news to your people?"

"I will find my men on Dracor and give them the news. I'm sure they are still looking for me."

"Would you like me to bring the RF-34 with me and administer it to them?"

"That would be great. I expect they'll be suspicious after what the Council did. However, if they see that I received it, most of them will give it a chance."

"I'll let Dr. Watts know of our intentions when he returns."

"This could change all Andoran lives as I knew them. We have suffered for some time and the disease just gets worse."

"How old are you in regards to an Andoran's lifetime?"

"I am still a young adult. We usually don't live to be elders. I knew one elder who lasted quite a while before dying. He told me interesting stories about our people."

"Perhaps you'll be telling stories about how you saved your people."

"That would be an honor greater than dying in battle."

Dr. Watts entered the room with a wide grin on his face. "Well, this is a happy day for us all. Your blood is completely clear of the bacterium. I'm amazed at how fast your body reacted to the RF-34."

"This is great news!"

"Dr. Watts, Ramador and I have been discussing how to break the news to his people. I would like to escort him back to his unit with a batch of RF-34 for his men."

"How many soldiers are in your unit, Ramador?"

"Twenty-two."

"I think we can accommodate that request. Can you give me a few hours and I'll prepare the package?"

"We've waited this long. I'm sure a little longer won't matter."

Ramador shook hands with Dr. Watts. "Dr. Watts, thank you so much. You've saved my whole race with your antidote."

"It's my pleasure to be of such help."

"Someday, I hope to repay you and Dr. Smith for your kindness."

"Peace and friendship would be a great gift."

"I'll do my best to make that happen."

"We're going to Conference Room B for breakfast and to discuss our other plans," said Doc. "I'll stop back later for the package." Doc and Ramador left the lab and anxiously headed for the conference room.

Maggie hung up the phone as Doc and Ramador entered the room. "I was looking for the two of you. Is Billy coming?"

"He should be on the way," replied Doc.

"How did the test go?"

"Excellent. The disease was just a simple virus left unchecked and the RF-34 erased all traces of it. Basically, it was a poor man's plague."

That's great. Congratulations, Ramador."

"Thank you, Mrs. Smith."

"Please, call me Maggie."

The door opened again and Billy walked in with Ginea. Doc and Maggie were stunned by Ginea's appearance. "Good morning, everyone," said Billy.

"It's a very good morning, Billy," replied Doc cheerfully.

"Let's sit down and eat while the food is warm," suggested Maggie.

"The RF-34 did the trick," announced Doc. "Ramador is cured!"

Billy was relieved and exclaimed, "That's great!"

The door opened again and Xerxes entered. "Good morning, everyone."

"Ramador is cured! We have an olive branch," Doc anxiously informed him.

"Excellent. What is your next move?"

"I'll escort Ramador back to his unit on the Dracor world. We're going to give RF-34 shots to any of his men who trust us enough to receive it."

"Then what?"

"We'll return to the battle star and I'll give them the news," answered Ramador. "We'll figure out how to get the others vaccinated later. I'll contact Pendragon and try to get your friends back. I'll also try to persuade him to cancel the attacks pending further investigation. I think we can resolve the issues peacefully."

"I can only apologize for what the Council did. I am new to the Council but I would like to punish those who were involved in the assassinations," Xerxes said sincerely. "I would also like everyone to know the truth about the Council. They aren't the group of guardians that they claim to be."

"I think that's fair," Ramador commented. "There's been enough pain and suffering."

"Where do I fit into all this?" asked Billy.

"You can accompany the *Luna C* to the portal and investigate what happened. I don't think it's very smart to go racing off to the mining colony when we are about to break the good news to Ramador's people."

"Your friends have to stop at one of our battle stars for supplies and fuel first. If they are still there, we can work on their release. If you go out there too soon, they'll kill you," he warned.

"I get it. So, when do we leave on the *Luna C?*"

"At noon," replied Doc.

"One more question that's been bugging me," Billy mentioned.

"What's that?"

"Who names these spaceships? I mean, who would name a ship the *Luna C?*"

"The dock monkeys have that honor. Since they were in charge of the docking bay, they were allowed to name several of the craft."

"Great. I can hardly wait to hear the other names." Everyone chuckled and ate their food.

"Ginea, what would you like to do?" asked Billy.

"I would like to stay with Sam for now. There's no point in going back to Dracor since there's nothing left of it. I wouldn't be of any help to you on your mission. At least I can help Sam with his research."

"I understand."

When breakfast was finished, Dr. Watts and Ramador left for Dr. Watts' office to pick up the package of serum. Doc, Maggie and Xerxes remained at the table to discuss additional issues.

Billy walked Ginea to Sam's lab. "Ginea, I…"

"I know what you're thinking. I will hope for your safe return."

He hugged her. "Goodbye, Ginea. I really wish that things could be different for us."

Ginea kissed him passionately and teased, "I learned that from TV."

"Wow! That was unexpected."

She hugged him and said, "Be safe, Billy."

"I will." Billy left them.

CHAPTER 6

REBELLION

The cargo hold of the Andoran cruiser was full of Firenghian and Dracor prisoners. About forty of the men and women sat quietly about the bay.

Penny and Seneca huddled in the corner. Seneca held her hands over her bruised eye. "Isn't there something we can do? Since we docked, there aren't that many Andorans hanging around," noted Penny.

Seneca surveyed the bay and thought for a moment. Cassius sat against the wall across from them dejectedly. "Cassius, come here," Seneca called to him quietly.

Cassius got up and approached the girls. "What is it, Seneca?"

"This might be our chance to take over the ship. I don't think they're expecting us to fight back."

"Do you have a plan?"

"I think so. Can you capture the Andoran called Lucien?"

"Why Lucien?" he asked, curious.

"Lucien is one of the pilots. We'll need him to fly us out of here?"

"I'll take care of it."

"Good. The other ship should be docked nearby. Send some of our people to take out the guards and secure the hatch. I'm going after

Pendragon. I want him dead." Cassius met with six Firenghi men and women to arrange backup.

"I'm going, too," added Penny. "We've got to put an end to this mess."

Seneca looked over her people, searching for someone. "Tarkus, where are you?"

A tall, blond Firenghian man stood up. "Over here, Seneca. What is it?"

"Come here. I need your help."

"Yes, my Queen." Tarkus noticed Penny and hastened his approach. "Come with us. We have work to do."

Tarkus ogled Penny playfully. "Who is this fine young specimen?" he inquired.

"This is Penny, a very close friend of mine," replied Seneca. "That's not important right now so I need your attention."

Penny admired Tarkus' physique. "Wow, where have you been during my visits?" she asked coyly.

"This is a hell of a time for you two to let your hormones run wild," chastised Seneca.

"But Seneca," Penny muttered, disappointed.

"Stay focused. You can talk to Tarkus later."

"I'm looking forward to it," Tarkus responded enthusiastically.

Cassius returned, looking very nervous. "Well?" asked Seneca.

"The Andorans are either very arrogant or very stupid."

"What happened?"

"We took out four sentries on the deck and three inside the ship."

"Let's move before someone notices that they're missing." Eight of them left the ship and crossed the dock.

Another Andoran returned and approached the second ship. Four Firenghi easily overpowered the guard and dragged him down to the cargo bay. Three more Andorans entered the transport bay. Seneca, Penny, Cassius and Tarkus ducked behind crates. When the soldiers passed, Tarkus and Cassius ambushed them from behind. Tarkus grabbed two of the Andorans and snapped their necks. Cassius slammed the third Andoran into the wall and punched him in the face. The force of the blow shattered the Andoran's skull, killing him instantly. Four more Firenghi left the Andoran ship and joined them.

"Anyone comes into this bay, take them out," Seneca ordered.

"That's the sister I know and love," Cassius remarked proudly.

Seneca searched the hatch area and saw no one. "It's clear. Let's go." She led her friends up the stairs to the main deck and through the steel doors. They followed her down the dimly lit corridor to another stairwell. Seneca ascended the stairs alone to and paused outside the battle star's control room. Three Andorans sat at the table, angrily discussing the destruction of their battle stars.

Seneca returned to the bottom of the stairs and whispered, "There are only three. I think we can take them."

"With what?" asked Penny.

"I'll distract them; blindside them; and get their weapons."

"I'll cover the rear," said Cassius.

Seneca ascended the stairs and discretely crossed to the opposite side of the control room. She brazenly pulled up a chair and sat facing the Andorans. The Andorans were startled to see her there. They jumped out of their seats and drew their guns.

"What are you doing up here?" shouted one of the officers. "Get back to the cargo bay!"

"Come on, boys. I'm sure you could use some company. It's boring down there."

"That's it! I'm calling security to escort you back to the ship. They'll shackle you to your seat." The Andoran turned around to reach for the intercom and was promptly knocked out by Tarkus' fist.

Penny grabbed the gun and fired two quick shots. The second Andoran fell to the ground lifeless. Tarkus picked up the remaining Andoran and held him against the wall. "Where's Pendragon?" Seneca questioned.

"I don't know."

"Give me the gun, Penny. I see this is going to be a slow torturous process," said Tarkus arrogantly. Penny handed him the gun. Tarkus placed the barrel against the side of the Andoran's head. "Who are you?"

"I'm Lucien."

Tarkus grabbed Lucien's jaw. He squeezed until the Andoran's mouth opened. Lucien shuddered as Tarkus forced the barrel of the gun into his mouth. "I'll ask you one more time. Where's Pendragon?"

Tarkus pulled the barrel from Lucien's mouth and Lucien quickly relented. "Alright, I'll tell you where he's at."

"I see you're a smart Andoran," quipped Seneca.

"I'm dead either way. Pendragon will kill me if you don't."

"Then you won't mind helping us," she suggested.

"What are you doing, Seneca? You can't trust him!" exclaimed Penny.

"What do you want me to do?" asked Lucien.

"Tell us where Pendragon is."

"And then what? I'm sure that's not all you want."

"Then you'll fly us back to Firenghia."

"And what if I don't?"

"Then I'll kill you, slowly," answered Tarkus. "You'll wish that Pendragon finished you when you see what I'll do to you."

Seneca glared at Lucien hungrily. "No, I think I should like a piece of him."

"Why should I fear you?"

"You asked for it," replied Seneca fiendishly. Seneca transformed into her alter-shape. As a mythical creature, her body was muscle-bound. Her long black mane was smooth and shiny. She stepped out of her clothes and bared her fangs at Lucien. Penny and Tarkus chuckled at Lucien.

"You should have seen what she did to the last Andoran she attacked," taunted Tarkus. "She tore out his insides and dropped them on his face while he was still alive! She shredded him to pieces until there was nothing left."

"Pendragon won't even know it was you. He'll think you abandoned the ship like a coward," ribbed Penny.

Seneca placed her face close to Lucien's and licked his cheek. She stared into his eyes and snarled. "I give up!" cried Lucien. "Call her off." Tarkus and Penny gently rubbed Seneca's mane.

Lucien watched in horror as she transformed back into her Firenghi form. Seneca smiled slyly at Lucien as she dressed. "You're lucky, Lucien. Sometimes I lose control when I'm that close to killing someone."

"Does Pendragon know you can do that?"

"I doubt it. My people aren't sheep either. We can be nasty fighters when we need to be."

"Okay, I get the point. He's up in the control room. He's upset about losing four of his battle stars at the portal so it's probably going to be messy up there."

"We'll see about that." Seneca took the guns from the corpses and handed one to Tarkus. "How do we get there, Lucien?"

"Follow this hall to the end. Make a right into the main hall. Look for the stairs and go up one floor. You'll hear him."

"Now was that so hard?" she quipped.

Tarkus pulled the Andoran into the hall. "Take him back to the ship. We won't be long," Seneca instructed. He took Lucien by the collar and pulled him toward the transport bay."

"When we get back to the ship, prepare for a quick escape back to Firenghia. I'm sure we'll be leaving in a hurry," Cassius informed him. Lucien cooperated fully.

Seneca, Penny and Tarkus crept down the corridor to the main hall. "I didn't know that you had such a mean streak, Seneca. Where did that come from?" inquired Penny.

"When you're a queen, you have to show what you're made of sometimes. This was one of those times."

"You should see her when she's in a bad mood. This was nothing," quipped Tarkus.

"I'm impressed. I never imagined this side of you before."

"That's enough talk for now," Seneca said sternly.

They turned the first corner and nearly collided with two Andorans. Tarkus immediately fired at them. They fell to the floor with smoking holes in their chests.

Penny kept watch while Seneca and Tarkus stowed the bodies inside a small room. When they reached the end of the main corridor, they encountered three more Andorans. The first quickly drew his weapon and fired. Tarkus pushed Penny out of the way and returned fire. Seneca fired twice and killed the Andorans. Tarkus pushed the bodies under the stairs where they wouldn't be noticed. Penny breathed a sigh of relief. "Thanks, Tarkus. I owe you one."

"Yes, you do and I'll be collecting for it."

"Will you two children please concentrate," Seneca snapped at them. Tarkus and Penny grinned at each other. They sensed Seneca's discomfort with their fondness for each other.

The three of them ascended the stairs and stood outside the control room doorway. Seneca peered inside and watched as Pendragon hosted a meeting with several of his officers. Tarkus and Penny grinned coyly at each other as Pendragon spouted expletives about the incompetence of his military.

"I will not tolerate insubordination or incompetence by any of my men. Jerrin, stand up!" ordered Pendragon.

"Yes, Pendragon."

"Why did we lose four battle stars?"

"I don't know, sir."

"Wrong answer!" Pendragon drew his gun and fired at Jerrin's head. After a brief flash, the headless body fell to the floor.

"Someone else answer the question."

A voice from the back of the room called out, "They were negligent. The incident should not have happened."

"Very good. Now, I don't want any more incidents. I have zero tolerance for negligence and failure." Pendragon resumed the meeting and divulged details for a new weapon capable of wiping out any resistance from the Earthers, the Council and that entire region of the universe.

"We have to warn my people as soon as possible," whispered Penny to Seneca.

"After we take care of Pendragon," she replied, adamant.

"We can't afford to die in a shootout," Penny reminded her. "We should go now."

"And what about Pendragon? We can't just let him go."

"We'll get him later. This is more important."

Seneca looked flustered. "Let's go before we're spotted," she relented.

They hurried down the main corridor and found two sentries investigating the bodies underneath the stairs. They fired first and struck Tarkus' arm and leg. He stumbled and fell to one knee. Seneca fired and killed both instantly. Penny helped Tarkus to his feet. Penny and Seneca escorted him to the ship.

When they reached the ship, they found Cassius waiting with Lucien in the pilot's seat. "Get us out of here as fast as you can," ordered Seneca. "We have vital information for Penny's people."

"You heard her. Get us out of here," Cassius directed him. Lucien pushed buttons and turned switches. "Contact the other ship. Tell them we're leaving," ordered Cassius.

"Can one of you sit next to me and help fly this thing?" requested Lucien.

"Why? Can't you do it by yourself?"

"Yes, but it'll take longer."

Cassius reluctantly agreed and took a seat next to Lucien. "These seats are very uncomfortable, Lucien. Can't your people find descent furniture for your ships?" kidded Cassius.

"I'm going back into the cargo hold to inform everyone what's going on," interrupted Seneca.

"I'm fine up here," replied Cassius. "I don't think Lucien will give us any trouble."

Lucien looked down at the gun pointed at his side. "It will be a peaceful trip," he assured them. He turned on the monitor and waited for the second ship to respond to his signal. The ship slowly pulled away from its mooring in the bay and drifted away from the battle star.

"How long before they realize we've left," inquired Cassius.

"I don't think anyone's worried about two transports full of prisoners when four battle stars have been wiped out. "

Seneca returned a short while later. "Lucien, what do you know about the new weapon your people are working on?"

"You heard about that, huh?"

"Yeah. It sounds like Pendragon's ready to use it."

"It's an insane idea by Pendragon that creates a large vortex of energies, violently reacting together. The result is a black hole, which absorbs and destroys everything within its range. Whatever it swallows is destroyed forever without a trace."

"Did he design this weapon?"

"No. One of the alien races we conquered designed it for Pendragon. They agreed to do this in exchange for their freedom."

"How close is this weapon to completion?"

"He can use it now if he wanted to. The only problem is that it can't be controlled. Once the black hole starts, it will migrate like a parasite through space devouring everything it reaches. He calls it 'Dark Horizon'."

"Would he really be crazy enough to use it?"

"As I said, you don't really know him. Ever since his offspring were killed, he hasn't been rational."

"Cassius, have you seen Penny?" asked Seneca.

"No, I haven't."

"I'll be back," Seneca replied and stormed down the steps to the next level. After searching most of the main deck, she checked several of the quarters, not realizing what she might find. She reached the last quarters and pressed the door switch. She waited impatiently as the door opened. "Penny, are you in here?" she called.

Seneca entered the quarters without thinking. To her surprise, Penny and Tarkus were lying together on a table, wrapped in each other's arms. Each was partially undressed. The two of them stared wide-eyed at Seneca. Penny was embarrassed.

"What's wrong, Seneca?" Tarkus asked.

"I need to speak with Penny immediately."

"We weren't hurting anything, were we?" Penny asked innocently.

"Screw your pathetic behavior. It's about Pendragon's doomsday weapon."

"I'll be right out," stammered Penny.

"I told you two to stay focused," chastised Seneca. We have a job to do and you're not helping matters by entertaining your desires." Seneca left the quarters.

Just when they thought she was gone, Seneca's voice echoed one more time, "Tarkus, I'm disappointed in you. We'll talk later."

"Are you in trouble?" asked Penny.

"No, she just doesn't approve of my behavior."

"Oh, so this is a regular thing for you: meeting a female and jumping into the sack with her."

"Well, as a matter of fact, it is. Is that wrong?"

"In my book it is."

"Then we aren't going to finish this?"

"No, not unless you make a commitment."

"A commitment. Why?"

"Because I don't like to share my toys."

Tarkus chuckled at her response. "Is that a fact? Would you swear to that?"

Then Penny remembered that the Firenghi read each other's minds. Tarkus knew about her relations with Seneca, Billy and maybe even Jarret.

"Why don't we start from here with a clean slate?" she suggested.

"That's not fair," complained Tarkus. Penny stood before him and dressed tantalizingly. "Well, I guess it would get me out of Seneca's doghouse."

"That's not good enough, Tarkus. I want to hear 'Penny I want to make a commitment to you'."

"And you're not going to stop until I do?"

"That's right."

"And if I do, what do I get in return?"

"I'll make you the happiest man alive."

"But I'm not leaving Firenghia."

"And neither am I."

Tarkus considered what he was doing and reluctantly declared, "Penny I want to make a commitment to you."

"That's better. I'll let you know when I've decided to make a commitment to you."

Tarkus felt duped. "Hey, that isn't right!"

"Behave yourself and it won't be a problem."

Seneca's voice came over the page, "Penny, I'm waiting! This is important."

"Let's go, lover. Duty calls," she teased. The two of them returned to the upper deck.

"Ah, now I have your attention," Seneca scolded them.

"This isn't funny, Seneca."

"That's my point. This is a bad time to satisfy personal needs."

"Why are you so upset about this? Is it because of Billy?"

"That's your business. Look at our situation and what's at stake. I can't do this by myself!"

"Who is Billy?" inquired Tarkus.

"Nobody important."

"How can you say that after everything he did for you?" bellowed Seneca.

"Stay out of it, Seneca. It's over."

"Now I'm seeing a side of you that I never knew," said Tarkus playfully.

"Drop it, now! I don't want to talk about it."

"You used me just like you used Billy. You couldn't care less about me or anyone else. You're a selfish whore!" cried Seneca.

Tarkus laughed at the girls. "Gee, Seneca. You didn't just hit a nerve; you ripped it out."

"Tarkus, shut the hell up. You talk too much."

Tarkus took the hint and went down to the cargo hold.

Cassius exited the flight deck and glared at them. "Why don't the two of you go sit down somewhere and cool off? Perhaps you both need a rest. I'll be fine here with Lucien."

"Thanks, Cassius. Call me if anything important arises."

"Sure, Sis."

Penny slipped away without muttering a word. She couldn't understand why everyone worried about her business. She and Billy were done, whether everyone else liked it or not.

— X —

Pendragon descended the stairs from the control tower and saw the dead Andorans on the floor. "Lucien! Where the hell are you?" he shouted. Pendragon stormed down to the transport bay and saw that the transport ships were missing.

"They'll pay for this! They'll all pay," he swore angrily.

Pendragon returned to the control room and stood before his officers. They looked up unaware of what had transpired. He drew his pulse pistol and shot each of them in the head. "I hate failure and I hate incompetence."

— X —

Ramador shook Billy's hand and thanked him for helping to cure him.

"Ramador, I need to know something."

"What is it, Billy?"

"Where do you think the prisoners were taken?"

"If they already left the battle star, then they are on their way to Orpheus."

"Can you give me the location of Orpheus?"

"I will write down the coordinates for you. Please don't go there unless we know that Pendragon refused peace with your people."

"I just want to know where they are in case something goes wrong and I don't see you again."

"I understand."

Ramador scribbled half a page of numbers and letters. When he finished, he handed Billy the paper. "Any of the Council's pilots will know how to get there. It's a very long journey and a very lonely part of the universe."

"Thank you Ramador."

Doc Smith entered the room. "Are we ready Ramador? I have the case with the RF-34."

"Yes, Dr. Smith."

Ramador stared respectfully at Billy. "Good bye, Billy."

Billy waved half-heartedly and watched his friends leave for the transport bay. He walked down the hall and got on the elevator. He sensed something bad was happening and needed to get control of the situation somehow.

The elevator stopped on the second floor. When the doors opened, John and Seamus stepped on. "Where are the two of you off to?" asked Billy.

"The same place as you," replied John.

"You're going on the *Luna C* with me?"

"No, two ships are going. We'll be on the other ship, the *Trav ST.*"

"When did this change occur?"

"I requested it from Xerxes. Ronnie and Randy are on the *Specter* and if there's a chance of finding them, we want to be there."

"That makes sense. There's been no word from them?"

"None. The Council received information from a passing freighter that there is a lot of wreckage from the battle stars. They didn't see anything that belonged to the *Specter* though."

The doors opened and they proceeded down the long corridor to the transport bay. "Do they know what caused the battle stars to explode?"

"No, but I studied the maps of the area and I have an idea what might have happened," replied Seamus.

"I'm listening."

"There is a large asteroid located in the vicinity of the portal. The Andorans may have been hiding behind the asteroid and attempted to ambush the *Specter.*"

"Why would they use four battle stars?"

"I think they wanted to access the portal. The Council controls the portal like a switch track. If the Andorans got into the portal with four battle stars, they would create major problems for us and the Council."

They reached the deck and stopped in front of the *Luna C.* It was longer than the other ships previously docked in the transport bay. Further down was the *Trav ST,* equally long and just as splendid.

"Wow! Xerxes mentioned that these were newer and more advanced, but look at them!" he remarked as he marveled at the ships.

On top of the craft were two tinted bubbles; on the underside were two more; and one each on the nose and tail. "How come so many bubbles?" inquired Billy.

"Those are the new cannons," answered John. "They can fire automatically at short range but for longer distances, we have to operate them. The sensors give us data but we have to compensate for things like the density of the target and energy fields between us and the target."

"How many gunners on a ship?"

"Usually two. In this case, Seamus and myself."

"No way! You guys are trained on these things?"

"Sure. You don't believe it?"

"It's not that. I'm surprised, that's all. I thought that swords were your gig."

"I guess we outgrew them."

A tall, slender woman in a teal uniform and a black belt approached them. Billy was amused by the way she wore her dark hair in a bun. She reminded him of a librarian without the glasses.

"Are you getting on board or do you need an invitation?" she asked Billy sarcastically.

John and Seamus chuckled at him.

"That's Tera. Word is 'stay out of her way'. She's deadly with a gun and tough as nails," warned John.

"Thanks, guys. I'll remember that. Good luck." The men shook hands and parted.

Billy rushed to catch up with Tera at the hatch. "Sorry to hold you up, ma'am."

"Save it. We have work to do. What's in the bag? This isn't a vacation, you know."

"I brought a CD player and some music. I hoped that I could plug into the speaker system."

"In a bag that big?"

"Well, I have something else that I carry for protection."

"Like what, a security blanket?"

"No, it's… Never mind. I don't think you'd understand. My name is Billy. Billy Brock." He extended his hand to her but she smirked at him.

"I'm Tera. If you stay out of the way and do as I tell you, we'll get along fine."

"Yes, ma'am."

"Don't call me that. Tera is fine."

"Okay, Tera."

"These containers have to be stowed before we can take off. Open that door and place them on the shelves. Make sure the markings on the shelf match the markings on the container."

Billy opened the door to the supply room and stowed the containers as Tera disappeared up a set of stairs. He was taken aback by her. She obviously had a chip on her shoulder and he wondered if they would get along. His mind wandered to Penny and how she suddenly ended their relationship. *That's twice in less than a year my heart was broken. I never want to date another woman again,* he thought pathetically.

Billy stowed the last plastic container and took a seat. He drifted off in a daze as he stared at the outside monitor. He watched technicians go back and forth to the different ships in the bay. "Hey! Wake up. This isn't a joy ride," shouted Tera.

"Oh, Tera," Billy said after being startled. "I'm sorry. What do you need?"

"When we clear the portal, I want you to take a seat in one of the turrets up top."

"Sure. Is there a problem?"

"Just precautionary. They may have ambushed the *Specter* when she passed through the portal."

"I'll be ready."

"Do you know how to operate the cannons?"

"No, but I'm sure I can figure it out."

"I'll give you a quick run down."

Billy followed Tera up to the turret and listened intently as she explained. When she finished, she asked, "Do you have any questions?"

"No, it seems pretty easy."

"Right! And you know everything."

"Haven't you heard of Play Station?" Billy joked.

"What are you talking about?"

"Never mind. I promise I won't disappoint you when the time comes."

"I'd really like to see that from a man."

"What do you have against me? I've known you for all of two hours and you've talked down to me ever since," replied Billy, irritated by her attitude.

"Just be glad I talk to you at all."

"I'm honored, your highness."

"Bite me, Brock."

"No, you bite me!"

Tera walked nonchalantly away from him as if his words didn't matter at all. The more he thought about her, the madder he got. "I hate women!" he shouted.

To his surprise, Tera's voice rang back from the top of the stairs, "Grow up, Brock."

Billy slammed his fist against the hull. He sat in the turret and waited to reach the second portal.

— ✕ —

Ramador and Doc exited the portal and approached Ruger's castle. The daylight faded and a cold breeze swept down from the mountains. "That castle reeks with evil, Dr. Smith."

"I couldn't tell you how right you are, my friend. That's where Diomedes and Ruger worked their evil from."

"Pendragon doesn't know what he consorted with," Ramador remarked. "It seems that she created quite a bit of trouble for your people."

They entered the castle and proceeded to the main chamber. Most of the torches had burnt out, leaving only a few to flicker. "Ramador, do you remember where the portal was?"

"Yes, I do. It's near the far wall."

Doc nearly slipped on the stone floor. He looked down at wet piles of translucent ooze.

"What's all this slime on the floor?"

"I think the species we took captive from here had just finished some sort of morphosis. They were covered with this stuff when we got here."

Ramador felt along the wall until he found the portal. "Here it is." He passed through the portal first. Doc followed behind, lugging the case with the RF-324 inside. They emerged inside the cave and carefully wound through the dark maze to the Dracor world.

"I guess nobody uses light around here," complained Doc.

"That was ideal for Billy and his friends. We never saw their portal in the dark."

When they reached the bottom of the mountain, Ramador let out an eerie howl. Doc shivered and asked, "What was that all about?"

"That's so my men can find us. It won't be long."

They walked for another fifteen minutes. Ramador put his hand out and stopped Doc. "They're here."

"What do you mean? I don't see anyone."

Seven Andorans suddenly landed on the ground around them. Doc asked in surprise, "Where did they come from?"

"Andorans are good at this."

"Ramador, where have you been?" asked one of the Andorans.

"Pendragon has been up our tails to find you and get you back to the battle star."

"Yes, I'm sure he has."

"Who is this, a prisoner?"

"He is the bearer of good news for our people."

"How is that possible?"

"The Earthers aren't like the others. They have a cure for our plague."

"I don't believe it. It's a trap."

"No, it's not. I am the proof. I slept for the first time in a long time and I had no problems, no degeneration, and no pain."

"But how could they find it so fast?"

Ramador turned to Doc. "Why don't you explain it to them?"

"Well, it's like this. Your blood is very similar to ours. What you have is a bacterium that, if left unchecked, creates the symptoms that you experience. It's very similar to bacteria that we have on Earth. When we gave Ramador a dose of it, we figured that the worst thing that would happen is nothing. Fortunately, he recovered quickly."

"I understand that many of you will not want to take this serum because of what the Council did to some of our leaders," explained

Ramador. "The Earthers didn't know of the existence of the Council until Diomedes screwed their world up."

"But how could she do that? She was Pendragon's mate," asked another Andoran.

"Diomedes used Pendragon for bigger things. She was a very evil creature."

"Does Pendragon know this?"

"No and I'm sure he doesn't want to."

"Will you tell him?"

"Yes, and I'll also tell him about the serum. This gives us good reason to stop the invasion and reevaluate what's going on."

"Pendragon will never go for that!" the Andoran blurted.

"Then it is time for Pendragon to step down as leader of his people," announced Ramador.

"We will follow you, Ramador."

"I won't fail you. Now, anyone who would like to receive the serum, come forward and Dr. Smith will give it to you." Ramador was surprised that all of the men but two received the shot.

"We will rest until morning. I believe Dr. Smith will return to his people and we'll return to the battle star tomorrow to meet with Pendragon." After administering the serum, Doc and Ramador spoke for several minutes before shaking hands and parting.

When morning came, the Andorans were ecstatic. Most of them had no lingering effects at all from their ailment. A few had chills and a bit of nausea but the improvement was significant. The two Andorans who rejected the opportunity to receive the RF34 were bitter over their comrades' good fortune. Ramador offered to contact Dr. Smith for more of the RF-34 but they elected to pass. They were still quite suspicious of the serum and the fact that humans would help them.

The Andorans boarded their ship and took off to rendezvous with their battle star. During the trip, Ramador conversed with his troops about the failed battle plans. One of his officers questioned, "How is it possible that the humans could take out four of our battle stars so quickly. There was no report of an attack or heavy damage."

"If the battle stars were clustered too close," he explained, "then a tactical hit on one or two of them could result in a chain reaction, thus destroying the others. Do we know if there is any chance of survivors?"

"I've heard that one battle star is somewhat intact but totally disabled. Survivability is possible but unlikely."

"Has Pendragon sent rescue ships to check for survivors?" Ramador inquired.

"I don't know. He called a big meeting at his battle star. I haven't been able to reach anyone since."

"I'm sure he's going through the roof and there will be some bloodletting. How many fighters did we lose in the aerial assault on Earth?"

"Most of them. Only about a dozen made it back. Their fighting machines were most efficient. We never expected that."

"Another reason we should settle for peace with the Earthers."

"But Pendragon is talking about unleashing Dark Horizon."

Ramador looked shocked. "He can't! There's no way to control it once the reaction starts. Hell, it could engulf our world as well."

"What can we do?" the Andoran asked, growing nervous.

"If I can't change his mind, we'll have to stop him physically."

As the Andorans spoke of the circumstances and possible plans of action, the two, who passed on the serum, exploited their bitterness as traitors to their comrades. They contacted Pendragon and revealed Ramador's actions to him.

When the transport ship reached the battle star and docked, there was a unit of Andoran troops waiting for Ramador and his unit. Ramador led his men from the ship and greeted the troops.

"Fellow Andorans, I have great news that will change all of our lives."

"Stay where you are, Ramador," ordered one of the Andoran officers. "You and your men must surrender or die."

"We received word that you are leading a rebellion against Pendragon," announced another.

"Listen to me first before you carry out your orders," Ramador requested.

"What news could you have that is so important?"

"There is a cure for our affliction," he said enthusiastically.

"Can you prove that?" challenged the first officer.

"Most of us have received the serum and are cured," he revealed. "We have slept well the last two sleep cycles with no side effects."

"How did you come across this 'cure'?"

"The Earthers are not like the others. I have been there and met with them. They ask for peace."

"They have destroyed four of our battle stars and most of our fighters. They came aboard this ship and slaughtered many of our officers."

"All but Pendragon. Imagine that," Ramador replied with a smirk.

"You don't think he killed them, do you?" asked one of the troops.

"It won't be the first time. He's irrational and insane. Perhaps it's time for him to step down."

"But he has always been our leader."

"Yes, but unless he gets the cure, he'll go mad. He'll massacre everyone, especially if he detonates Dark Horizon."

"So, what do you intend to do?" questioned the first officer.

"I want to talk to him first. Perhaps he'll listen. Are you going to help us or interfere?"

The Andoran was unsure and looked to his men for support. They were interested in the cure and supported Ramador. "See if you can raise him on the tele-link. I'll talk to him," requested Ramador.

The Andoran obeyed and left for the communication room. Ramador ordered his men to bring forth the two traitors for questioning. "Why would you do this? Many Andorans could have died fighting each other because of you."

"You've sided with the humans. They are our enemy," answered one of the traitors.

"If they can cure our people, I hardly think that makes them the enemy. You've overstepped the limits of your rank. Without proper authorization, you passed on incomplete information in a reckless manner. I must sentence you to death."

The two Andoran traitors pleaded for mercy but Ramador raised his arm signaling their execution. Two of his men raised their guns. When he lowered his arm, the men each fired once. Two well-placed shots penetrated each one's skull and killed them instantly.

A voice blared from the page system, "Ramador, Pendragon is waiting to speak with you."

Ramador went to the communication room and sat in front of the screen. "Pendragon, it's been a while."

"Yes, you traitor. What are you doing to my forces?"

"We have a cure. It works fast and is very effective."

"I don't believe you."

"My men and I have received the serum and we have slept well the last few cycles."

"Who gave you this serum?"

"The Earthers. I have met with them and discussed the situation surrounding us all."

"You are a traitor!"

"No, Pendragon. You have been deceived by Diomedes and now you are blinded by your madness. I'm offering you a way back to sanity and what we were."

"I will never bow to the humans. They killed my children, and my Diomedes. I will kill them all."

"There is no bowing, only friendship," urged Ramador.

"Then there will be no one!" shouted Pendragon. The screen went blank.

Ramador stared at it dejectedly until the communication officer interrupted him. "What do we do now? He's going to use Dark Horizon."

"My men will stay here and control the battle star. Have all remaining fighters assemble here. Your men can return with me to receive the antidote if you like. I must speak with the Earthers before anything else happens."

"What about Pendragon?"

"He's going to Arterius to get Dark Horizon," answered Ramador. "It should take him a while to get there."

"How will you stop him?"

"The humans have very good portals. Perhaps we can head him off."

"It certainly sounds risky."

"I know. Instruct the pilot to take the battle star to the portal."

"Why the portal?"

"Because that's where Pendragon will want to strike if he returns. Your mission will be to stop him at all costs."

"Yes, sir."

"When you get to the portal, look for two ships with the names *Luna C* and *Trav ST* on the sides. If you see them, do not fire at them. Contact them and tell them you're with me." The Andoran seemed uncertain but obeyed Ramador's orders.

Pendragon arrived at the battle star *Pernicious* and docked inside the transport bay. Four Andorans awaited him when he exited the hatch. "Where's your crew, Pendragon?"

"The traitors have joined the humans and sided against us."

"There is a rumor going around about a cure for our disease."

"That's a lie and if I hear one more word about it, I'll kill the pathetic creature who speaks of it!"

"Yes, sir."

"Where are our fighters right now?"

"They've returned to the *Ciphones*."

"Get them back here now!" he screamed in a rage.

"Sir, there are only about two dozen left."

"Is that a problem?" Pendragon shouted.

"No, sir. I'll arrange that immediately."

Pendragon entered the control room. Seven Andoran officers immediately came to attention. "We're going to the seventh quadrant," announced Pendragon. "I want that portal taken by storm, if necessary. If you encounter any resistance, destroy them."

"Sir, what if they are Andoran?"

"Do I stutter? Destroy anyone or anything that gets in your way. Do you understand?"

"Yes, sir."

"I must leave to pick up an important component. I'll join you at the portal." Pendragon left the control room for the transport bay. Two Andorans intercepted him and saluted.

"Pendragon, we've received word that there is a truce to the war and there's a cure as well. Is this true?" asked one of the officers.

Pendragon sneered and looked away for a moment. As he turned to face them, he drew his gun and shot both Andorans in the face. The smoldering bodies fell lifeless to the floor. "They just don't get it, do they?" he uttered as he marched away.

Pendragon boarded a transport and departed from the *Pernicious*. Once underway, he contacted the commander on Arterius. "This is Pendragon."

"Good day, Sir. This is Commander Jaxton.

"Prepare Dark Horizon for loading. I'm on my way."

"But, Pendragon, it isn't ready. If you launch it now, there's no telling what it will do."

"Did you hear what I said, Commander! It seems that my people are developing hearing problems and I do have a cure for it."

"Yes, sir! It will be ready when you arrive."

"I'll contact you when I clear the Thorus Nebula." Pendragon turned off the tele-link and leaned back in his chair. He tried to recall how long it had been since he last slept. A cure would be so welcome. Unfortunately, he could never give in to the humans, not after what they did to him. He would appear weak to his people. The humans killed his family, destroyed half of his battle stars and most of his fighters. He couldn't ask his allies for support because he couldn't trust them. If the Andorans appeared weakened, they would turn on him. No, Dark Horizon was the only solution. He had to show that he was merciless and powerful beyond anyone's imagination.

I can't let those two humans (Billy and Penny) get away with this. They must pay for what they've done to Diomedes, he thought desperately as he considered how to exact his revenge on them. Pendragon changed the coordinates of his ship and headed for Firenghia. He would go after the escaped prisoners and hunt Penny down.

The *Luna C* and the *Trav ST* circled the wreckage area and looked for signs of the *Specter*. A male voice came across the page, "This is Prax, your pilot. We're getting a distress signal from a small planet not far from here. It may be from the *Specter*."

CHAPTER 7

NEW FRIENDSHIPS

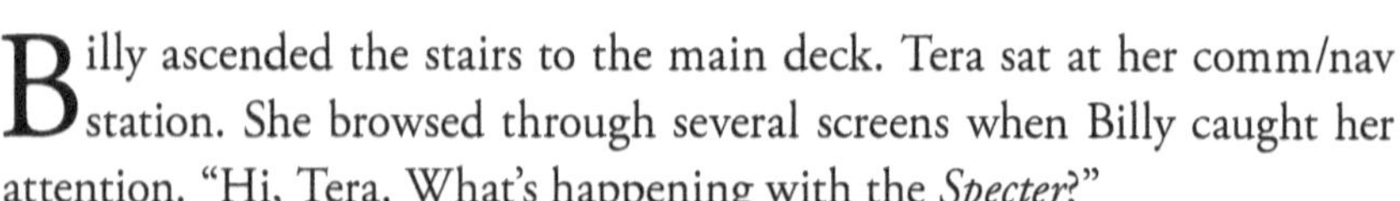

Billy ascended the stairs to the main deck. Tera sat at her comm/nav station. She browsed through several screens when Billy caught her attention. "Hi, Tera. What's happening with the *Specter*?"

"You don't belong up here. Return to your seat."

"I have friends on board the ship. Can't you show some compassion?"

The pilot entered the cabin. He was in his late twenties and about the same height as Billy. He had thick, black wavy hair about shoulder length. "I'm Prax," he said in a friendly manner. "You must be Billy."

Billy shook hands with him. "Yes, I am. It's nice to meet you, Prax."

"Tera's been telling me all about you." Before Billy could respond, Tera interrupted, "I don't think so, Prax."

"How would you know anything about me?" he asked Tera, curious of Prax's remark.

"I don't, so it doesn't matter," she muttered.

Prax was amused by Tera's behavior. "I heard you asking about your friends," Prax mentioned. "The *Trav ST* is investigating a distress signal from a nearby planet. It may be them. Meanwhile, we're checking out the battle star. I'll let you know if I hear anything more on your friends."

"Thanks, Prax."

"What are we supposed to be looking for anyway?" asked Tera.

"Survivors and hopefully information we can use to negotiate with the Andorans," answered Billy.

"Is it safe to go onboard?" asked Prax.

"I hope so."

"Courtney, my co-pilot is going to stay on board and watch for uninvited guests," Prax informed them. "I'll be joining you."

"How long before we dock?" Billy inquired.

"Oh, about half an hour by your time. It's probably wise to buckle up in the meantime. We've never docked on an Andoran battle star before."

"Thanks, Prax. I appreciate the information." Billy returned to his seat downstairs.

Tera punched Prax in the arm. "Why did you say that?"

"Well, you do seem to know quite a bit about him. Does he know who you are?"

"No and I want to keep it that way."

"I can tell you like him," teased Prax.

"He's not my type."

"Face it, Tera; there aren't many men in the universe who are your type," he joked.

"And why is that?"

"Because you're downright scary. I mean look at the way you dress up off-duty. And that music you listen to - it's bone chilling. No wonder Earth is the only place that it's played."

"That's my business. After what Xerxes did to my mother, I feel that way inside."

"You can't still blame him for that."

"He left my mother heart-broken. When the aliens attacked and took her prisoner, he did nothing to save her."

"What should he have done?"

"Fight for her! She died rather than face imprisonment at the hands of the Boromeans. I watched it all happen and I was a child. How am I supposed to feel?"

"Hey, I was there, too, you know," Prax reminded her.

"I'm sorry. It gets me so mad when I think about it."

"Have you ever talked to him about it?"

"Are you kidding? He's too busy solving everyone else's problems to worry about me."

"Does he know you've been sneaking to Earth all this time?"

Tera laughed at the question. "No, and I'm sure he's not interested. "I have a lot of respect for the Earthers."

"Is that why you like Billy?"

"I didn't say I like him."

"You don't have to. I can see it."

"I doubt it."

"We'll see about that. I have to help Courtney dock the ship." Prax returned to the flight deck and prepared for docking. Tera resumed monitoring the navigation and communication equipment.

— X —

Billy climbed into the turret and gazed at the stars. When he thought about Penny, a tear welled in his eye. He put his head down on the dash and thought about all the things that he and Penny went through together. He recalled the happy experiences he had with Seneca. Even the thought of his son, Will, was not enough to give him hope.

Tera paused at the bottom of the turret's ladder and looked up. "Hey, Brock. Are you okay?"

Billy was startled. "Uh, yeah. How long have you been there, Tera?"

"Not long." Tera climbed up the ladder and poked her head inside the turret. "I didn't mean to be so hard on you. I came to apologize."

"Thank you."

Tera noticed tears in his eyes. "You're crying. What's wrong?"

"It's just a tear."

"You've been dumped, huh?"

"Yeah, it's a recurring theme in my life."

"I know how you feel. Whenever I'm alone, I feel that way."

"You've been dumped, too?"

"In a way. It's a long story and I'm not about to go into it. When we dock, you and I will check out the battle star. I've mapped out the compartments that are still intact using sensors. We'll don oxygen masks and pulse pistols. Prax will guard the hallway leading to the transport bay and Courtney will stay aboard. We'll have radio contact if she picks up anything hostile on the monitors."

"I'll be ready."

"We'll talk later. I've got to get back to my station."

"Thanks, Tera. I appreciate your understanding."

"I'm sorry. I've always been bitter, so don't take it personal."

"You've got it down pretty good."

Tera smiled for the first time at him and descended the ladder. Billy wondered what she knew about him and why discuss it with Prax. If she did know, then how?

The *Luna C* rocked several times as it bumped the transport bay dock and settled into the nest. Sounds from the hydraulic latches broke the silence. Hissing from air solenoids in the ceiling reminded Billy of a train pulling into the station. He climbed down from the turret and entered the main quarters.

Prax and Tera descended the stairs with some equipment. "Last chance to back out, guys," said Prax hopefully.

"Always the brave one, aren't you?" chided Tera. She strapped her oxygen pack on and attached the pulse pistol to her belt. Billy and Prax weren't as quick as Tera and rushed to keep pace.

"Ready, Billy?" she inquired. "Do I have to dress you, too?" Billy frowned at her while Prax cast a sly smile at her.

When Billy was fully suited, he and Tera donned the oxygen masks and tested them. They tested the radio devices, which strapped to their heads. Once everything checked out, they stepped into the inner hatch. "Billy, are you okay with your gear?" Tera checked with him once more.

"Yeah, I'm good. Let's go."

Tera pushed a red knob, the size of a mushroom. The cabin depressurized and the hatch opened. Billy and Tera passed through the hatch and entered a long corridor leading from the transport bay. Prax remained at the entrance from the transport bay in case he needed to cover them for a quick escape.

Tera climbed the stairs and proceeded down another long corridor. Billy followed about ten feet behind her, watching for any sign of danger. When they reached the end of the corridor, they found the control room. Tera's attention was drawn to the big table with several charts and a logbook spread out. Instinctively, she went to the table without looking.

Billy saw the door near the corner of the room open slightly. An Andoran crept out and aimed his gun at Tera. "Tera!" shouted Billy. He rushed at her and knocked her to the floor. The room was filled with a bright flash. Billy howled in pain. He rolled off of Tera and fired three shots from his pulse pistol at the Andoran. It screeched and fell to the ground, wounded.

Tera quickly got up and kicked the gun away from the Andoran. "Get up!" she screamed.

The Andoran sneered at her and replied, "I can't. I'm wounded, you fool."

Billy lay on the floor, writhing in pain. Tera knelt by him and looked concerned. "Are you okay, Billy?"

Billy pulled his mask off. "I think it's just a graze but, damn, it hurts."

"Let me help you onto a chair." As she lifted him, she yelled at the Andoran, "Don't give me a reason to put a hole in your head."

"Can't you see, I'm trembling." He mocked her. "Just shoot me and get it over with."

"So, you're a comic, too," Billy taunted him.

"Shut up, Earther."

"I'll shut you up permanently, Andoran," warned Tera.

"Who are you?" Billy interrupted.

"What do you care?"

"I'm a friend of Ramador's," Billy informed him.

Tera removed her mask and was surprised by the conversation that transpired before her. "Ramador? What do you know of him?" she asked Billy.

"He and I have developed a friendship."

The Andoran scoffed at Billy. "Why would he do that?"

"Because we have a cure for your affliction. Ramador's trying to give the cure to everyone but Pendragon wants to keep fighting."

"What does that do for me?"

"Maybe we can help each other. We can get you out of here and get you medical attention."

"And what do you want in return?"

"There was a small ship out here before your mishap. I had friends on board. Do you know anything about it?"

"No, I never saw the ship."

"What happened out here?"

"There were four battle stars. We waited behind the asteroid C5P for the portal to open. There was a report of a small ship sitting idly by when we left the asteroid."

"What caused your ships to explode like this?"

"The ship fired projectiles into the exhaust vents of two of the battle stars. By the time we realized what happened, it was too late. The explosion was incredible. My guess is that their ship was hurled away from us toward the planet Dorinos. We lost power to most of our systems and now I'm here."

"Are there any other survivors on board?"

"No. Two of our transports escaped in a hurry but when they left the bay, they were destroyed by the shock wave."

"You can come back with us if you like. Ramador will be meeting with us soon and you can return with him."

"Why would you do that for me?"

"Why not? We don't have to hate each other."

"Then why did you assassinate some of our leaders?"

"A small group of people were responsible for that. You can't blame everyone for the actions of a few."

"What is Ramador doing about it?"

"He wants to get everyone vaccinated but he also wants to end the fighting."

"Is that happening?"

"It's hard to tell. I haven't spoken to him since he returned to his men."

"Alright, I'll go back with you. It beats dying here. Besides there isn't much backup power left for the life support systems."

"Can you walk, Billy?" asked Tera worriedly.

"I think so."

"You saved my life."

"You'd have done it for me."

"How do you know?"

Billy forced a smile and said, "I know."

Tera wondered what he meant, but opted not to pursue the conversation further. "Can you walk?" she asked the Andoran.

"Yes, I can. Your weapon was only set to stun." The Andoran stood up and teetered.

"You look pretty wobbly for just a stun," kidded Billy.

"I have a few spots in my eyes but other than that, I'm okay. For what it's worth, my name is Cirrus."

"This is Tera and I'm Billy."

"You wouldn't be the same Billy that Pendragon is looking for?"

"It seems that good news travels fast."

"You know he won't stop until he kills you."

"I've heard."

"What could you possibly do to Pendragon that he wants you so badly?" inquired Tera.

"It's a long story," Billy replied somberly.

Cirrus was amused by Billy's response to Tera's question and interjected, "Billy terminated Pendragon's witch spouse."

"You weren't fond of her, were you?" asked Billy.

"No, she was evil and we all knew it. Pendragon was blind to what she really was. Besides what human woman in her right mind would mate with an Andoran?"

Billy was shocked. "She did what?"

"Yeah, she mated with him. She went through a horrible transformation and mutated. I'm glad she's dead."

"That's enough talk," interrupted Tera. "We should leave before the oxygen runs out."

Billy stood up and hobbled toward the door behind Cirrus. Tera moved next to Billy and put his arm around her. "Thanks, Tera."

"No, thank you."

When they approached the corridor to the transport bay, Tera ordered Cirrus to stop. He looked back at her in surprise. "What's wrong?"

"One of our people is guarding the corridor. I don't want you to get shot."

"I see." Cirrus stepped aside and followed them.

"I can't believe we're rescuing the Andoran. Are you sure you know what you're doing?" Tera whispered to Billy.

"You'll see why when we get back."

"Does Xerxes know about this business with serum and Andorans?"

"Yeah, why?"

"Just curious. Since when do Andorans speak our language?" she asked, curious.

Billy countered, "When did you learn to speak my language? Earth has a multitude of languages."

"I've been through a very long training course to become an officer. I needed to learn all of your languages as part of it."

"So, you can speak every language on Earth?"

"Well, most of them. But what about him?" she asked as she pointed to Cirrus.

Cirrus overheard and answered, "I have a translator box here on my neck. It allows me to speak your language. I also have an implant in my brain that allows me to interpret what you say very quickly."

"Does Xerxes know about all this?" Tera asked Billy.

"How well do you know Xerxes?" Billy asked.

"What's that got to do with anything?"

"Did I hit a nerve or something?"

"No, just drop it."

"You humans talk too much and you talk about the stupidest things. That conversation made no sense at all," complained Cirrus.

"Then don't listen," Tera replied sarcastically.

"Typical female," he remarked cynically.

Billy laughed and drew an angry glare from Tera. "Don't look at me. He said it."

"And you found it funny."

Billy warned Cirrus, "Don't get her mad at you. It's not a pretty sight."

Tera grabbed Billy's side and squeezed. He cringed in pain. "Ouch! What are you doing?"

"Don't think you're exempt from my wrath, Brock, just because we talked for a little bit."

Cirrus laughed. "What a fate for you, Billy. I can see you killing another evil woman in your future."

Tera turned and put her pulse pistol into Cirrus' face. "Do you really think so? My pistol is set for 'kill', not 'stun'."

"That was an attempt at Earth humor. I give up, already," said Cirrus dryly. Billy chuckled as they turned the corner.

Prax approached them with his pistol drawn. "What's going on?"

"It's okay. He's coming back with us," answered Billy.

"Am I missing something, Tera? That's an Andoran."

"Yeah, I know. These two shoot each other up and now their best friends. I always said that men were screwed up." Prax looked confused as they entered the *Luna C* and removed their equipment.

Billy sat down on a crate and leaned back against the wall. "Lay down flat so I can fix your wound," ordered Tera.

"It'll be okay."

Tera glared at him. "Brock, don't you ever listen!"

"Okay, okay," he muttered.

Cirrus curled up in the corner and stared at the monitor. It showed the battle star as they pulled away. Tera ripped away Billy's shirt and washed off his wound. "It looks like more than a flesh wound."

"It'll heal fast. Trust me."

"Don't play that macho crap with me. That's how infection sets in."

Billy forced a smile and said, "You do care."

"Don't push it." Tera bandaged Billy's side. "I've got to go upstairs. I'll check on you later. Besides, I'm sure Cirrus will keep you company." Billy laughed cynically.

"Are all Earth women like her?" inquired Cirrus.

"I'm starting to believe that. Are Andoran females like that?"

"Oh, yes. That's why the males stay away on the ships. We only go home to mate."

"I think I like that idea."

"Even that's a chore sometimes," Cirrus complained.

"I guess female behavior is universal," Billy remarked and chuckled.

"Watch yourself," warned Cirrus. "I wouldn't trust her."

"I don't think she can hurt me any more than I already have been."

Prax' voice came over the page, "Fasten your seat belts. Alien fighters approaching from the starboard." Billy instinctively hobbled to the ladder and climbed into the turret.

A dozen lights approached the ship quickly. He strapped himself in and studied the controls for the cannon. He lowered the visor over his eyes and gripped the joystick. "Prax, can you feed me coordinates for those fighters?"

"Sorry, Billy. I can't, but I think Tera can. Hang on for a moment. I'll ask her." Prax' voice came back on the headset: "Billy, Tera's going to handle it. Do you know how to use the cannon?"

"It's just like Play Station. No problem."

Prax and Courtney looked at each other in bewilderment on the flight deck. "What's Play Station?" Prax asked Courtney.

"Beats me. One of those Earth games, I think."

As soon as the coordinates streamed onto Billy's visor, he fired. He missed his first seven shots, but finally hit one of the fighters. Tera's voice rang over the headset: "It's about time you hit one! I can see I'm going to have to teach you how to shoot." Before he could reply, the *Luna C* shuddered and jerked to the right.

"You'd better start hitting them fast, Billy. That last one took part of the hull and one of our sensors with it," Prax advised nervously.

"Here we go. I'm warmed up," Billy said confidently. He disregarded the coordinates and lined up his shots as if he were playing a game. He picked off three of the fighters that circled around them. Suddenly two more exploded and a third one was damaged.

Billy looked across at the other turret and saw Tera there. "Hey, what are you doing? Leave some for me," he kidded.

"Just shut up and fire," she ordered. "This isn't a game."

A shot sailed dangerously close to the top of the *Luna C* and warmed the temperature in the turrets. Billy wiped the sweat from his head, thankful that the ball of energy missed him. Now he felt a sense of urgency and chased the remaining fighters with cannon fire. He hit another and watched as two more exploded nearby. The last one peeled away and disappeared.

Prax voice blared in their headsets, "Nice shooting! You two make a great pair."

"Can it, Prax," replied Tera.

"Come on, Tera. You know what I mean."

"How's the ship, Prax?" asked Billy.

"Some damage but nothing serious. If that shot were ten feet lower, we'd have been history, though. It was that close."

"I thought you said you could shoot?" asked Tera.

"I did. I wasn't that bad, was I?"

"Typical male. All talk."

"I'm checking out of this conversation," said Prax. "Nice job, Billy."

"Thanks, Prax." Billy descended the ladder and met Tera as she climbed down the other one. "You shot really well, Tera. Were you trained as a gunner?" inquired Billy.

"No, it came naturally."

"You did great up there. I was really impressed."

"Well, how about that - a complement," she remarked cynically. "I suppose I should be grateful."

Billy was disappointed. He thought they were past the sarcasm. "No, just forget I said anything." He walked toward the front of the quarters and wondered, *What ails that woman?* He felt light-headed so he lay across the crate.

Cirrus commented, "Boromean."

Billy looked over at Cirrus. "What's that?"

"The fighters were Boromean, not Andoran."

"What does that mean?"

"Other alien groups are entering the area now to attack the humans."

"Is there an alliance between the Andorans and these other races?"

"Kind of. They know that the Andorans are vulnerable right now without four of their battle stars so it's likely void."

"That's just great. So even if we take care of Pendragon and the Andorans are happy with the serum, the other races are still going to fight the war?"

"That's exactly it. Pendragon's theory was that Dark Horizon would guarantee that the Andorans wield the power so no one will ever think of turning on us. Your people set us back quite a bit. If the others believe the Andorans are weakened, they could turn on us, too."

"So, if we were to destroy Dark Horizon, then the power that protects you from them is gone."

"Now you're learning."

"What is Dark Horizon?" asked Billy.

"I don't really know? Pendragon has captured some specialists from Archaenia. He's holding some of their family members hostage until they develop the weapon."

"Oh, great! What else could possibly happen?"

"Don't ask, Billy. You might not like the answer."

"Thanks, Cirrus. You're a wealth of comfort."

— ☓ —

The *Trav ST* approached the small planet, Dorinos, and zeroed in on the signal. Once the ship descended through the thick layer of clouds in the upper atmosphere, the visibility was very good.

John and Seamus sat anxiously in front of the monitors and searched for any sign of the *Specter*. The terrain was covered with barren mountains, dried gulches and riverbeds. As the ship hovered past two pointed peaks, the *Specter* came into view.

The pilot's voice came over the page, "Gentleman, the *Specter* is in our sights. We'll be landing shortly."

"Isn't it strange that no one's outside the ship? I'm sure they can hear us," John asked Seamus.

"I hope they're alive."

The *Trav ST* set down close by the *Specter* and shut down its engines. Commander Gordon briefed the men before opening the hatch. He warned them to be wary of any unforeseen dangers. In addition, he issued each man a pulse pistol.

The hatch opened and they stepped out onto the hard rocky surface. The *Specter* was a battered wreck. Part of the tail and the wing sections were missing.

Gordon kept a wary eye while Seamus and John hurriedly worked the hatch open. After several anxious moments, the hatch squealed and broke loose. They jumped aside as it fell to the ground with a bang.

The men entered the *Specter* and searched for any survivors. When they reached the top of the stairs, they tried to enter the flight deck but the door was barricaded from the inside.

John picked up a broken piece of conduit and beat on the door. They heard a scraping sound from inside the cabin, followed by a loud thud. The door opened slowly, but no one came out. John pushed it open and leaned in.

Ronnie, Randy and Tur lay on the floor, in a weakened state. Their faces were ashen and drawn in. John lifted Ronnie up and hugged her. "Thank God you're alive."

Ronnie struggled to speak. "Get out of here. Get out before they come back," she uttered weakly.

"Who?"

"Get out, John. Please."

"Quickly, let's get them back to the ship," Gordon ordered. "There's still a threat in the area." John and Seamus carried the girls while Commander Gordon assisted Tur back to the ship.

The ground suddenly moved as if it were alive. The men hustled to reach their ship but Gordon stumbled and fell. He quickly picked up Tur and stepped inside the ship. He pressed the knob and closed the hatch. Suddenly, he fell to the floor screaming. He grabbed at his leg and shook violently.

John rushed to his aide and held him down while Seamus cut away at the pant leg. They were horrified to see seven brown, leach-like creatures with tentacles attached to Gordon's leg. The tentacles were pulsing as blood and fluids were drained from his leg. Seamus quickly sliced each of the creatures in half and cut out the tentacles from Gordon's leg. Gordon became unconscious and delirious. He quickly developed a fever and sweated profusely.

John shook Tur until he came to. "Tur, we've got to get out of here. We need your help."

Tur opened his eyes. "Is it really you? Are we safe?"

"Yes, but not for long if we don't get out of here. The pilot's unconscious. I need you to help us fly the ship."

"Get me into the seat and I'll show you."

John and Seamus carried him up the stairs to the flight deck and seated him. Seamus returned to check on the girls. Tur instructed John how to fly the *Trav ST*. Soon they were in the air and darting through the thick layer of clouds.

Seamus returned to the flight deck and handed Tur a container with water. "How are they?" asked John.

"They'll be okay. They've lost a lot of blood, though."

"What the hell were those things?"

"They're like little vampires," replied Tur. "They're attracted to anything with moisture in it: blood, water, anything at all. The ground is covered with them, but when they dehydrate, they lay dormant. The moisture from our bodies sparked them back to life. It's horrible what they did to the other pilot."

"I have to get the others some drinking water. I'll be down there with them. Holler if you need me."

"Thanks, Seamus."

"Did you come alone?" asked Tur.

"No, the *Luna C* is waiting out by the battle star wreckage," John replied.

"Here is the comm-link. Call them and let them know we're coming."

John gladly reported to the *Luna C* that the survivors were aboard and they were returning home. He descended the stairs to see his friends.

Ronnie sat up and drank from a flask. Seamus cradled Randy in his arms. She opened her eyes and forced a smile. "You saved me."

"Of course, I did. You're my sweetheart." She nestled against him and sipped water from a flask. John knelt by Ronnie and kissed her forehead. "I was so worried."

Ronnie smiled at him. A tear rolled down her cheek. "I thought we were going to die."

"I wouldn't let you. I need you." John hugged her.

"What about Gordon?" asked Seamus.

"He'll need medical attention," said John somberly. "He's bad." Seamus tried to give him water but Gordon was incoherent.

$$— \mathbf{X} —$$

A female voice came over the intercom: "Billy, this is Courtney. Just wanted to let you know that your friends have been rescued and are onboard the *Trav ST* as we speak. They are returning."

"Thanks, Courtney. I appreciate that."

"So, things are okay now for you?" Cirrus asked.

"No, they're never okay for me," Billy complained. "Ever since Diomedes and Ruger screwed up my life seven months ago, things have never been okay."

"I'm sorry to have brought up that issue."

"When we get back, if you like, I'll have the doctor give you the serum."

"I'd love to sleep peacefully again."

Tera returned a short while later. "Hey, Brock. How're you feeling?"

"Tired, but not bad."

"Let me check the dressing."

"Tera, it's okay. You don't have to do this."

"Why not?"

"Because you'll only bitch at me when you're done."

Cirrus laughed. "Smart boy. You learned fast," he joked.

Tera took her pulse pistol and pointed it at Cirrus' head. "Do you really want some of this?"

"Yeah, yeah. I know. Shut up, Cirrus," he said, mocking.

Tera removed the dressing and was surprised how fast the wound healed. "I don't believe it!!"

"I told you I heal fast."

"What are you?" she asked, stunned.

"I'm part Firenghian, you know, shapeshifter. I have some of their other traits, too."

"I heard stories but..."

"What stories?" he interrupted.

"Never mind. It doesn't matter."

"Tell me," Billy demanded. "What are you hearing and from whom?"

"I just heard that you've been through a lot and did some interesting things to stay alive," she explained innocently.

"That's not it," he challenged.

"That's all I'm telling you."

"Why?"

"When I'm ready, you'll know."

"Look, Miss Priss, I'm getting tired of your games. I'm not a pawn and I won't play anymore."

Tera smiled at him coyly. "That's a shame," she crooned, tossing the dressings in the trashcan. "I guess, since you're a fast healer, you don't need me anymore." She tweeked his nose playfully and then ascended the stairs. Cirrus laughed uncontrollably.

"What's so funny, Cirrus?" asked Billy, annoyed.

"The devil woman has your number. I pity you."

"Well, I pity you the next time you crack a joke around her. She will shoot you. She's a cold-hearted bitch."

"You should be an expert on them by now."

"As a matter of fact, I am. Just about every female I meet is an inconsiderate deceitful pain in the ass!"

"And the truth comes out. I see you have a history of evil witches," Cirrus remarked.

"Don't remind me."

Tera stood at the top of the steps, listening with a big smile as Billy and Cirrus conversed back and forth. Prax tapped her on the shoulder and startled her. "What's going on?"

"Oh, nothing. I was just eavesdropping on Billy and Cirrus."

"What are you doing now?" questioned Prax. "I know you're causing trouble."

"Who me? Never."

"Does Billy know that you have it for him?"

"Have what? Oh, shut up. You have no idea…"

"Come on, Tera. I've never seen you like this before. You've smiled three times on this trip. That's three more times than I've ever seen you smile."

"Don't you have something better to do?" Tera asked defensively.

"You're right. Got to get back to my seat."

Tera reluctantly descended the stairs again to the lower level. Cirrus couldn't resist antagonizing her. "Well, well. It's the Grim Reaper."

"Andorans have one of them, too?" Billy asked humorously.

"We do now."

Tera checked Billy's pulse and pulled down a first aid kit from the cabinet above. After rooting around in the case for a few minutes, she took out a syringe and a vial.

"Look, Cirrus. That's for you. I told you she would get you," Billy teased.

"No, my friend. I think it's for you."

Tera's face turned red as the two laughed at her. She gave Billy a shot of an antibiotic and put the kit away. She stormed back to Billy and leaned over him, her face just inches from him. Before she could say anything, they locked their eyes on each other. She leaned forward and kissed him, gently at first, then more passionately. Suddenly, she jumped back and shouted, "That won't work with me, Brock. You're dead meat when we get back!"

Billy was amused and responded calmly, "Okay."

"I'm not kidding!"

"Okay."

"Ooh, you're going to pay for this!"

"Okay."

She raced up the steps and sat down at her station.

Prax heard the shouting and hurried down to her station. "Are you okay?"

"Yes, why?"

"How's Billy?" he inquired, grinning.

"What are you talking about?"

"We heard you all the way up in the flight deck."

"Oh," she muttered, embarrassed by her loss of control.

"I'm serious. Are you okay, Tera?"

"Yes. I'm fine."

"What happened down there?"

"I kissed him."

"Did he force you to?"

"No, I did it."

Prax laughed hysterically as he returned to the flight deck. Tera laughed as well when she thought about the whole episode. She remained upstairs for fear of what might happen next.

— X —

"Would you mind explaining to me what that was about?" asked Cirrus.

"I'm not sure myself," replied Billy.

"Does she have an interest in you or something?"

"I think so, but I'm not sure. Do Andorans kiss?"

"No. Our mating rituals are a little different. We rub our tails together and stroke the area between the ridges on our backs. Was this part of your ritual?"

"This wasn't a mating ritual, Cirrus."

"Sure, it was."

"No, it wasn't. That was an 'I'm a woman and I'm really confused' ritual."

"Humans are very unusual creatures. Are all of you like that?"

"What do you mean 'all of us'?"

"I mean all of the human species around the universe."

"For some reason, I don't think so. I think our planet is different from all the rest." Billy stared at the monitor in silence. Cirrus studied Billy for a while. He found Billy and Tera quite entertaining.

The two ships arrived without further incident in the transport bay of the research center. Two medical teams were on hand when they docked. They placed Gordon and Tur on stretchers and inserted IVs into their arms. Gordon regained consciousness, but looked like a frightened child. The med-techs promptly took the men to the infirmary. John and Seamus escorted Ronnie and Randy to the infirmary as well.

Doc came down to greet everyone. He was amazed to see another Andoran. "Billy, where do you keep finding these stray Andorans?"

"Cirrus is my new friend. Can you get him a shot of the serum?"

"Of course."

"Will I be able to sleep after I get this shot?" asked Cirrus.

"Ramador slept very well after receiving it."

"Good. Find me a place I can sleep afterward. I haven't slept in hundreds of cycles."

"Follow me and we'll get you started."

"Good luck, buddy," Billy said to Cirrus. "I'll see you when you wake up."

Cirrus shook Billy's hand. "Thank you, Billy."

"Anytime, Cirrus."

Tera crept behind Billy.

"Look out for the witch!" warned Cirrus.

Tera looked about to ensure no one was watching. She held up her middle finger to Cirrus in an obscene fashion.

"What does that mean when a witch points her middle finger at you in a vertical manner?" Cirrus asked Doc.

"Um, nothing of importance. Just disregard it."

Billy turned around and noticed her. "Yes, Tera. You want something."

Tera wanted to comment on the kiss but then relented and muttered, "No, never mind." She walked away leaving him alone on the dock.

Xerxes entered the bay and greeted Billy. "How did your flight go?"

"I suppose it was successful. We got Ronnie and Randy back and we rescued an Andoran from the crippled battle star."

"Did you find out anything of value from him?"

"Yeah. Have you ever heard of Dark Horizon?"

"No, why?"

"Well, you'd better find out fast. Pendragon has what sounds like a doomsday weapon and he's capable of using it."

"That isn't good."

"I also know that the alien alliance is shaky at best. The Andorans hoped that Dark Horizon would make them the superior alien power. Without it, the other races could turn on them. Boromeans attacked us on the way back already."

"Boromeans! Interesting. Maybe we can use that to our advantage somehow."

"In the morning, I'd like to go back. Pendragon's out there somewhere and the sooner I find him, the faster we can put a stop to this insanity."

"I agree. How about the same crew and the *Luna C*? I see it sustained only minor damage."

"Sure. Will it be ready?"

"I'll have the dock monkeys start repairs immediately. How was Tera?"

"Fine. Why?" Billy asked, surprised.

"She has the ability to be abrasive sometimes, especially to strangers."

"She is different."

"Be patient with her."

"I have all the time in the world," Billy kidded. He wondered why Xerxes was interested in Tera.

"I'll speak with you later, Billy. It's good to see you back safely."

"Thanks, Xerxes."

Xerxes then discussed the repairs with the dock crew.

Billy walked up to the infirmary to check on Ronnie and Randy. After getting strange looks from several people, he realized he wasn't wearing a shirt. His shoulder wound was healed but the bandage still covered it securely.

When he entered the infirmary, it was a full house. Ronnie couldn't wait to chirp at Billy. "Well, it's nice of you to come in and say 'hello'."

"I'm here. How are you doing?"

"What about me? Boy, you're some friend," scolded Randy.

"I'm getting to you. Give me a chance."

"So, I'm second fiddle to Ronnie," taunted Randy.

Billy put his hands up. "You win. I have nothing."

"Can you answer one question?"

"For you, Ronnie, anytime," he said playfully.

"What happened to your shirt?"

"I got burned and it had to be cut off."

"What was her name?" asked Randy. "Give us the sordid details."

"There are no details. Nothing happened."

"I'll bet you your sword and scabbard and your skull that something happened with a woman."

Billy looked guilty as sin. "No, I'm not a betting man."

"Ah, something did happen," Randy blurted giddily.

Ronnie took a hospital gown from the table next to her bed and threw it at Billy. "Here. Cover yourself up. We can't control ourselves when we're around you."

"Stop it," Billy uttered, embarrassed. "That ain't right."

"John, hold me back," teased Ronnie. "Billy's here and I can't control myself. He's such a babe magnet."

Billy grew red-faced and shouted, "Enough! I'm glad to see you're all doing better."

"They'll be fine after a few days of hydration," replied John, amused.

"Thanks, John, for helping to rescue them."

"And what about me?" asked Seamus.

"You, too, Seamus. Thank you."

"Billy, can I ask you something?"

"Sure, John."

"Why is it that these girls get so riled up when they see you?"

"I wish I knew."

They were on their last breath until they saw you. Suddenly, they're so full of life."

Billy shrugged his shoulders. "I have no idea."

"Yes, you do!" teased Randy.

"I'll be back later to see you all. Good bye." Billy laughed as he exited the room.

"Come back, my babe magnet! Don't leave," Randy called to him, giddily.

Everyone laughed as Billy hurried up the hall. He couldn't get away fast enough. For some reason, he was an easy target for women. Why, he never understood.

When he returned to his room, he took a hot shower. Afterward, he turned on a CD and lay down on the bed. The sound of Rob Zombie's "Feel So Numb" relaxed him to the point where he nearly fell asleep. Shortly after, a knock at the door woke him up. Billy sat up in bed and reached for the remote control. He pressed the button for 'door' and the door slid open.

Tera entered, with her long black hair hanging down near her waist, carrying a vinyl black bag. Billy wondered if he was in trouble again. She wore a black leather skirt and vest. The vest had a six-inch gap in the front and was tied together with black shoestring. On her feet were black boots extending up to her knees with pointed studs around the bottom and up both sides. Black straps with studs decorated her neck and wrists.

Billy was stunned. "Is that you, Tera?"

"Is there a problem, Brock?"

"No, no. I just want to be sure who I'm talking to." Billy pushed the button and closed the door. He stared at the pentagram earrings and a flat silver skull with red ruby eyes for a pendant.

"What's wrong, Brock. Haven't you seen a Goth chick before?"

"Uh, no. That's not it. I just didn't think you were the Goth type. Your hair. It's..."

"You talk too much. What kind of music you got?"

"All kinds."

She walked over to his CD player and pushed play. "Let's see what you listen too. Is it going to be Country Western, Rap, or Blues? No, you aren't a Blues kind of person. Easy listening, yeah, that's you." She crooned as the beginning of 'Sinister Urge' played. "No, way! I love Zombie." She pulled out a plastic bag with three bottles of champagne and ice. "Got glasses?"

Baffled, Billy stood up and went into the bathroom. Tera turned off the music and opened a bottle. Billy returned with two glasses and set them on the table. He grew uneasy as Tera poured the champagne. "Tera, what's going on?"

"Shut up and enjoy yourself. You saved my life. I can never repay you but I can show my gratitude."

"Where did you learn to be a Goth?"

"I've been to Earth a number of times. I'd go there just to hang out in Goth-style night clubs."

"What made you do that?" he asked, curious.

"Your planet is the only place where humans are exciting. They know how to live and die. Besides, it helps me relate to the anger inside me."

Tera held her glass up. "What do we toast to?" she asked.

Billy wasn't sure what to say. He was overwhelmed by her appearance.

"Okay, Brock, I'll help you out. How about a toast to us?"

"Sure. Then I'll get dumped again. Why not?"

"Don't wine. Don't screw me over and I promise I won't screw you over."

"Deal."

"This is what I really am. Can you live with that?" she asked.

"I think so. You aren't going to use me for a human sacrifice, are you?"

"Don't be a creep. I'm serious."

"Yes, I can."

"Good. Then this toast is to us." They tapped glasses.

No sooner had Billy sipped his champagne, Tera pulled him to her and kissed him. It was a wild, passionate kiss with an exclamation point on it. His head spun as he tried to comprehend everything that was happening. *Is this Tera, the wonder-bitch?* he thought. In a strange sort of way, she was what he wanted: no games; right to the point.

They continued to kiss, but then Tera stopped and pushed him back a step. "So, what do you want to do next, Billy?"

"I'd like to get to know you."

"What, no sex?" she asked, surprised.

"No, not now," he admitted. "That would ruin things before they ever started."

"Billy, I believe you passed the test. I'm so happy you said that."

"No, I'm not done yet. There are other issues."

"Don't worry. I can't have kids. That's part of being a female officer in the Council's Force."

"That solves part of the problem. There's more."

"I'd better have another glass of champagne," she responded uneasily. "This should be interesting."

"Well, I've inherited several not so human traits," he confessed.

"Oh, boy, and how did you do that?" she asked.

"A close friend of mine, Seneca, is a Firenghian shape-shifter. When we were up against the wizard Ruger and the creature Diomedes, some things happened between us. As a result, she has a son by me and I inherited many of her traits."

"What kind of traits did you inherit?" Tera inquired with interest.

"I have the keen senses of animals like night vision, smell, telepathy and some other rather unusual things."

"Like "

"Well, like I can change into an alter-shape."

Tera's eyes widen in surprise. "You what?"

"I don't like to do it but when I need to, I change into a wolverine."

"Wow! Now I've heard everything."

"Look, Tera, you don't have to believe it. I hope you never see it happen. All I know is that I don't like it and I hope it never happens to me again."

"Is there something else?"

"Yes. If we make love, you might inherit some of these traits as well. Penny, my ex, inherited them directly from Seneca and she changed, but not for the better as far as I'm concerned."

"What happened?"

"She became too attached to her alter-shape. That's what came between us and killed our relationship."

"I'm sorry. How do you stand with Penny and the other woman now?"

"Penny and I are finished. She wants to stay friends but it hurts me to see her so I'd just as soon avoid her. Seneca has become more like family; like a sister since we parted ways in the old world. I'm sure we'll stay close friends, especially since she's the mother of my son."

"Why do I believe you?"

"You don't have to. You can walk out that door right now and forget you ever met me."

"Too late. You ruined me."

"How did I do that?"

"You embarrassed me on the *Luna C*. Then you caused me to lose my temper. And worst of all, you coerced me into kissing you."

"I did not," he responded, amused. "You wanted me."

"Regardless, you got to me. Then you and your lizard friend started with the witch stuff and I got so mad that I flipped him off in the bay."

"What's so bad about that?" Billy asked, entertained by the thought.

"I've never lost my cool before, let alone three times in one day. That's how I knew I wanted you."

"I'm flattered. So now it's your turn to answer questions for me."

"I guess I could."

"Can you read my thoughts?"

"No! Why would I be able to do that?"

"Don't worry. That works for me."

"Oh, so you don't want a telepathic woman."

"Nope. Too much trouble. Now, how did you hear about me?"

"I need to use the bathroom first," she replied nervously.

"Help yourself," he said and pointed toward it.

Billy leaned back on the bed and smiled at his good fortune. The door buzzer startled him back to reality. He picked up the remote and pushed the 'door' button.

When it opened, Xerxes rushed in. "Billy, I've got to talk to you about what's going on." Xerxes noticed the champagne and the two glasses. The sound of running water from the bathroom sink also caught his attention. "Did I come at a bad time?"

"No. Me and a friend were conversing."

"What happened to your neck? Did you get burned?"

Billy stood up in front of the mirror. There was a large passion mark on his neck. *Damn. Tera left her mark already*, he thought. "No, I must have scraped it or something."

The bathroom door opened and Tera walked out. When she saw Xerxes standing there, she was shocked. "What are you doing here, father?"

It was Billy's turn to be shocked. "Father! Xerxes is your dad?"

"Uh, yeah."

"You didn't tell me that!"

"I was working on it."

"So that's how you knew about me."

Xerxes was stunned. "Tera, look how you're dressed! Your hair – it's, it's like your mother's."

"I didn't want you to see me dressed like this. Besides, when did you care?"

Xerxes turned to Billy. "What's she doing here?"

"Oh, boy," muttered Billy. "It's a long story."

"You didn't care about mom, so why should you care about me?" she remarked sadistically to Xerxes.

"Your mother and I had issues."

"Is that what you call them? I watched her die at the hands of aliens when I was just a kid. You didn't even try to help her."

"You wouldn't understand."

"Oh, yeah! Try me."

"When your mother and I met, she dreamed of becoming an officer like you in the Council's Force. When she became pregnant, that ended any chance she had of being accepted."

"So, it's my fault, now!" Tera shouted.

"No, it's not. Your mother hated me for it. She loved you. What made it worse was that you look nothing like me. You're not an albino at all. You have eye brows and olive skin, just like your mother." Tera began to shake and cry. Billy put his arm around her for comfort.

Xerxes continued, "Your mother swore that if she were taken prisoner, she wanted to die fighting like an Officer of the Council's Force. If I would have interceded, I would have been killed and you'd be an orphan. If I rescued your mother or we both became prisoners, she would have been disgraced and probably killed herself and maybe me, too. I've lived with that pain all my life. I loved your mother more than you'll ever know. If it wasn't for that damn Council, we would have been happy."

"Why didn't you tell me before?"

"You didn't want to know. It was easier to hate me." Tera went to her father and hugged him. Billy walked to the window and stared into the evening sky, hoping to grant them some privacy.

"Billy, later on tonight we should meet and discuss your mission. I've received some very important information from your friend Cirrus."

"How about ten o'clock?" Billy suggested.

"That's fine. In the conference room."

Tera trembled and looked away from both men. Xerxes added, "Tera, you, too." He left and the door closed.

Tera hugged Billy and, with tears streaming down her cheeks, assured him, "I was going to tell you. I swear."

"I believe you."

"I need another glass of champagne," she said, relieved.

"Me, too," Billy replied, still stunned by this latest revelation.

Tera sat in bed next to him and nestled against his shoulder. Billy kissed her forehead. "Your father noticed the mark on my neck right away."

Tera lifted her head to see it and giggled. "I'm sorry. I was marking my territory."

"It's marked – right here." Billy pointed to his heart.

"That's so sweet." She kissed Billy over and over.

CHAPTER 8

MESSAGE OF DOOM

Two Andoran cruisers approached the two transports. Lucien pressed several buttons and watched the monitor change. He pressed another and the tele-link came on.

"What are you doing?" asked Cassius.

"There are two ships closing in on us quickly. I'll notify the other transport that we're landing on a nearby planet to hide." Lucien turned on his transmitter.

"How are we going to do that?" asked Cassius.

"The sensors show that the surface temperature is below freezing. There is significant snow and ice buildup as well. I'm sure we can disappear for a while."

"Alright. I'll inform Seneca of the change in plans."

Cassius stepped off the flight deck into the stairwell. He focused on Seneca and communicated telepathically. Seneca stirred from her sleep on the steel floor. "Seneca! We have a problem."

Seneca quickly scrambled to her feet and hurried up the stairs. Cassius returned to the flight deck and sat in the co-pilot's seat. Seneca entered and noticed the ships on the monitor. "Who are they?"

Lucien replied, "Andoran cruisers."

"Lucien thinks we can hide on the surface of a nearby planet," explained Cassius. "It's ice and snow on the surface."

Seneca glared at Lucien. "I assume you know what I'll do to you if you try any tricks."

"I'm too far into this. I can't go back."

"Very well, then."

When the transport descended through the clouds, they flew right into a snowstorm. The ship rocked violently as they glided toward the surface. The winds were incredible and made the ship difficult for Lucien to maneuver. He kept a steady eye on the monitor and quipped. "Nothing like flying blind."

"Then pull out," ordered Cassius.

Lucien noticed a narrow opening in the surface. "There's a canyon. I'm going for it."

Cassius was puzzled. "Why do we want to go there?"

"The two ships are still approaching. It'll be difficult for them to follow us." Lucien carefully navigated the ship down through the narrow crevice and followed its winding path. He checked the display above the monitor. "The sensors show that the intruders are still back there. We'll have to try something else." Lucien craned his neck back and forth, often checking each of the monitors, targeting the sides of the canyon.

"What are you looking for, Lucien?"

"A cave or something. We have to hide somewhere."

They cruised further until Lucien spotted a dark opening in the ice and pointed to it. "There's something over there. I think it's a cave." He steered the craft toward the opening.

"Are the others still with us?" asked Cassius.

When he pressed two switches on his left, lights on the front of the ship illuminated the cave. Lucien checked the monitor. Another green dot followed their dot. "Yes, they are." He turned off the exterior lights and noticed brightness ahead of them.

When they exited the other end of the cave, they entered a beautiful subterranean world. Fluorescent fungus illuminated the high ceiling. Trees covered most of the landscape and the air was surprisingly warm.

Lucien landed on a sandy beach next to a stream facing the cave. He watched as the other transport landed nearby, facing the cave as well. "There's no sign of the cruisers on the sensor screen."

"So, what do we do now?" asked Cassius.

"Looks like a good place to wait them out."

"How long?"

"Maybe a while. We have time to kill until those ships give up and go away. Why not give everyone a break?"

"That's a good idea."

Lucien shut down the engines and followed everyone out through the hatch. "I would stay close if I were you. I don't know how fond our friends are of you," Cassius warned.

"No problem. I'm going to get a drink from the stream."

"I'll keep an eye on you."

"Thanks, Cassius."

The underworld was a beautiful place. It was so peaceful with small forms of wildlife all around and comfortable temperatures. Seneca met with Cassius and Xanther by the stream. Penny and Tarkus had other things on their mind. They disappeared into the trees. The Firenghi and Dracor rested near the ships.

"What do you think of this place, Cassius?" asked Seneca.

"It's beautiful."

"How about you, Xanther?"

"I love it. Why?"

"Perhaps we should consider staying here. I mean we need to check out the area for any dangers, but Firenghia has been ruined and the Dracor don't have any place to call home. This could be a new beginning."

"If the area is safe, then I'd just as soon stay here and not return?" Cassius replied.

"Penny and I have to return to warn Billy's people about Pendragon's new weapon," Seneca informed him. "Besides, I have to find Will and Rena."

"I understand. What about Billy?" he asked.

"I'd also like to tell Billy where we are."

"I'll organize everyone and have them spread out to inspect the area. We have two ships. Take one of them when you're ready. If anything goes wrong, we can fit everyone into the other one."

"Are you sure, Cassius?"

"Yes, sis. Your son is important. Go to him."

"Thanks, Cassius." Seneca left them and searched for Penny and Tarkus. She was reluctant to use her telepathy out of respect for their privacy. She knew Tarkus all too well.

Seneca returned to the ship, where she found Lucien sitting with two other Andorans from the second transport. "Lucien, can I have a word with you and your friends?"

"What is it?"

"We're considering starting over on this planet. Our homes have been destroyed and this place is beautiful. Cassius is taking some of our people to inspect the area for any dangers."

"And what do you want of me?"

"A few of us need to return to Firenghia for a short time. Then you can do as you please. I'd like one of you to stay until Cassius has determined that it's safe here. Once that's done, we won't need the second ship."

"That's reasonable. I don't know where we'll go since we're now branded as traitors, but at least we have a choice. I'll take you."

"Perhaps it would make sense for your friend to meet you where you found us. Then we'll know if they're safe here or if they had to flee. While you're waiting, we can find out what's going on with the war. Maybe things have changed."

"I doubt it, but it's worth a try. When do we leave?"

"As soon as I find Penny and Tarkus."

Seneca went to the stream for a drink of water. She stared at her reflection in the crystal-clear water and thought about Billy and Will. Clearly, Penny had fractured their friendship. Things would never be the same. Billy was right to be concerned about Penny inheriting her traits. Penny was losing control of her emotions and it was her fault. Perhaps she cared too much for both of them. She couldn't understand why? A tear rolled down her cheek and she wondered if things weren't better when Ruger was the only enemy.

"Seneca, what are you doing?" Penny's voice startled her.

Seneca wiped the tear away and faced Penny. "I was just thinking." She could smell Tarkus' scent all over Penny. She felt even more distant than before. "Where's Tarkus?"

"He went for a walk. He'll be back."

"We're leaving for Firenghia as soon as Tarkus returns."

"Great! I can't wait to get back there."

"We're not staying, Penny. There's nothing left for us to go back to, just memories and a ruined land."

"What? Where will all these people go?"

"They're going to settle here. Cassius and several others are scouting the area now. If there's a problem, they'll join us later."

"I could get used to this place. You don't need us to go, do you?"

"Penny, that's your world back there. You have to explain to your people what's going on."

"I guess you're right."

"I'll be waiting on board the ship. Please find Tarkus so we can go."

"Seneca, things have changed between us, haven't they?" Penny asked, uneasily.

"Yes, they have."

"Things weren't right between Billy and me."

"I realize that but you handled it poorly."

"This thing with Tarkus bothers you, doesn't it?"

"Yes. You don't realize what you've gotten into. Tarkus has never been faithful to anyone. If you conceive a child, he'll leave you. Even worse, you could bear a child in five moons. Your body requires a longer period of time as I understand it. It will be a painful pregnancy."

"I never thought of that."

"And you left me no opportunity to tell you."

"I'm sorry. Maybe Tarkus has changed and things will be alright."

"I hope so, for your benefit. You'll need his support."

Cold reality hit Penny square in the face. Seneca was right. Penny let her emotions run away with her and she lost control of her new self. "I'll find Tarkus immediately and we'll leave." Penny walked upstream a short way and found Tarkus talking to two of the Firenghi women. He seemed to be enjoying himself until Penny showed up. "Well, Tarkus. I see I'll have to keep you on a tight leash."

"Oh, Penny. What do you want?"

"Hello, ladies. Is my boy-toy causing problems?"

"Oh, we were just talking. Is he yours?" A young brunette inquired.

"Absolutely. Isn't that right, Tarkus?"

Tarkus tried to artfully dodge the question. "Is something wrong, Penny? I got the impression you wanted to tell me something."

"Spoken like an unfaithful, I mean a true male. Let's go. We're leaving."

"I'll catch up with you later, girls."

"Tarkus, we're leaving now. Seneca is waiting at the ship for us."

"What about everyone else?"

"They can stay here and start their lives over. You and I have much work to do."

"But you don't need me to go, do you?"

"Look, Sweetheart, get on the ship and stop whining. You agreed to this relationship and you are going to stick to it. If I have to stay with you every waking moment, I will. Don't tick me off."

"Alright, I'm coming." The two of them returned in silence to the ship. During the entire trip back, neither spoke. The giggling and handholding ended already. Seneca could tell that Tarkus was already up to his old games. She chose not to get involved in either's business anymore.

When she approached the stairs, Penny asked, "Where are you going?"

"Why? Does it concern you?"

"No, I just wondered."

Seneca continued up the stairs. Penny felt as though she didn't have a single friend in the universe. She screwed over everyone she knew, just like others had done to her when she was younger. *How ironic? I've become what I always hated most.*

— X —

Seneca entered the flight deck and inquired if there was any sign of the enemy ships. "By the time they could pick us up on their short-range sensors, we were underground," replied Lucien.

"Any idea how to find Billy?"

"We were able to contact the Council of Guardians. They relayed our message to Earth," answered Cassius.

"Have you heard back from them yet?"

"Sure have. We have the coordinates to their portal."

"How much longer?"

"We're close to the portal now," said Lucien.

"I think they'll give us another set of coordinates once we clear the portal or maybe the portal will take us right into their headquarters."

"I'd be surprised if it did," replied Lucien. "That would leave them vulnerable if someone follows us."

"Maybe they alternate the coordinates. Then you'd only know what they are if the humans contacted you."

"That's possible. I wouldn't expect them to be that sophisticated. I mean, after all, they're only human."

"I guess we'll find out," commented Seneca.

— X —

When Ramador and his troops reached the Dracor world, he ordered them to camp out for the night. "I'll inform the doctor that we need more serum. I'll be back as soon as I can," Ramador told his lieutenant. The Andoran nodded and saluted him.

Ramador ascended the side of the mountain and entered the cave. He felt his way around in the dark until he felt the tingling of the portal and then passed through it. The brightness of the transport bay in the research center startled him. Several soldiers drew their weapons and surrounded him. "Don't move! Who are you?" Two soldiers quickly disarmed him.

"I'm Ramador. I need to speak with either Doc Smith or Xerxes?"

"I don't think so. You'll come with us."

"I'm working with them to quell the Andoran violence."

One of the soldiers whispered to the sergeant, "He's the Andoran vice-commander. He's close with Dr. Smith and Bill Brock."

The sergeant nodded. "My bad, Ramador. I'll contact them and let them know you're here."

"Thank you."

Ramador waited patiently with the soldiers until Doc passed through the double doors. He was excited to see him. "Ramador, how are you?"

"I feel excellent. The serum works well. We have more important issues to discuss, though."

"Talk to me."

"I have forty-one Andorans who need injections. I also have some very bad news about Pendragon."

"I'll call Dr. Watts and have him prepare a package of RF-34. I'll also contact Xerxes and we'll discuss your findings." Doc picked up a nearby phone and spoke for several minutes. After hanging up, he announced, "Watts is taking care of the RF34. It'll be ready in a few hours."

"Thanks, Dr. Smith. My men are camped outside the cave. What happened to the second portal? I was surprised to enter the transport bay right away."

"Xerxes had the two portals reconfigured so that there is only one now. I'm scheduled to meet with Billy and a few others in a little while. This is good timing to discuss things."

"I could think of better things to discuss, Dr. Smith. Pendragon has a doomsday weapon called Dark Horizon."

"A doomsday weapon?"

"Yes. It's not fully developed and the reaction can't be controlled. If he detonates it, much of the quadrant will be annihilated. The worst part is that it could spread beyond the quadrant. Its capability is extensive."

"Why would he detonate a device that isn't fully developed?"

"He's mad."

"Are you sure of this?" Doc asked, concerned about the consequences.

"Yes, and I'm positive that the reaction cannot be controlled."

"This is terrible. We'll have to do something soon."

"I have some ideas on how to stop Pendragon, but it won't be easy."

The Andoran transport ship passed through the portal and landed inside the research facility's transport bay. "Well, I'll be. Look where we're at," said Cassius pleasantly. They exited the flight deck and descended the stairs.

"Are we there?" asked Penny.

"Yes," Seneca replied curtly. She opened the hatch and exited.

Cassius and Lucien descended the stairs to the main quarters. Penny and Tarkus sat at opposite ends of the quarters, ignoring each other. "Are the two of you coming?" Cassius inquired, amused by their behavior.

"If I must," Tarkus remarked cynically.

"You'll stay right by my side since I can't trust you to go ten feet from me," ordered Penny.

"Yes, Master."

"Oh, shut up, Tarkus, you big baby!"

Cassius and Lucien exited the ship followed by Penny and Tarkus. Several soldiers approached them and surrounded them. "Who are you and what do you want?" asked the sergeant.

"Xerxes gave us the coordinates to come here. He's expecting us," replied Seneca.

"Take the elevator to the third floor. He's in Conference Room A."

"Thank you." Seneca, Cassius and Lucien proceeded toward the elevator.

"Where's Billy Brock staying?" Penny asked the sergeant.

The sergeant checked his logbook. "Fifth floor. Room 511."

Penny and Tarkus hurried after the others.

"What do you want with him?" asked Tarkus.

"I need to make sure he knows about Dark Horizon. Besides, if Pendragon wants both of us dead, I think he should know about it."

"So, you're going to get me killed, too."

"Come on, Tarkus. You're a big boy. I'm sure you can handle one Andoran."

"But Pendragon is insane. That's a whole different thing, altogether."

The elevator doors opened. Everyone entered and waited. Seneca pressed 'three' on the panel. Penny reached past her and pressed 'five'.

"What's on 'five'?" asked Seneca.

"Billy."

Seneca suggested to Cassius, "Why don't you and Lucien go ahead on 'three' and look for Xerxes?"

"Sure. Will you be okay?"

"Of course. I'd like to see Billy, too."

The elevator doors opened on the third floor. Cassius and Lucien exited.

— X —

Tera lay next to Billy on the bed. They were nestled in each other's arms. "Are you going to the meeting dressed like that, Tera?" asked Billy.

"Now that Xerxes, I mean my dad, has seen me, I guess it doesn't matter. Do you care?"

"No. I can't wait to see the reaction on some faces, though."

They got up and held each other close. "Are you sure?" she asked. "I'll change if you want me to."

"No, you're fine. There is one thing bugging me though."

"What's that?"

"Why didn't you tell me that Xerxes was your father?"

"Because no one else knew it, either. I wouldn't acknowledge him as my father."

"He never told you what happened with your mother?"

"No, this was news to me, too. I never knew my mother wanted to be an officer in the fleet."

"It's ironic that you did."

"You know what's ironic, Billy?"

"What?"

"You and me."

They stepped into the hallway. Billy pressed the button, which closed the door. Tera pushed Billy against the wall and kissed him. She started with his neck and finally his lips. Billy was overjoyed by her impulsiveness. "I love when you handle me like this, Tera."

"I'll bet you do." They wrapped their arms around each other and kissed a little while longer.

Penny, Tarkus and Seneca got off the elevator and entered the hallway. Penny saw Billy with Tera and became enraged. "Just great, Billy! It didn't take you long to get over me, did it?"

"Penny! Seneca! What are you doing here? I thought you were captured."

"We escaped, no thanks to you."

"What's with you?"

"So, you go out and find the nearest available tramp for a quick fling?"

Tera took exception to Penny's statement and stepped in front of Billy. "Excuse me."

"You heard me, tramp."

Tera grabbed Penny by the jaw and shoved her against the wall. When she made a fist, four metal spikes stood out dangerously from her gloved hand. "I'm not a tramp. If you say it again, I'll rearrange your face." Penny realized she was overmatched and backed down very quickly.

"Please don't hurt her," requested Seneca. "We've been through a lot and we're a little edgy."

Billy put his hand on Tera's arm. She glanced at Billy and he nodded. She reluctantly released her hold on Penny.

"A lot of help you are," Penny mumbled to Tarkus.

"Well, you started it."

"Enough, children!" Seneca scolded them.

"Hello, Seneca. It's good to see you," said Billy.

Seneca hugged him. "Hi, Billy."

"This is Tera. She's…"

"My replacement, right?" Penny interjected.

Billy became irritated. "Yes, and a damn fine one, too."

Seneca extended a hand to Tera. "Hi, I'm Seneca."

Tera was receptive to Seneca's friendship and shook her hand. "Hi. I've heard a lot about you."

Seneca smiled at her. "I hope it was good."

"It was. How is the baby?" asked Tera compassionately.

"I don't know. We're going back to Firenghia to find him."

"Who's watching him?" asked Billy.

"Rena had him. Neither was captured so I'm hoping they escaped."

Penny grabbed Tarkus' arm and ordered, "Come on. We're going back to Firenghia."

"But we just got here."

"Shut up and walk."

"What about the meeting? We have important things to discuss," Seneca reminded them.

"You handle it," Penny blurted sarcastically. We're out of here."

"Let's get to the meeting," Billy instructed them. "We'll figure out a plan without them."

On the way to the conference room, Tera asked Seneca, "When you have time, can we talk?"

"Sure. What about?"

"Billy and You."

"Don't worry. Billy and I know where we stand on things."

"No, I understand that. Billy told me about the traits and I'd like to know how it might affect me."

"As far as what?"

"Will I be like Penny? I understand she changed quite a bit after the traits affected her."

"Penny already had emotional problems, plus she inherited her traits directly from me. If you get them from Billy, it will be a little different. If you are concerned about having children, the pregnancy will be tough on you."

"That's not an issue. I can't have children."

"Then you'll be fine."

They entered the conference room where everyone was waiting. "Sorry we're late," apologized Billy. "We had a little problem in the hall."

"Grab a seat and get comfortable. We'll be here for a while. What happened to Penny and her friend?" asked Doc.

"It's a long story."

"Yes, it usually is."

Prax and Courtney sat in the back and waved to Billy. Cassius sat next to them.

"I was afraid Tera tied you up someplace," kidded Prax.

Billy chuckled and placed his arm around her. "No, it was worse."

Courtney noticed the passion mark on Billy's neck. "Oh, dear. Billy, your neck."

"Yeah, Tera branded me."

"What a change I see in you, Tera," remarked Prax.

"Shut up before I come over there."

"Now that's the Tera I know and love."

After three hours of hashing out the information from everyone regarding Dark Horizon, Ramador made a recommendation. "I think it would be prudent to send someone to Archaenia and find out about Dark Horizon from those who created it. If they can tell you how the weapon works, we might be able to disable it before Pendragon gets his claws on it."

"Where is Pendragon now, Ramador?" asked Doc.

"We're not sure. I'll send scouts to find out."

"What would it take to go to Archaenia?"

"One ship. One crew. Can you set up the portals to get that ship to Archaenia?" requested Ramador.

"I can arrange that with the Council," said Xerxes.

"What if they can't get to Archaenia before Pendragon?"

"Then we go to his battle star. We'll have to stop him before he launches the weapon."

"That sounds considerably more dangerous."

"It is. The battle star will be expecting you and Pendragon will make sure they don't have thoughts about defecting."

The phone rang, interrupting the meeting. Doc reluctantly answered it. After thirty seconds, he said, "Thanks, I'll be right down." When Doc hung up, everyone paused to hear what happened.

"That was Sam. He and Ginea may have a breakthrough on the ore. I'm going down to his lab. Continue the meeting without me."

"What about this new group of aliens, the Boromeans?" asked Seneca. "They could cause a problem if they're already in our quadrant."

"My people will handle them," Ramador said confidently. "I've already ordered one battle star to the portal for protection. The fighters should be reporting there shortly. We'll keep the Boromeans busy."

"Are the two of you ready to go again tomorrow?" Xerxes asked Prax.

"We're always ready to go."

"Good. Billy and Tera will team up with you. You'll travel to Archaenia and find out what you can about Dark Horizon. Ramador will supply the coordinates for you."

"How will we know if we find the Archaenians? What do they look like?" inquired Billy.

"Don't worry. They'll make sure you know who they are and where to go," Ramador informed him.

"Why doesn't that make me feel very good?" Everyone laughed at Billy.

"I'll contact them and let them know you're coming."

"Now, that would help," Billy remarked.

"If necessary, we can try to slow Pendragon down for you," offered Xerxes. "Hopefully, Ramador's scouts can locate him for us soon."

"If you're done with my crew, we'd like to leave," requested Billy.

"Yes, we'll want to get an early start," added Prax.

Xerxes pressed several keys on a device he wore on his wrist while everyone watched curiously. "I've asked the Council to set up a portal to get you as close as possible to Archaenia," he explained. "I'll be able to tell you where it exits before you leave. Obviously, we'll need you back here as soon as possible."

"I'm going to the cafeteria to grab a midnight snack," said Billy.

"Would you mind if I joined you?" asked Seneca. "There are some things we should discuss."

"Sure, I think Tera and the others would like to come, too."

"Billy, can I have a moment with you?" asked Xerxes.

Billy cast a worried look at Tera and answered, "Sure."

The others left the room and went to the cafeteria, leaving Billy with Xerxes. "Look, Billy, I don't know what your relationship is with Tera, but she's my only daughter. Please, look after her for me."

"I will, Xerxes. She hasn't done anything to embarrass you and I surely won't. She's a good girl."

"Thanks, Billy. I'm sorry you didn't know about our relationship sooner."

"It was just really awkward. I felt like I did you wrong."

"If she's happy with you, then so am I."

"Thanks, Xerxes."

Xerxes returned to the table and spoke with Ramador and Cirrus. Billy left the room to catch up with his friends.

— ⟨ —

Doc entered the lab and pulled up a chair next to Sam and Ginea. "I hope you have something good for me today, Sam." Sam looked at Ginea and the two burst out laughing.

"What's going on?" asked Doc, looking befuddled.

"We stumbled upon this by accident," Sam announced. "You're not going to believe it."

"Try me."

"Well, we were eating some fries for dinner," Sam started.

Doc rolled his eyes and said, "I can tell this is going to be a good one."

"The ore sample was under a black light in the glass tank. See the lines of yellow streaming out of the sample at random intervals. I got a salt shaker and set it on the table near the glass and we saw something very strange."

Ginea took a salt shaker from another table and brought it over. She set it down by the glass. The yellow lines suddenly steered toward the saltshaker.

Doc was surprised. "What the heck just happened?"

"The salt is drawing the radiation from the ore. It's literally neutralizing it."

"But how?"

"I don't know, but it sure works."

"What happens to the salt?"

"I don't know. Maybe nothing."

"I wouldn't use that salt until we analyze it."

"But, Doc, what could possibly happen to the salt?" Sam asked.

"Do you want to find out the hard way?"

"No, I guess not."

"This is still great news!"

"Perhaps we can jam the portal using salt," suggested Ginea.

"That would be convenient but how would you do that?"

"There are a few ways," explained Sam. "We could make a cluster bomb filled with salt pellets. When it explodes, the salt would create a cloud that disables the portal."

"Cluster bombs - I like that. Are you doing any other tests?"

"We're going to test the sample in the presence of inert gases to see what else happens. If we find anything more, we'll call you," promised Ginea.

"It seems like the two of you are always here. Don't you ever call it a night?"

"We're having fun with this stuff," Sam said excitedly. "Ginea knows a whole lot of things that I can apply to our weapons and equipment."

"Do you think you two can design a cluster bomb that can scatter salt?" Doc inquired.

"We'll come up with something, Doc," Sam assured him.

— X —

Seneca followed Cassius, Tera, Prax and Courtney through the fast-food line. They each got a soda, ham sandwich and fries. Neither Seneca nor Cassius had ever seen food like this. In Firenghia, they lived off of nuts, berries, meat and fish.

Seneca sat down at the table first and Tera took a seat next to her. They conversed about different things and seemed quite happy with their new friendship. Billy entered the cafeteria and proceeded to the fast-food counter. As he waited for his order, he watched the girls converse. He was pleasantly surprised to see Seneca and Tera get along so well. He noticed that Prax and Cassius conversed in a friendly manner as well. In the back of his mind, he hoped that Seneca didn't have thoughts about passing traits to Tera. Things were never the same with Penny after she got them.

As if on cue, both girls looked up at him. He realized that Seneca must have read his thoughts. It had been so long since he used his telepathic abilities that he forgot about them. When Billy came to the table with his food, Seneca moved down so Billy could sit between them.

"Am I missing anything good?" he asked, curious.

"Just girl talk. And no, it doesn't have anything to do with passing traits."

"I was just wondering. It's not like you consulted me last time."

"I know and I regret that," Seneca reminded him.

Prax invited Billy to their end of the table and introduced him to Courtney. Billy excused himself and moved down to their end of the table. "Hi, Courtney. I wondered who the mystery woman on the flight deck was. It's nice to finally meet you."

"Thanks, Billy."

"Did you and Prax grow up together?"

"Oh, no. I'm not from his world. I'm a Narean."

"Women on her planet are anatomically different than human women," mentioned Prax.

"No kidding."

Prax leaned over and whispered in Billy's ear. Tera was amused when Billy blushed. "You're kidding, right?" asked Billy.

"Nope. That's why I spend so much time with her on the flight deck."

"I wish I had a picture of the look on your face," said Tera, giggling.

Already briefed by Tera on Courtney's anatomy, Seneca grinned and looked down at her fries, amused by Billy's reaction as well.

"Am I the only one who didn't know this or am I the butt of a joke?" complained Billy.

"It's true, Billy," affirmed Courtney.

"Okay, that's too much information."

"How are you and my cousin getting along, Billy?" questioned Prax.

"Fine, why?"

"Were you surprised to see her out of uniform?"

"I didn't see her out of uniform," Billy replied defensively and then realized he misinterpreted the question. "Oh, you mean the way she's dressed?"

"Of course. What were you thinking about?" Prax asked, curious.

Tera poked Billy and inquired, "Yes, what were you thinking?"

"I just thought he meant something else."

"I bet you never thought she'd be a Goth," kidded Prax.

"No, I was quite surprised. It does seem to befit her attitude, though."

"I had my reasons," remarked Tera. "If you don't like it, you can…"

"No, I love it." Billy put his arm around her and kissed her cheek. Now it was Tera's turn to blush.

"I think it's time to go. We have an early start tomorrow," Prax suggested to Courtney.

The two stood up and excused themselves. Everyone bade them a good night.

"So, what are your plans, Seneca?" asked Billy.

"Cassius will go back to the ship and I'll go with Lucien to Firenghia to find Rena, Will and the other children. Once we're all together, we'll leave for the new world we found. Penny and Tarkus will go, too, I'm sure."

Billy took the orb from around his neck and handed it to Seneca. "Use it to come back whenever you can. If you ever need anything, I'll be there."

"Thanks, Billy. When Will gets older, he'll need you."

"I'll be there for him."

Billy shook Cassius' hand and cautioned him to be careful.

"Well, I guess we'll get going, too," Seneca said sadly. "The two of you have a big mission tomorrow. Good luck."

"Thanks, Seneca. I appreciate all your advice," replied Tera. "How will you get back to this new world?"

"An Andoran named Lucien will fly us there," Seneca replied. "He brought us here."

Billy hugged Seneca and wished her a safe trip. Seneca hugged him back. Billy felt something stir in him as she walked away.

Tera noticed and became concerned. "Are you all right, Billy?"

"I'll never see her again."

"Sure, you will."

"No, I have a bad feeling."

They left the cafeteria and walked down a long white hall to the elevator. The door opened and they entered. "This trip's going to be dangerous," Tera mentioned to Billy.

"Yeah, it is."

The doors closed. "Are you scared?" she asked.

"Yeah, but not for me," replied Billy solemnly.

The elevator door opened and they proceeded down the hall. They reached Billy's room first. Tera hugged him tightly and offered to stay with him for night. Billy graciously accepted her offer. They entered his room and sat down on the bed.

"What were you and Seneca talking about?" asked Billy.

"Why? Are you worried?"

"No. Well, just a little. One night, Seneca and Penny…"

"I know."

"She told you about that?" asked Billy, surprised.

"Yes. She's hurting over Penny's behavior as much as you are."

"I guessed you talked to her about passing traits."

"No, not really."

"Then what could be so interesting? Did you talk about me?"

Tera giggled at him. "You don't really want to know, do you?"

"Yes, I do. Now I'm curious."

"We talked about requirements."

"For what?"

"For you. I want to make you happy and by the sound of it, you've had a very exciting life. don't want to bore you."

"Oh. I don't think you will."

"Billy, I'm serious. I will only give my heart away once and this is it. I couldn't survive being hurt."

"And I'm serious. I couldn't survive getting hurt again either. I think that's what makes our relationship good. I've always wanted to settle down with one woman and it's never worked out."

"This time it will," she promised. They snuggled together on the bed and fell asleep nestled in each other's arms.

— X —

Seneca passed through the portal and stepped into the green field. Behind her were mountains and trees; in front were the rolling fields and hills that she grew up around. This was her land and she was going to leave it behind. She felt like a part of her was dying as she walked away from the portal.

"Lucien, would you remain here. I should be back by midday tomorrow," she requested.

"Sure. It'll give me time to see if the humans' cure really works. I haven't slept in ages."

"Thank you. I'll see you then."

Seneca continued into the mountains. She had an idea where Rena would hide with the children. Rena was very reliable and helped Seneca on a number of occasions. If anything happened to Seneca, Rena would be an excellent replacement for her. Had it not been for her father, Ruger, she would have been a queen over part of the land.

When darkness set in, Seneca grew tired and found a nook in the rocks to lie in. She was nearly asleep when she heard a rustling sound above her. She jumped up and hid by a tree as several stones trickled down the side of the mountain.

Seneca moved to a better vantage point and saw something move near the ledge. When she crept to a higher ledge, she recognized the six-year-old girl from her village named Maya. "Maya!" she called.

"Queen Seneca! We've been worried about you."

"Where's Rena?"

"She's in a cave at the top of the mountain."

"What are you doing out here in the night?"

"Every night I look for the path to Billy's home. Rena said that if we found him, he might be able to rescue you."

"You did well, Maya. Take me to her."

Maya led Seneca up an obscure trail to the top of the mountain. The little girl crawled into a narrow opening in the rocks. Seneca got down on her knees and squeezed into the cave behind Maya. The cave opened into a small cavern. Seven young children slept on the ground. In the corner, an adult female slept against the rocks. Seneca looked around at all of them.

One by one, the children woke up. They were so excited to see Seneca. Rena was stunned when she saw her. "Seneca! What are you doing here?"

"We escaped from the Andorans. We're leaving here for another land."

"Are the others safe?"

"Yes, they are already there. Have you seen Penny or Tarkus?"

"No, but we saw firelight at the temple."

"I'll find them in the morning."

Maya tugged on Seneca's arm. "What's wrong, Maya?"

"Last night, I saw a flying machine land on the other side of our home."

"Are you sure?"

"Yes. It hovered around for a while before it landed."

"Let's get some sleep. Tomorrow we're going to a beautiful new world."

CHAPTER 9

PENDRAGON'S REVENGE

Ramador and the medical technician followed the rocky path down the mountainside to the Andoran camp. Andoran guards surrounded them.

"At ease. It's Ramador," called out one of the sentries.

Ramador recognized the voice as one of his longtime friends. "Dornan! How is everything?"

"Something isn't right."

"Why do you say that?"

"I sent two scouts out to investigate strange lights in the distance. They haven't returned."

"Get everyone up. We have the cure for their ailments. We'll do this quickly in case there's danger lurking in the night."

"That's great!" The Andorans anxiously lined up for their shots.

Dornan looked to the west, expecting an attack to happen. He rubbed his arm after the shot and stared into the darkness. Several flashes appeared nearby and two Andorans fell to the ground. "Boromeans! Return fire!" ordered Dornan. The number of flashes increased and several Andorans fell to the ground.

"Retreat up the mountainside!" ordered Ramador. "We'll take a stand on the ledge."

Twelve Andorans remained when they reached the safety of the ledge. Ramador was stunned at the sight of hundreds of Boromean fighters with torches gathered at the bottom of the mountainside.

"What do we do now?" asked Dornan, concerned.

"Get everyone into the portal. Where's the human?"

"He was hit in the first volley of fire. He didn't make it."

"Let's go, before they spot us." Ramador led them with a distinct sense of urgency into the cave. After some difficulty, he found the portal and guided his soldiers through. When they reached the transport bay, armed soldiers immediately surrounded the Andorans.

"I'm Ramador. You must close the portal immediately and notify Dr. Smith."

One of the soldiers stepped forward and asked, "Who put you in charge?"

"There are hundreds of hostile Boromean creatures coming. If you don't close that portal, they'll be picking your bones clean. Now, you make the choice!"

The soldier looked around for a consensus. The other soldiers nodded. "Close the portal, quickly!" he ordered.

"Please, contact Dr. Smith and Xerxes. Let them know we're back and we have important information for them."

"Stay put until we confirm your authorization."

— X —

Penny and Tarkus sat in the damaged temple on a marble bench. Tarkus lit candles on the altar and placed the torch in an iron bracket mounted on the wall. Penny informed him that they needed to discuss something. Tarkus feigned interest and pretended to be concerned. She mentioned that Firenghian women have shorter pregnancies than human women do. "Is that so?" he remarked nonchalantly.

"Yesterday I began to show signs of being pregnant," she revealed.

"You're a Firenghian. That can't be."

"Not entirely. I have a number of traits that your race has, but I'm a human."

"What! Why didn't you tell me that?"

"Would it have mattered?" she asked, annoyed by his sudden concern.

"Firenghian women can only conceive during short intervals. Human women are fertile almost all the time."

"I thought it was interesting listening to Seneca tell the other women about you," she related. "Well, Tarkus, it seems that you're going to be a father."

"But, Penny, I can't be a father!" he exclaimed in a near panic.

"Tarkus, my insides aren't ready for a short pregnancy. It's going to be tough and I'm going to need you."

"This wasn't part of our arrangement," he complained.

"Tarkus, we're in this together. What about the fun we had?"

"That was all it was – fun. You weren't supposed to get pregnant. This is your fault!"

"Tarkus, how can it be my fault?"

"You wanted to make love."

Penny's insides cramped up. She doubled over and fell to her knees. "Help me, please, Tarkus."

"You'll be okay in a little bit. I'll go find some fire wood."

"Tarkus, don't leave me. I need you. I need someone," she cried.

Tarkus stood there dumb-founded. He wanted to leave but he didn't want to abandon Penny while she was in trouble. Penny staggered to her feet and fought back the tears. "All right, Tarkus, run away you coward. I'll get through this without you." She knelt down and covered her face to hide the tears.

"Maybe tonight..." Tarkus started.

Penny heard a loud snap and Tarkus' voice stopped. When she looked up, Pendragon's arm was around Tarkus' broken neck. He released him and Tarkus' body fell lifeless to the ground.

Penny screamed and retreated from him. He grabbed Penny by the neck and threw her against the wall. Her body crumpled to the ground like a broken doll. Her eyes filled with warm, red blood. Her vision blurred and she became disoriented.

"How convenient? You are with child," Pendragon taunted.

"Leave me alone," she pleaded tearfully.

"Your people killed my children and I should leave you alone. You and your partner killed my mate and I should leave you alone. And now my empire is disrupted. Do you really think I should leave you alone?"

Penny crawled under a broken beam, but Pendragon grabbed her ankle and held her upside down. "Now I'll have my revenge!" Pendragon raised his clawed hand and punched Penny's stomach. She heaved horribly as she gasped for air. Pendragon tossed her body into the corner in a contorted, twisted pile and watched her quiver violently. When a pool of blood formed by her groin, he was satisfied that he exacted his revenge and left.

— X —

Maya shook Seneca several times until she awoke. "What's wrong, Maya?" asked Seneca.

"I heard a woman's scream."

"From where?"

"Down in the village. It sounded like it came from the temple."

Rena sat up and asked, "What's going on?"

"Maya heard someone scream. It could have been Penny. I'm going down there."

"It'll be daybreak soon. Why don't you wait? It'll be safer then."

"No, she's in trouble now," Seneca replied. "Get the children ready in case we have to leave in a hurry." She rushed from the cave and hurried down the mountain. As she approached the abandoned village, she thought about the spaceship Maya saw earlier and wondered if it could be Pendragon. Everyone was sure he was on his way to retrieve his doomsday weapon Dark Horizon but perhaps they were wrong.

When she reached the edge of the village, the sky brightened. She scanned the area and saw no sign of danger. The temple was the only building with any remaining walls intact, so she made her way toward it. She saw the flickering light from a torch inside and peered through the window. She grew nauseous and trembled when she saw Penny's feet quivering from behind a bench. Seneca looked further and saw Tarkus lying a short distance away, his head contorted grotesquely. Seneca knelt next to her and comforted her. "Penny, it's Seneca. Can you hear me?"

Penny's eyes were rolled halfway back in her head. Seneca had no choice but to get Penny back to her world for medical attention as soon as possible. She lifted her up and carried her out of the temple. Along the way, she tried to communicate telepathically but Penny didn't comprehend. She could feel Penny's pain as one of her traits allowed her to feel what another of her kind sensed or felt. Penny's pain was unbearable.

When she was halfway to the mountain, Maya rushed out of the trees. "Queen Seneca, what happened?"

"We have to go in a hurry. Get Rena and bring her to the portal. Remember the portal?"

"Yes, I do."

"Hurry, Maya. Penny's dying." The young girl disappeared in the trees.

Seneca felt the growing dampness on Penny's clothes and realized that she still bled. Her legs tired, but she pushed on.

When she reached the big field near the portal, she heard a buzzing sound. She looked back and saw strange creatures approaching in the distance. From the other direction, Rena came with the children. Lucien appeared from behind the rocks and rushed toward Seneca with his gun drawn. She was confused as to why he was attacking her. When he fired at creatures behind her, she realized they were being pursued from behind.

"Keep going, Seneca! I'll slow them down," shouted Lucien.

Seneca reached the portal entrance and passed Penny to Rena. "Get her to the other side. They'll help her there. Take the children, too."

"Aren't you coming?"

"I'll help Lucien hold them off. Tell the men on the other side to close the portal."

"What are you doing?" Lucien hollered at Seneca.

"I'm staying."

Lucien tossed her a pulse pistol. "You'll need this. Good luck."

Rena struggled with Penny but managed to get into the portal with the children. Maya stood at the entrance to the portal and watched. Seneca and Lucien valiantly fought off the attackers. Maya heard Lucien scream, "They're Boromeans!" She saw Lucien stagger backwards as he was hit several times by pulse fire. After firing three more shots, he fell to the ground dead.

Seneca continued to fire and killed several of the approaching aliens. One of the creatures crept in from the left and fired three shots at her. The blasts of energy struck her thigh, shoulder and arm. She fell to the ground, her arm nearly severed. Struggling, she fired back at the Boromeans. Two more of the creatures fell to the ground with lethal wounds. Another shot struck her head and she staggered awkwardly several feet before falling to the ground. She fired one last shot and died.

Maya shivered at the sight of Seneca's bloodstained hair and lifeless body. The Boromeans saw Maya next to the boulder and rushed toward her. She fled through the portal and yelled, "The monsters are coming!"

The soldier at the door immediately pushed a black knob after she exited and shut down the portal. A group of men took Penny from Rena and left the bay. Rena took Will from one of the girls and cradled him. Maya ran to her and cried, "They killed Queen Seneca!"

Rena's eyes filled with tears. "Are you sure, Maya?"

"They shot her and her friend a bunch of times."

Rena dropped to her knees and hugged Maya. She couldn't believe her cousin was gone. Seneca was like a big sister to her since she returned from her imprisonment in the castle.

Doc and Xerxes entered the bay and approached the new visitors. "Who are you?" inquired Xerxes. Rena introduced herself and the children. Then she explained what had happened.

"They are Boromeans," fretted Xerxes. "This is going to be a big problem."

Doc picked up the telephone and called Maggie. He broke the news to her about Penny. Xerxes ordered one of the guards to get Rena and the children a room until they figure out what to do with them.

"What do we do now, Xerxes?" asked Doc.

"Pendragon may have given us the time we needed because of his thirst for revenge."

"Let's just hope that Billy's mission is successful. We may have gained some time, but we still have to take advantage of it."

"Have Sam make arrangements to build those cluster bombs with salt pellets. At least we can try to disable the Andoran portal. Too much is happening here and we have no control over anything right now."

"I'll go talk to him. I'll call you later, Xerxes." Doc hurried to the medical clinic. When he arrived, Maggie was in tears. Ronnie and Randy paced the floor like mad women. John and Seamus sat quietly in prayer. Maggie threw her arms around Doc.

"She's not going to make it. She's a mess," Maggie sobbed.

"What did they say, Maggie?" She could only cry. "Did you hear what the doctor said?" Doc asked Ronnie.

"Yeah. They're bringing a specialist. They're trying to keep her alive long enough for him to try and help her."

"What happened to her?"

"She's got several lacerations on her head, a bleeding concussion and internal injuries. She was pregnant and received a severe blow to her midsection. She miscarried, and her insides are a mess. She's lost a lot of blood."

"Was it Billy's child?"

"I don't know."

"How far along was she?"

"They don't know. Probably not very far. She had marks on her neck from a large, clawed hand."

Doc thought for a moment and recited what Ramador told him, "A lack of sleep, because of their ailment, would eventually lead to insanity. Pendragon has gone mad! If he gets his hands on Dark Horizon, he'll use it."

"Not if I get my hands on him first," yelled Ronnie.

"We're going after him," said Randy. "He can't be that far ahead."

"Nobody does anything until Billy gets back," ordered Doc. "We have to know what the Archaenians' instructions are."

"If Penny dies, Pendragon's going to wish he was dead when I get done with him," Ronnie vowed.

Doc pulled out his pager and checked for a new message. "What is it, Doc?" asked John.

"Xerxes. He says Boromeans attacked Ramador's unit. They suffered many casualties."

"We can't do anything about it, can we?" asked Randy.

"Damn it!" shouted Doc. "We're losing this one in our own back yard"

"Do you have any suggestions, John?" asked Xerxes.

"I think it's time that we take the battle to Pendragon and the Boromeans."

"And how can we do that?"

"This Dark Horizon is probably a projectile of some sort. Therefore, he'll need to have a launch platform."

"Then he'll probably need to go to a battle star for that," Randy suggested. "Their transports aren't designed to make a missile launch possible."

"We need to know where his battle stars are," replied Doc. "Once we have that information, then we can sit back and wait for him to return with his weapon."

"I agree," said John. "Once he's on board the battle star, we'll board it and do whatever it takes to dismantle it and destroy him."

"Do you think you can do that?" asked Doc.

"There should be two Andoran transports available to us: the one that Penny and Seneca escaped on and the one that Ramador's troops used to arrive on Dracor," John responded. "We'll have to fight our way to them, but so be it."

"But once you get on the ship, how will you know where to go?"

"Our team can go on one transport while Ramador, and whatever men he has left, take the other. He'll know where to go once we're on board."

"And Dark Horizon?"

"Let's hope Billy has the answer to that," Doc replied.

"That's the closest thing to a plan I've heard yet."

"I'll meet Ramador and discuss your plan with him."

"Would you mind if I joined you?"

"Not at all."

"I want to talk this over with Seamus and the girls. I'll meet you later," said John.

CHAPTER 10

NEW ALLIES

The *Luna C* sped through the portal on its way to Archaenia. Prax and Courtney piloted the ship, wary of any unknown objects on the sensor screens. This was new territory for humans and there was no history of the regional alien populations.

Tera completed uploading the coordinates into the computer at the navigator's station. She sighed and opened the curtain to her bunk. It wasn't the most comfortable place to sleep but, it became adequate for rest. She sat down on the bunk and contemplated her new relationship. Images of her and Billy flashed through her mind, still overwhelmed by how fast things happened between them. She never thought she'd open up to anyone ever, but the stories about Billy intrigued her, particularly his steadfast love for Penny.

Billy's ambitious quest for adventure was something else she craved to be part of. When she heard that Penny ended their relationship, she felt some of the pain that Billy felt. It brought back the agonizing memories of her mother's death.

Billy grew weary of the stars as he gazed from the gun turret. He knew something tragic would happen to Penny and Seneca. Perhaps it was a new trait surfacing in him or maybe he was just edgy about things. After

Penny's performance in front of Tera, he no longer thought of Penny in the same light. She had become someone else that he didn't want to know.

Billy climbed down from the turret and pondered what Tera was up to. She proved to be so different than he expected: tough as nails but capable of sharing her feelings and emotions. He hoped that they could build the kind of relationship he always wanted.

Yes, Tera was different than most girls. Her black, leather attire and spikes seemed appropriate when he got to know her. She was wild but disciplined, which was something Penny lacked.

Billy arrived in Tera's compartment and pulled up a chair. "Yes, Mr. Brock," she said with a smile.

Billy couldn't help thinking how cute she was out of uniform. "Aren't you going to get into trouble for not wearing your uniform on a Council sanctioned mission?"

Tera smirked at the comment. "I quit. The Council isn't running the show any more. Your people and my dad are."

"You seem pretty confident of that."

"I've heard enough of the Council's crap for one lifetime. They are pompous, old goats and they play God from their space station in the sky. Got a problem with that?"

"No, not at all," Billy replied, impressed by her fire.

"Do you miss the uniform? I'll wear it if you prefer," she offered.

"Well, actually I like you in leather. In fact, you look quite sexy dressed like that."

Tera blushed until she regained her courage. "Did you bring your music with you?"

"I sure did."

"What else you got in that bag of yours?"

"My security blanket."

"You're kidding, aren't you?" she teased.

"Well, it's really my protective skull."

"Oh, Gosh. You're really kidding now, aren't you?"

"Come on, Tera. You're a Goth chick. You should have an affinity for things like that."

"I may be Goth, but I'm not a fanatic. Put something good on your CD player and shut up."

"What kind of mood are you in?"

"Can you read my mind?"

"Maybe."

"Did you run your checks on the weapons systems?"

"Not yet."

"Bad boy. Make sure you do it later."

"So, what kind of music do you want to hear?"

"Something to fit the mood."

"What mood?"

"This mood." Tera sat on Billy's lap and kissed him. First, she kissed his ears; then his neck and finally his lips. Billy's heart raced and he returned her affections. When Tera unbuttoned her leather vest, he paused and pushed her away.

"What's wrong, Billy?"

"I've got just the song." He reached into his CD case and pulled out the last one. He eagerly inserted the disk into his small CD player. "Who is it, Billy?"

"I'm sure you've never heard of them before."

"Try me. I know a lot of Earth songs."

"Pretty Poison - Closer."

"Hmm. You're right. I've never heard of them."

As soon as the song started, Tera knew she was going to enjoy it. The sound of the saxophone lulled her into a fantasy. She pulled Billy's shirt over his head and tossed it onto the floor. "What are you doing?" asked Billy.

"It's time."

"For what? Oh, never mind," he said, embarrassed.

The two of them slid under the covers and were soon tangled in each other's arms. Their motions coincided with the rhythm of the music and they drifted together in a romantic spell. They kissed and caressed gently until Tera whispered, "I'm ready. I want you now."

Billy made love to Tera purposefully and methodically, ensuring that she enjoyed every second of it. Afterwards, she giggled and licked his cheek playfully. The door to Tera's compartment opened and Prax poked his head in. "The sensors are picking up visitors. They could be…" Prax froze as he realized Tera and Billy were together under the blanket, with bare shoulders showing. "Oops. Excuse me, kids."

Tera chastised him. "Don't you ever knock?"

"I hope I didn't ruin your big moment, cuz'."

"No. As a matter of fact, it was more than a moment and it was so good, I was thinking of more." Billy blushed and ducked behind Tera's head.

"So, what were you saying about the sensors?" she asked.

"There are a dozen or so objects tracking us. They're still pretty far out, but I thought I'd give you a heads up."

"Thanks. Hey, Prax."

"Yeah, Tera."

"The flight deck is your territory, this is mine. Next time knock."

"Sure." Prax stepped out but quickly stuck his head back through the doorway again. "Hey, Billy."

"Yeah, Prax."

"You the man!"

Billy pulled the covers over his head. Tera laughed and dressed herself. "Don't mind Prax. He's a pervert. He and Courtney are perfect for each other. Why do you think they never leave the flight deck for very long?"

"Does this have anything to do with her anatomical differences?"

"It sure does."

"Oh, boy. I really didn't need to know that."

Tera chuckled at him. "You should get on your weapons checks soon. Turn the power bank on and let it charge up."

Billy sighed and got out of her bunk. "Yeah, I'll get right on it." He finished dressing and opened the door to leave.

"Billy, wait."

"What's that, Tera?"

"Come here." She reached her arms out and pulled him toward her. She kissed him passionately for several minutes and hugged him. "Thanks. That was everything I hoped it would be for the first time."

"You mean that really was your first time?"

"Yeah."

"I hope I didn't disappoint you."

"No. I'm looking forward to the next time."

Billy smiled and kissed her. "I'd better get my chores done. See you soon."

"By the way, good music. It was perfect for the mood."

"I thought you'd say that." Billy kissed her again and descended the stairs.

— ⧗ —

Ramador exited the elevator when Doc and Xerxes spotted him. "Ah, we found you!" exclaimed Xerxes. "We've been discussing our situation and we have some ideas."

"Good, because the Boromeans have become a bigger problem than we expected. Pendragon's alliance is coming apart and now everyone's in danger."

"Ramador, I have a few questions about Dark Horizon. Can you tell me if it's a projectile?" inquired Doc.

"I haven't seen it but I've heard Pendragon talk of launching it into other star systems."

"Is there any way he could launch it from a transport or a fighter?"

"No, that's impossible. I've heard it's nearly the length of an Andoran fighter, so a fighter couldn't possibly carry that big of a missile."

"Then he'll either have to launch it from your planet or he'll need a battle star."

"That's correct. Don't forget, though, he could launch it through one of our portals, which gives him significant range."

"If Sam can develop a simple cluster bomb that would neutralize the portals, then Pendragon has but one choice left – to get to a battle star," Doc surmised.

"How many battle stars do you have left?" asked Xerxes.

"Four."

"How many do you have control of?"

"Two. One is on its way to the portal. The other is near the mining colonies."

"So, he has two battle stars to pick from. Do you know where they are?"

"One should already be at the portal. The other is stationed near my world for protection at home. My men will try to persuade them to turn their allegiance to me."

"Then he really only has one logical choice, especially with the Boromeans on the attack. He'll go for the battle star at the portal."

"Now that we figured out where he's going, what options do we have?" asked Ramador.

Doc explained, "We considered going onboard the battle star and disabling Dark Horizon."

"That's dangerous, Doc. What if we fail?"

"We can't fail. Do you know where he would attempt to launch Dark Horizon from on the battle star?"

"Yes. We have three missile launch bays. Only one is large enough to accommodate something that size."

Xerxes elaborated, "We want to send you and your men, accompanied by Ronnie, Randy, and Seamus, to the battle star. You'll guide them to the bay where they'll try to disable it. Then you and your men will attempt to apprehend Pendragon or drive him out."

"But how will they disarm the weapon?" asked Ramador, somewhat baffled by their plan.

"That's where the team on the *Luna C* comes in," explained Xerxes. "Their mission to Archaenia is critical."

"And if they don't make it?" asked Doc.

"If I can get to a transport, I can contact the battle stars. Perhaps they can provide some protection for Billy's ship," suggested Ramador.

"We'll have some of our soldiers support you in getting past the portal," Doc committed.

"If you can summon them now, I'll go immediately."

"Xerxes, can you arrange that?" asked Doc.

"Yes, I can."

— X —

Tera sat in one of the turrets as Billy performed his startup procedure for the weapons power bank.

Prax' voice came across the page; "Hey, lovebirds, we've got bigger problems on the monitor. Better make sure the cannons are ready."

"Don't worry about us," replied Tera. "You just fly this tin can."

"Shall we take them on manually like last time?" asked Tera.

"We make a heck of a team, Tera. Let's show these aliens a thing or two."

Tera felt at ease with Billy's confidence. "Hey, Billy, a candlelight dinner says I get more kills than you."

"That's not fair. You've had training on this system."

"Like hell! Your friends got the training. I'm like you – a free-lance gunner."

"Then I suppose that's fair." Billy climbed into the other turret and placed the headsets on.

Tera tested her headset first. "Prax, can you hear me?"

"Loud and clear."

"How about you, Billy? Are you on?"

"Yeah, Tera. I hear you loud and clear."

"Here's what we have," announced Prax. "Thirteen coming from the left at high speed. I'm sure you can handle them. It's what's behind them that I'm worried about."

"Are you going to tell us or will we have to die from the suspense?" joked Billy.

"Well, it looks like the whole Boromean force is headed this way. I see seven very large ships; perhaps twenty medium-sized cruisers; and countless numbers of fighters."

"I wonder what brings them after us," Billy pondered aloud.

"How long before we reach Archaenia?" inquired Tera.

"If you can get rid of this first wave, we can probably outrun the rest. Going home is going to be a problem, though."

"First things first," Billy declared. "You get us there as fast as you can and we'll take care of the rest."

"Are you ready for coordinates, kids?"

"No, Prax. Billy and I have a little wager. We'll wing this in 'manual' mode."

"Tera, I know you feel like a woman now, but..."

"Prax, stuff it."

"Okay, but don't screw up."

"Prax, aren't you and Courtney due for some down time?" she teased.

"That's not funny. You just take care of those fighters and let me worry about Courtney."

Billy chuckled. "Nothing like a little family feud."

"Don't make me come over there, Brock," Tera warned.

"Uh, oh. We're back to 'Brock' again. I'm in trouble."

"Here they come!" Prax announced excitedly.

Billy picked groups that were in a line and keyed in on the lead fighter. He squeezed the trigger and watched proudly as three of the alien fighters exploded into flames and disintegrated.

"All right, wise guy. Watch how a lady shoots." Tera sent a spiral of fire toward the approaching fighters and opened a hole in the formation by taking out three more.

"They're in firing distance," warned Prax. "I'm going into maneuvers."

The *Luna C* began to weave left then right. Billy and Tera kept firing and the number of attacking fighters dwindled to four. Two of the fighters disappeared under them, so Prax took the ship into a barrel roll and steered toward the approaching fighters.

Billy and Tera fired a steady stream at the trailers but couldn't put them away. Suddenly the ship lurched, tossing them sideways against their armament panels. The turrets filled with a bright flash and a wave of heat hit them. The ship leveled off and resumed a steady course.

"Are you okay back there?" asked Prax.

"What the hell did you do, Prax?" asked Tera, fearing damage to the ship.

"A simple little maneuver."

"Where are they?"

"Gone," Prax said proudly. "I got all four in one move."

"You jackass!" shouted Tera. "You could have killed us."

"And you had everything under control, right?"

"We did, didn't we Billy?"

"Yeah, except that the power bank had dropped to ten percent. We were about to shut down, Tera."

"Well, that's just great. Why didn't they put a low power alarm on this system or something?"

"Nice flying," Billy praised Prax.

"Thanks. By the way, Archaenia just appeared on the monitor. The Boromeans seem to be hanging back, now."

"That's odd," Billy remarked.

"So, who won, Billy?" Prax asked, curious.

"I did."

"No way! How?" questioned Tera.

"Because I have you."

"That's not what I meant."

"You did well, Tera. I'm proud of you."

There was no answer so Billy put the headsets down and unbuckled his harness. When he climbed down from the turret, Tera was waiting for him. She pushed him against the wall. "I think I won because I have you, too." They kissed passionately.

Prax descended the stairs and interrupted them. "Can't you two get a room?"

"Don't you have a spaceship to fly?" replied Tera.

"No, we've been locked onto by a tractor beam. The Archaenians are bringing us in."

Courtney descended the stairs. "Where did the two of you learn to shoot like that?" she asked excitedly.

"Play Station," replied Billy.

Courtney was in the dark and shook her head. "I never heard of it."

"I have," answered Tera.

Billy glared at her. "Where did you hear of Play Station?"

"I told you I've been to Earth lots of times."

"I thought you meant once or twice."

"No, it's been much more than that."

"So that's where you learned to shoot."

"Uh, yeah. Well apparently, you did too."

"What else have you done on Earth?"

Tera grinned sheepishly. "Not nearly as much as I've done on this ship."

"Alright, that's enough," complained Prax.

"Don't we have some time before we land, Prax?" asked Courtney.

"Yeah, I think we do," replied Prax.

"Imagine that," said Tera coyly.

Billy smiled and suggested. "I think we earned some down time as well. Let's go, Tera." They raced up the stairs.

A half an hour later, Prax' tired voice came across the page. "We're landing, kids. Time to get real again."

"Bummer," complained Billy.

"It'll give you something to look forward to when we go back," Tera reminded him.

— ⧗ —

Ramador drew a rough sketch on the whiteboard and defined the major parts of the battle star. He highlighted a large hatch hidden on the left side of the megaship. "This is where Pendragon will try to launch Dark Horizon from."

"Where could he initiate the launch from?" asked John.

"Most likely from the Command Control Center, which is located in the central portion of the battle star. That's where the brains are for the whole ship. From there he can oversee everything."

"He's not just going to sit back and let us on board without a fight," Ronnie commented.

"First, he'll send troops to the bay to investigate every transport that enters the ship."

"How many troops would he send?" inquired John.

"I would expect about twenty Andoran soldiers to greet us. I'll try to talk to them and hopefully we'll avoid a firefight. Then I'll lead my troops in first to clear the way. We'll get you to the missile bay and you'll take over from there. My next move will be to apprehend Pendragon."

"Why not lead him off of the battle star and deal with him out in the open?" suggested Randy.

"I'll consider that option if the opportunity arises."

"Can Dark Horizon detonate while we're on board?"

"Yes. If that happens, we'll all be leaving the ship in a hurry."

"When can we expect to hear from Billy?" Ronnie asked, anxious.

"I think it will take about three Earth days," replied Ramador.

"What do we do until then?"

"We need to get the transports from Dracor and from Firenghia."

"Our soldiers are ready to support you when we reopen the portals."

"Thank you, Doc. I'd like to do this as soon as possible."

"Meet me in an hour in the transport bay." Doc exited through the doorway and hurried down the hall.

Xerxes asked, "What portal do you want me to open first, Ramador?"

"Let's do Firenghia first. I think we need another day before we should enter the Dracor world. The Boromeans aren't very patient, but they aren't stupid either."

"Ramador, we'll go with you to Firenghia," volunteered Ronnie. "I'd like to see what these Boromeans look like. I hear there are a few carcasses lying about near the portal."

"Boromeans are ugly creatures. I'm sure you won't forget them once you've seen one."

"Do you know where to find the ship?" inquired Xerxes.

"No, but I have a sensor that picks up a beacon emitted by each craft. It's like a homing signal."

"I have nothing further at this time," Doc announced. "Just remember, we need you for the assault on the battle star, so come back in one piece."

"We'll gather some weapons for the trip. How about we meet you in the bay?" suggested Ronnie. "That will give you time to roust your men, I mean your Andorans."

"I'm sure they've taken full advantage of the opportunity to sleep since they received their injections," Ramador commented, satisfied.

Ronnie led her friends from the conference room to the armory. "Is it necessary for us to risk our lives with the Andorans, Ronnie?" asked John.

"I'd like to see what these Boromeans are like since we'll probably be fighting them in the future," she explained.

"Ramador says we'll never forget them once we've seen them. I don't know if I like this," complained Seamus.

"Come on, Seamus. How bad can they be?" chided Randy.

"I'll remember you said that."

"It'll be fun. Just like old times," remarked Ronnie.

"Whose old times?" quipped John.

Ronnie leaned her head against John's shoulder and promised, "I'll protect you, Honey."

"You'd better."

Randy followed along and pressed Seamus against the wall. "Come to mama. I'll take good care of you," she teased.

Seamus became red-faced but pulled her close to him. He kissed her and whispered into her ear, "I love you, Randy."

"I love you, too."

"All right!" bellowed John. "That's enough, already."

They reached the armory and buzzed the attendant. A grizzled old man appeared and leaned across the counter. "What do you want?"

"Pulse pistols. Four to be exact. What do you have in grenades?"

"What do you want?"

"Eight incendiary will do," answered Ronnie.

The man scanned the guns and each of their badges. He scanned the serial code on the grenades and placed them in a mesh bag. "Have fun."

"Don't be so enthusiastic," taunted Ronnie.

The man walked away but not before he mumbled, "Bitch."

"I could kill him with one finger," replied Ronnie indignantly.

"Keep walking," John ordered as he pushed her forward. "He's harmless."

— X —

Prax' called from the page, "Why don't the two of you come up here? I think you'll want to see this."

"We won't be embarrassed, will we?" asked Tera.

"No, I'm serious. This is something to see."

"Do we have to?" he complained. Tera leaned forward and kissed him slowly on the lips then on his neck. "Oh, alright. There's no sense starting something we can't finish."

Tera smiled at him as she quickly dressed. She pushed her hair back and began to hum a song. Billy was amazed at how feminine she looked without the Fleet uniform or the black leather outfit. He finally pushed aside the sheets and dressed himself.

They entered the flight deck and were immediately taken in by the view. The Archaenian planet was in full view with nine rings of various colors surrounding the orange and blue planet. The *Luna C* was pulled smoothly toward the planet, under the control of the Archaenian tractor beam. They were amazed as they were drawn to the strange new world.

Courtney broke the silence first and asked, "Do we know what to ask the Archaenians or how to ask them? I mean, how do we communicate with them?"

Billy shrugged his shoulders. "Beats me. Ramador didn't think it would be a problem, otherwise he would have mentioned it."

"Billy, do you know anything about bombs?" asked Tera.

"Not really."

"How is it that the Archaenians know how to do this?" she continued.

"Ramador said that some of their people were taken captive and forced to build the device," explained Billy.

"They are supposed to be a very intelligent species, I assume."

"It sounds like it. They're giving us a smooth ride in, so I have no complaints yet."

As the *Luna C* glided through the misty gray skies, Billy and his friends gazed in awe at the huge metropolis before them. It was a single complex with long, pointed spires ascending high above the city. A large platform extended out to their ship. The *Luna C* landed on the deck and was retracted inside the complex. A large door closed behind them and sealed them inside.

Prax pushed several buttons and watched the monitor as information scrolled from top to bottom. "Well, it's safe to go out. The sensors indicate a breathable environment," he announced.

"Let's go meet our new friends," replied Billy.

"Hey, Tera, the Archaenians are going to love your outfit," kidded Prax. "I hope they don't think we all dress like that."

"Hey, Prax, don't take any of their women onto the flight deck. We don't need an intergalactic sex scandal."

"Tera, that's cold!" he muttered.

"Courtney, don't you have a leash for him?" asked Tera.

Courtney giggled. "No, I like him like this."

Prax reached for the red knob and depressed it. The air cylinders activated and opened the door. His gaze was fixed as he stared out the hatch.

Tera crept behind him and shouted, "Boo!"

Prax jumped and hit his head against the bulkhead. "Holy crap, Tera! What was that for?"

"You've gotten soft, Prax. Once upon a time, you were like a rock."

"I've softened him up," confessed Courtney. "He's just cuddly now."

Tera rolled her eyes. "Oh, please. I'm going to gag."

Billy chuckled as he enjoyed being left out of the crossfire. He took the initiative and stepped off the ship first. The bay was empty except for the trace of a door on the back wall. There were no cutouts or controls, just trace marks. Tera followed Billy to the wall and waited.

"Well, they brought us here so I'm sure they know we're waiting for an invitation to come in," Billy commented.

The area inside the trace marks suddenly turned into vapor. Billy glanced at Tera for her reaction. She shrugged her shoulders and suggested, "I guess we go in."

Billy entered the doorway and stepped into another chamber. Tera followed him in, but Prax and Courtney hesitated just inside the doorway. Tera realized that they would only be a hindrance, so she suggested, "Why don't the two of you wait in the ship. We can handle this."

Prax and Courtney were happy to accommodate Tera's proposal but as they turned to leave, the doorway vanished, leaving only trace marks again.

Billy chuckled at them. "You see, Prax, the Archaenians are anxious to meet the two of you as well."

"I don't like this at all," Courtney complained.

"Don't worry. Ramador said they'd expect us. If not, I don't think they'd bring us on board."

Suddenly the room felt as if it were falling. Prax and Courtney drifted back against the wall, holding onto each other tightly. Billy and Tera spread their feet and maintained their balance. Billy was proud of Tera's fearlessness and her support for him.

When the room finally became still, the floor folded like foil under each of their feet. They tumbled down slippery tunnels like a giant water slide. Eventually, the four of them sprawled on a flat surface in a glass cavern. The walls were smooth and rounded without any color at all. It was like being inside a giant ice cube without the cold.

Billy helped Tera to her feet. Together, they inspected the area around them. Billy placed his hands across the transparent surfaces of the walls, looking for another doorway. Tera copied Billy's actions and searched other walls as well.

Prax and Courtney were content to stay put on the floor, next to each other. Suddenly, Courtney screamed and crawled on all fours to Billy and Tera. Prax quickly followed her.

Billy burst out laughing. "What the hell is wrong with the two of you?"

Courtney pointed up at the wall, trembling. A face resembling a mouse appeared on the wall as if it were on a huge TV screen. Billy and Tera walked toward the illusion for a closer look. Courtney sobbed and clung to Prax.

"We've got to get out of here!" muttered Prax.

"Shut your holes, both of you!" ordered Tera.

They froze in surprise at Tera's sternness. Prax had never seen that much intensity in her before. She was usually cold and didn't waste words. Sarcasm was her way of handling fear. This time, she demanded their obedience in a way that shook the two of them.

"Can you understand me?" Billy asked the image.

A low-pitched voice echoed through the cavern. "Welcome to Archaenia. You require information from us."

"Yes, we do," Billy replied.

The cavern reverberated. Billy fell to his knees and covered his ears. When he moaned, Tera rushed to his side and held him. "Please stop. You're hurting him," she pleaded.

"You require information," the voice repeated.

Tera felt the same feeling and crumbled against Billy. The two of them were immersed in the Archaenian world. Mouse-like creatures with bodies shaped like humans, surrounded them and studied them. One of Archaenians stepped forward and introduced himself.

"I am Gorich, the Archaenian leader. Welcome to our world."

"Where are our friends?" asked Billy.

"They're in the cavern. No harm will come to them."

"How are we here?" inquired Tera.

"The mind has many powers that you have not learned of. You have been sent by an Andoran."

"Yes. His name is Ramador," Tera responded.

"The Andorans have destroyed much of our planet," explained Billy. "

We were coerced into building a weapon for them," Gorich admitted.

"We've heard; Dark Horizon," Billy commented cynically.

"The Andorans invaded our planet by surprise. They killed many of my people. We developed a defense mechanism for our cities where outsiders can only penetrate using the powers of the mind. Andorans are barbaric creatures and could not solve our defenses."

"Why would you build a weapon that could destroy your world as well as everyone else's?"

"My children built the weapon. Pendragon has terrorized them into thinking that we are his prisoners and our race will only survive if they cooperate."

"How did they know how to build such a weapon if they are children?" questioned Tera.

"Our race is very advanced compared to any that you know of. We learn methods and universal laws at an early age. Applications are something that can be developed by any of us at any time. Pendragon told them what he wanted and they obeyed."

"So, you can tell us how to stop this weapon?"

"Yes. But you must free my children and the other Archaenians in return."

"We can try," Billy replied, unsure of how. "I don't know where Pendragon has imprisoned them, but I will do my best."

"The Archaenian prisoners are on the Andoran planet. We don't have the ability to rescue them because our strength is in our numbers."

"I don't get it, Gorich."

"We have the ability to channel energy from our minds to defend ourselves. We could not gather enough of us in one ship to funnel that same energy into an attack."

"If we can stop Pendragon, then Ramador would likely be the new Andoran leader. I think we can count on him for peace and the release of your fellow Archaenians."

"Ramador did communicate that to us."

"How do we disable the weapon?" asked Tera impatiently.

"We'll provide you with a component that you will install inside the projectile. The original component must be removed to disable it."

"Why do we need the new component?" asked Billy. "Why not just remove the old one?"

"The component controls the energy sources inside the missile," explained Gorich. "Without it, the reaction grows quickly and will destroy all of you. It must be swapped out quickly."

"Where is the new component?" Tera inquired.

"It will be waiting for you in your craft. Now you must go."

Billy and Tera felt lightheaded and stumbled to the ground again. Both rubbed their eyes and were slightly disoriented. Prax and Courtney helped them to their feet.

"Are you okay?" asked Prax.

"Wow, my head is spinning," complained Billy. Tera hugged him and buried her head in his shoulders. She was rattled by the experience.

"When can we get out of here?" asked Prax, uneasily.

Billy answered, "Right now."

"What about the Archaenians?"

"We've spoken with them."

"When did that happen?" questioned Prax, baffled.

"Enough. Let's get out of here," ordered Tera. Prax and Courtney lowered their heads sheepishly and followed. The cavern grew misty and visibility vanished. The four of them clung to each other.

"What's happening now?" cried Courtney.

"I think we're going back to the ship," guessed Billy.

When the mist cleared, the doorway opened before them. Prax and Courtney rushed to the ship as fast as they could. Billy and Tera walked calmly to the craft.

"What happened back there, Billy?" asked Tera.

"I don't know. It was like an out of body experience or something."

"Did that really happen? Did we really meet the Archaenians?"

"We'll see if the component is on board the ship."

When they boarded their ship, Prax and Courtney studied a strange black box just inside the hatch. "What is it, Billy?" asked Prax.

"This is what we'll use to stop Dark Horizon. We have to get back as soon as possible."

"What about the Boromean fleet?"

"Do whatever you have to do. Everything rides on us now."

Prax and Courtney entered the flight deck and started the ship's engines. The bay door opened as if on cue. Billy placed the black box on the table by Tera's workstation and studied it.

"What do you see, Billy?"

"Nothing. Nothing but a black box."

"How will you know what to do with it?"

"There's probably a panel on the side of the missile. I imagine we'll have to unstrap the old box and install the new box. The problem is getting to it."

Billy pressed the button for the page. "Prax, holler if you see Boromeans. We'll do our best to keep them off your tail."

"Roger, Billy."

Billy sat on Tera's bunk and leaned back against the wall. Tera sat next to him and laid her head on his shoulder. "Billy, I feel like I've aged twenty years."

"Me, too."

"I don't care about getting old so long as I do it with you."

"That's great, Tera, but I'd like to have the memories."

"Always a smart ass, aren't you?" she replied.

"That's why you fell for me."

They slept in each other's arms, exhausted from their experience.

Prax pressed several switches and guided the ship at full speed into the first of three portals they would need to pass through on their return. Courtney watched the monitors intently for any sign of the Boromeans. After a few hours, she began to tire. "Get some rest, Courtney. I'll be okay by myself," said Prax. Courtney tilted her seat back and slept.

CHAPTER 11

BATTLE PREPARATIONS

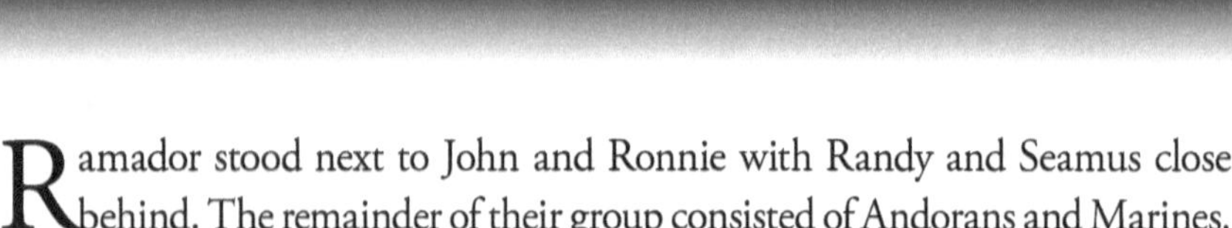

Ramador stood next to John and Ronnie with Randy and Seamus close behind. The remainder of their group consisted of Andorans and Marines. Everyone stood with guns drawn, ready to rush through the portal.

Xerxes stood by the portal and activated the controls until the screen came to life. He tapped the enter key and punched in an access code. "Is everyone ready?" Heads bobbed up and down in affirmation. Xerxes pressed a black knob and the portal energized. The orange mist formed and spiraled until it took on a three-dimensional look. "Go ahead, Ramador. The portal's operational," announced Xerxes.

Ramador led the group through the portal toward Firenghia. As soon as he stepped onto solid ground, he bolted to the left. The group split in half as troops went left and right, forming a wall in front of the portal.

A small contingent of Boromeans was camped in the distance. They immediately spotted Ramador's team exiting the portal. The creatures climbed onto mechanical devices that looked like metal chariots. A whirring sound filled the air as the machines roared to life.

"Fire at will!" ordered Ramador.

The sound of gunfire echoed across the plains as several of the Boromeans fell to the ground. The others raced toward Ramador's group, howling their blood-curdling scream. The twilight sky added to the terror as the Boromeans drew closer.

Ronnie noted that the Boromeans were only killed by shots to the head. "Headshots only! They've got body armor," she alerted everyone.

As the Boromeans got closer, they became easier targets. When they suffered mounting casualties, the remainder of the Boromean army turned and scattered.

Ronnie approached one of the wounded Boromeans and observed it. The creature raised its ugly head and hissed defiantly at her before taking its last breath. She poked at the dead creature with her gun.

Ramador pulled her back and warned her, "The tentacles on its head are poisonous. They will live until you place a hole in the center of its skull like this." He raised his gun and fired a pulse of energy through the back of the creature's head. The tentacles quivered briefly. "Now you can inspect it more closely."

Ronnie knelt down near the creature and studied it. She was mortified by its appearance. The tentacles had a moss-like substance that clung to them. The face might have been slightly human, but was grotesquely deformed. The mouth had no lips and the teeth were horribly crooked. The creatures weren't very tall, but they had a tough exoskeleton from the neck down, almost like a turtle shell. The arms and legs had spikes attached to the exoskeleton and were quite sharp.

"Be careful," warned Ramador. "Everything about those creatures is poisonous. You don't want to touch it."

Ronnie shuddered. "Thanks for the warning."

Randy spotted Seneca's corpse nearby and went to investigate further. Her body lay in a contorted position with part of her head missing. Her long black hair was blood-soaked. Her hands tightly gripped her pulse pistol. Ronnie couldn't help notice that the red light on the side of the weapon indicated that it had run out of power.

Seamus joined her and suggested a prayer for Seneca. Together they prayed for her soul. Seamus took off his long, wool coat and wrapped Seneca's body inside of it. "We'll take her back for a proper burial. I'm sure Billy would appreciate that." Together they carried Seneca's body back to the portal.

Randy looked on sadly. She couldn't help thinking about her experience with the dinosaur and the dragon. She could have been in a body bag had Ronnie not saved her life. *How sad that none of us could save Seneca*, she thought.

Ramador led the Andorans over the hill in search of their transport, while the soldiers followed Ronnie and Seamus back through the portal. When they returned to the transport bay, Doc and Xerxes waited anxiously for news. Both men grew concerned when they saw Seamus and Ronnie with a body.

"Who is it?" asked Doc.

"Billy's friend, Seneca. She was killed by the Boromeans."

"What about Ramador and his troops? Did they make it?"

"Yes. They're on their way to the ship."

Maggie entered the bay and approached them. "What's happened? Who is that, Seamus?"

"Seneca."

"Poor dear."

Seamus asked, "How is Penny's condition?"

"She's in a lot of pain and the doctors are keeping her very sedated."

"Those Boromean creatures – they are the most awful things I have ever seen," remarked Ronnie.

Doc and Xerxes were interested in her comment. "Can you tell me about them, Ronnie?" asked Doc anxiously. "What were they like?"

"Imagine your worst nightmare. I don't think I'll ever get a good night's sleep again. They are the consummate boogie men."

"Okay, already! Can you give me some scientific detail?"

"How about a Medusa with a face so horrible and no dental plan? I thought I was going to vomit."

"A Medusa?"

"Yes, except that it had poisonous tips at the end of their dreadlocks. I thought they were dreads at first but they were fleshy snake-like things. Oh, God! They were so awful."

"Would you like me to bring back a corpse for you to study?" offered John.

"No. I think I'll pass on this one."

"Ramador will be in touch when they approach the portal. Does he know how to communicate with you from outside the gate?"

"Yes," answered Xerxes. "I gave him coordinates to contact the Council for access to the first portal."

"Then phase one was successful," he concluded.

"Why don't we call it a night?" suggested Doc. "I'll shut down the portal if everyone is accounted for."

"Xerxes, where are Rena and the children?" Maggie asked.

"We moved them to a dorm next door."

"What will happen to them?"

"Their people were relocated to a small planet not too far from the outermost portal. When it's safe enough, we'll take them back there."

"Do they know?"

"Not yet."

"Then I'll go speak with Rena."

"What do we have to look forward to tomorrow, Xerxes?" inquired Doc.

"Hopefully we'll hear something from the *Luna C*. I do need to spend some time with Sam and Ginea in the weapons lab. I'd like to see how this cluster bomb is coming along."

"We'll be able to shut down the Andoran portal with three of them," Doc informed them.

"Are you sure?" asked Xerxes.

"Based on the tests in the lab, we should be able to de-energize the portal and possibly the source as well."

"Excellent. Then I'll call it a night. I'm beat."

— X —

Prax opened the door to Tera's compartment and yelled, "Billy! Tera! We've got trouble."

Billy rubbed his eyes and sat up. "What's wrong, Prax?"

"We've got big trouble!"

"You said that already," retorted Tera irritably.

"No, this is really big. The Boromeans are moving in from the Serphian galaxy and an Andoran battle star is approaching from the Corynthian Belt."

"Can we outrun them?"

"I doubt it. This will be like running a gauntlet."

"Tera and I will slow them down," replied Billy. "What are our best odds, the Andoran battle star or the Boromean fleet?"

"I don't think anyone in their right mind would give odds on either matchup."

Tera stood up and stretched. Her black leather outfit defined her slender shape. Billy tried to keep his sense of humor. "Damn, girl. You look good even when you just wake up."

"Save it, Billy. This is serious."

"Come on, Tera, we can take them."

"Yeah, right. Dreams over, Billy. We're in trouble."

"Do we have them on the monitor yet, Prax?"

"Which ones?"

"Both of them. I want to see where we are relative to their position."

"Tera, you can bring them up on your work station, can't you?" asked Prax.

"What are you thinking?" Tera asked Billy.

"If we travel at half-speed and stay midway between them until they get into close range, we might be able to escape."

"And you'll pull a rabbit out of your butt, too," she said cynically.

"No, think about this. They will both attempt to fire on us. Once we get into their firing range, we'll accelerate to full speed and shoot right between them."

"Just like running a gauntlet, right?" Tera commented sarcastically.

"No, this is better. When they fire at us, many of their shots are likely to be wide at first until they zero in on us. When one of them misses a shot, it has a chance of hitting the other. Perhaps we can turn the Andorans and the Boromeans on each other."

"And what if they hit us with their early barrage? If the ship is damaged, we're sitting ducks," Tera complained.

Billy pondered for a moment. "What if the Andoran ship is here to protect us?" he contemplated aloud.

"Why would they do that?" asked Prax.

"What if Ramador got word to them and they are here to make sure we get back?"

Tera mulled over the idea. "It could be, but how can we find out?"

"What if we glide away from both groups, and then drift toward the Andoran battle star," suggested Prax. "We can monitor their guns for tracking."

"Why don't we just hail them?" suggested Billy.

"What's that mean?"

"What do you mean 'what's that mean?' You're a pilot, aren't you?"

"Yeah, but I never heard of that expression."

Courtney's voice came over the page. The tone of her voice echoed her fear. "We'd better do something fast, Prax. They're getting close."

"Communicate with them, Prax! Ask them if they've heard from Ramador," ordered Billy confidently.

"Are you sure?"

"Do it now before it's too late!"

Prax hurried back to the flight deck. He turned on the transmitter and monitor. "Come in Andoran battle star. This is the *Luna C.* Do you copy?" To his surprise, they responded.

"This is the battle star *Promethius.* Ramador has advised us of your mission. We have also been warned of the Boromean insurgency."

Prax tried, in a husky voice, to sound like he knew what he was talking about. "Can you help us to pass the Boromean fleet?"

"Is Billy Brock on board?"

"Yes, he is."

"We must speak with him."

"Stand by." Prax muted the comm-link and pressed the page button. "Billy, you'd better get up here fast! Your friends want a word with you."

"I hope you know what you're doing," warned Tera.

Billy smiled, inspiring confidence in her. He raced up to the flight deck and knelt down in front of the monitor. Prax turned off the mute to the comm-link.

"Billy is here. Go ahead," he announced.

"Billy Brock?"

"Yes, what is it."

"Ramador has told us you have a cure for our affliction. Your people have an ample supply of the serum. Is this true?"

"Yes, it is."

"Ramador has told us that you can stop Pendragon. Is this true as well?"

"I believe so. We have information from Ramador and the Archaenians to help us stop Pendragon and Dark Horizon."

"Then you must pass. Tell Pendragon that Polypheus and his crew are loyal to him. Go now. We will take care of the Boromeans."

"Thank you, Polypheus." The monitor went blank. Prax gave Billy a strange stare.

"What's wrong, Prax?"

"You are the luckiest S.O.B. that I ever knew. Get back there and man the guns. We're going full speed for the portal."

Billy descended the steps to Tera's station and kissed her cheek. "How in the world can you be so relaxed at a time like this?" she asked.

"The Andorans are loyal to Ramador. They'll help us out of here, so get your cute little butt up to your turret. We're going to find out who the better gunner is." She grabbed his arm and stopped him. "What's wrong, Tera?"

"I love you."

"I love you, too." Billy kissed her passionately.

"I mean I really love you, Billy. I've never loved anyone before and if this is it, I want you to know that." Billy pinched her butt. "Get up there and shoot like the woman I know." He climbed the ladder to his turret.

Tera smiled and wondered what it would be like to spend some leisure time with Billy, without all the excitement and drama. She took Billy's CD player up to her turret and selected the song Closer from earlier. She put on the headset and pressed the play button. The sound of the saxophone calmed her nerves. "Billy, can you hear me?"

"Yes, I can. What's that sound in the background?"

"Listen." She turned up the volume and began singing the words."

"Interesting choice, Tera."

"In case we don't make it, I want to think about the most important thing that ever happened to me." Billy got a lump in his throat and searched for something to say.

"Stop it, you two!" interrupted Prax. "Courtney's in tears and I'm feeling nauseous."

"Here they come. It's show time," announced Billy.

Prax maneuvered the *Luna C* away from the Boromeans toward the shelter of the Andoran battle star. The cannon fire from the battle star sent reverberations through their ship. The Boromeans swarmed around the battle star and attempted to pursue them. Billy and Tera fired tenaciously at the fighters that evaded the battle star. Together they decimated large numbers of their attackers as they drew closer to the portal.

"Hey, Tera. You're fantastic."

"So are you. I think we're going to make it."

"Three to go and we're free."

"Best two out of three. Winner takes all," she challenged.

"Sounds like you played some cards on Earth, too."

"Once or twice."

"Oh, no!"

"What's wrong, Billy?"

"My gun's down."

"Hell, the power bank is under ten percent. No more guns."

"What are you talking about? Get them, quick!" pleaded Prax.

"We can't, Prax. The system is down."

"Get ready, then. Here they come." The *Luna C* lurched left, then right. Suddenly the main power failed.

"Back up power taking over. We've got damage," announced Prax.

They reached the portal followed closely by the Boromean fighters. As soon as they entered the portal, a large, fiery blast flung the ship through at an awkward position. Billy held on tightly inside the turret until the ship stabilized. He scanned the perimeter looking for the fighters. The *Luna C* wasn't moving and a Boromean fighter closed in. Billy heard a beep as the bank charged to eleven percent. "Hear that!" he shouted. "That's enough for one short burst." No one answered.

Filled with fear, Billy targeted the fighter with his cannon and squeezed the trigger. He breathed a sigh of relief as a short pulse struck the fighter, sending it into a fiery spiral. With no other attackers in sight, he unbuckled his harness and hurried over to Tera's turret. He panicked when he found her lying on the floor at the bottom of the turret steps. He helped her to her feet and escorted her to her compartment. She had a wound on the side of her head and blood trickled down the bridge of her nose.

"Tera, can you hear me?"

"Yeah, what the hell happened?"

"I don't know yet. I'm going to take you up to your workstation and then I'll check on Prax and Courtney."

After setting her in her bunk, Billy hurried onto the flight deck where he found Prax and Courtney slumped across the controls, unconscious. He gently shook Prax until he opened his eyes. "Are you okay, Prax?"

"I have a killer headache."

"I think we've lost the last of the Boromeans for now. Can we get the ship started?"

"I'll try. What about Courtney?"

"Let me get some water and a rag. I'll be right back."

Billy took two containers of water and some bandages from the supply cabinet. Then he took some rags from the maintenance cabinet. He stopped in Tera's compartment and dressed her wound first. He returned to the flight deck where Courtney awakened. Billy placed a wet a rag on her head. Courtney thanked him and leaned back in a reclining position.

"How's Tera?" asked Prax.

"She'll be okay. She's a real trooper."

"Are you okay?"

"Yeah, I'm fine. Can you start the ship up?"

"We'll know in a second," Prax replied, still reeling from the impact. "The computer is finishing the diagnostic check."

Tera entered the flight deck and put an arm around Billy's waist. "What's going on?"

"You should be in your compartment resting," Billy cautioned. "That's one heck of a knob you have on your head."

"I'll be okay. Why aren't we moving, Prax?"

"The diagnostic check is complete. We have damage to the ship but it should be operable."

Billy was concerned about the damage. "Will we make it back?"

"I think so. When we reach the next portal, I'll be able to give you an answer. We have no primary power so that means no more weapons system. Two of the four fuel cells burst and one of our oxygen supply tanks was blown away."

"How did that happen?" Billy asked.

"The tail was hit and the damage ignited a fuel line," Prax explained. "When the flame spread toward the supply tank, I ejected it along with the surrounding equipment before it exploded."

"What are our limiting factors?"

"Fuel should be enough to get us back but the oxygen is going to be limited."

"Then what are we waiting for? Get this ship going!" ordered Billy.

Prax punched a code into a computer and pressed two switches. The ship shuddered and sprang to life. The instrument controls illuminated and the ship finally moved. Billy and Tera returned to her workstation. She rebooted the navigation equipment and entered data into the computer. "Tera, do you need to do that now?" asked Billy, concerned by her injuries. "You should try to rest."

"I'm all right, Billy. This will only take a few minutes and then I'll lie down."

Billy massaged her shoulders and rubbed her neck. Tera finished loading the next set of coordinates and put on the headset. "Prax, the coordinates to the next portal have been loaded into the computer," she announced over the intercom. "You can select auto-pilot at any time."

"Thanks, cuz'."

Tera took the headsets off and took Billy by the hand. They entered her compartment and sat down on her bunk. Billy hugged her and cradled her against his chest. He gently laid her down and covered her with a blanket. Satisfied that she was resting, Billy returned to the flight deck and sat in the spare seat behind Prax.

"Can I ask you something, Prax?"

"Sure, Billy. Shoot."

"You don't say much about Xerxes, yet he's your uncle, right."

"Uh, yeah."

"Well, I understand Tera was pretty upset with him for a while, but you never talk of him or to him. How do you feel about him?"

"Why do you ask that?"

"I guess because I've been through a lot with Xerxes. Sometimes, however, I feel like he's not telling me everything."

"My father, I mean my uncle was good at that. He hid many things from his family. He didn't have time for us so he sent us to the Fleet academy. It must have run in the family because his brother treated me the same way."

"Tera said that it was pretty bad when her mother became pregnant," Billy commented. "I'm surprised that she had two children."

"That's the irony of it. She didn't have two children."

"But you and Tera are related, right? You keep calling her 'cousin' but I think you are brother and sister. Why do you deny it?"

"Yes, we're related but we have different mothers. My father was Xerxes and he wanted children. Since Tera's mom was opposed to the idea, he had a short relationship with my mother."

"Was your mother someone I would know about?"

"She was a member of the Council and he hoped for inclusion into the Council as a result of their relationship. When she informed him that their tryst was only a tryst and nothing more, he became angry. He returned to Tera's mom but shortly after, both women found out that they were pregnant. Tera and I both hated him for what he did."

"But all he wanted was a family. I don't agree with how he pursued it, but it doesn't seem all that bad."

"What about his desire to gain a seat on the Council?"

"Are you so sure of that, Prax?"

"Why else would he do that?"

"What does your mother say about it?"

"She won't speak about him at all."

"So maybe there was another reason for what happened."

"I don't know and I don't care. Now, the discussion is over."

"I'm sorry. I was just curious."

"Some things are better off left alone."

Billy left the cabin and returned to Tera's workstation. He knelt down next to her bed and laid his head on her shoulder. He wondered how far this would go and if it would ever end.

— X —

Doc and Maggie stood in the back of the room and watched as the doctor examined Penny. Ronnie and Randy sat in the corner with John and Seamus standing behind them. The doctor finished and motioned the group outside to the hallway.

"Her injuries are very severe," he explained. "The concussion is the least of her worries. She's bleeding internally from a number of areas. It's slowed down, but I don't think there is anything that can be done. We can move her to Bethesda, but all we can do is comfort her. It's just a matter of time before her body shuts down."

Tears ran down Maggie's cheek. "Is she going to die?"

The doctor lowered his head and answered, "Yes. There's no way to repair all of the damage. She sustained an unbelievable trauma to the stomach area. It's amazing that she's lasted this long."

Maggie buried her head in her husband's shoulders and sobbed.

"Can she hear us?" asked Ronnie.

"Yes. She's not comatose but she is very weak. As I said, it's only a matter of time before her body shuts down."

Ronnie and Randy entered the room. They each pulled up a chair and sat next to Penny's bed. Randy held Penny's hand. "Penny, can you hear me?" Penny opened one eye about half way and faintly squeezed Randy's hand.

"Can I get you anything?"

Penny turned her head slightly. "Billy. Where's Billy?" she whimpered.

"He'll be back soon."

Penny strained to speak but the words were faint. "I'm sorry. I'm so, so sorry," she murmured.

"Did Pendragon do this to you?" asked Randy. Penny pursed her lips and a tear rolled down her cheek.

Randy nearly cried. "I promise, Penny, we'll make him pay for this."

"Penny, you and Billy both received strange healing qualities from Seneca," Ronnie reminded her. "I don't understand them but if you can fight this until he returns, you might have a chance." Tears rolled with greater frequency down Penny's cheeks and formed a wet spot on the bed sheet.

Randy squeezed her hand and said, "We're here for you. As soon as Billy returns, we'll send him in. Please don't give up."

Penny seemed to slip away into a deep sleep. Randy wiped a tear from her eye and left the room. She recalled how scared and alone she was when she was thrown from the dragon. Her life was slipping away and no one was there to help her until Ronnie came. She wanted to be there for Penny. When she exited the room and saw Ronnie sobbing, she cried again.

"There must be something we can do for her," she uttered.

"They've given her blood. They've tried to stop the bleeding, but it's only slowed down. She has fluid on her brain from the concussion. She's a wreck," cried Ronnie.

Randy then realized something. "You might have a point about something, Ronnie."

"About what?"

"Penny and Billy inherited some strange things from Seneca."

"So."

"They've been giving her blood from ordinary donors. If Billy has the same blood type as Penny, perhaps his blood can help her."

"That sounds far-fetched, Randy."

"It's worth a try. Let's find the doctor and talk to him."

"Before they can do anything, Randy, Billy would have to have the same blood type as Penny."

"Let's get Doc Smith. He's in the other room with Maggie. He'll help us find out."

Randy rushed into the lab and interrupted Doc and Maggie. "We have an idea that might save Penny. Can you help us?"

"There's nothing we can do for her. You heard the doctor," said Doc dejectedly.

Ronnie persisted, "Penny and Billy had some things that they inherited from Seneca. One of them was their ability to heal quickly."

"Yeah, but it doesn't seem to be working."

"But they're giving her blood from ordinary donors. What if Billy could give her some of his blood? Perhaps she might begin to heal. The doctor said it himself that the bleeding has slowed down."

"So, you think that by giving her some of Billy's blood, she might recover?"

"Yes. Can you find out if they have the same blood type?"

"I sure can. It's worth a try."

"When is Billy due back?" asked Maggie.

"I believe by the end of the day. We haven't heard from the *Luna C* yet but we probably won't until they clear the second portal. I'll contact Dr. Watts and have him verify the blood types on record."

— X —

Xerxes returned from the Council and spoke with several of the technicians that worked in the transport bay. As he finished his discussion, the warning lights flashed over the primary portal, indicating an incoming spacecraft. He waited, hoping that the *Luna C* was arriving ahead of time. The portal glowed with a brilliant green gas as an Andoran transport emerged and docked in position number three.

Xerxes was somewhat relieved. At least Ramador secured the first of the two Andoran transports required for the attack. The bay vibrated as the turnstile rotated to the next empty dock in front of the primary portal. A loud hissing sound filled the air and the Andoran spaceship's hatch opened.

Ramador was the first to disembark from the craft, followed by several other Andorans. Xerxes approached Ramador and greeted him. "I see the first part of the plan went well."

"We had some resistance from the Boromeans but we managed to suppress them," Ramador informed him.

"When do you want to go after the other ship?"

"Right away. I'd like to get back as soon as possible. Have you heard anything from Billy yet?" Ramador inquired.

"No, but they should be on their way back by now. As soon as they clear the second portal, we expect to have contact with them."

"Is the portal ready for us to return to Dracor?"

"I can take care of it right now. Do you need military support from our people?"

"No, I think the Boromeans would have left by now. If not, we'll be back in a hurry."

"Well, good luck." Xerxes turned on the portal and Ramador led his troops to Dracor.

He felt better seeing that Ramador was making progress and at least one of the Andoran craft was recovered.

— ⏳ —

Prax voice carried over the page, "Billy, if you're awake, you might want to come up here. We have a problem."

Billy lifted his head when he heard Prax' voice. "Oh, not again," he muttered as he reached for the page. "Prax, I'm here. What's up?"

"Come on up. We have a problem."

"I'll be right there."

"What's going on, Billy?" asked Tera.

"We'll find out soon enough. I'm going up to see Prax."

"I'm coming, too."

Billy entered the flight deck followed by Tera. "What's going on, Prax?"

"See that spec on the screen that's coming toward us very quickly."

"Any ideas who it might be?"

"It's coming from Andora."

"Do their craft normally go that fast?"

"Beats me. I don't know enough about alien ships to tell you anything about their capabilities."

"Then we ought to get the heck out of here as fast as we can. It might be Pendragon."

"Why would he come looking for us?" asked Tera.

"If he knows the Archaenians gave us the information to disarm Dark Horizon, he might try to stop us before we get the information back to Xerxes."

"How long before we reach the portal, Prax?" Tera inquired.

"Not long, but if he catches us, we have no weapons."

"Will we make the portal before he catches us?"

"I think so. It's going to be close but I think we'll have him by about forty seconds in your time."

"As soon as we clear, get the Council to shut the portal. If not, we're done."

"What if we don't make contact with them?"

"Just do your best," instructed Billy.

Courtney awakened and stared at them. "What happened?" she asked.

"You fell asleep," Prax answered.

"No, really?"

"We're going home."

"Call me if anything changes," requested Billy. He and Tera entered the stairwell.

"Is there any way of manipulating the weapons system to make it work?" asked Billy.

"I don't know. The backup system powers only the essential systems for operation and life support."

"Well, we're missing several components here. I'm wondering if we can reroute some of the wiring for the systems that Prax ejected. Maybe we can get enough for one lucky shot."

"You'd have to get the power bank over ten percent for one shot."

Billy inquired about schematics for the ship. Tera promptly pulled out three binders from under her workstation. They thumbed through the folded drawings until they found the plans for the rear section. Billy pointed out four cables that they might use. They located the panel that fed the cables. After browsing through a few more drawings, Billy found the schematic for the weapons system power bank. "We can do this, Tera."

"Are you sure you know what to do?"

"I think so. This panel is fed from the backup system. We'll turn the power off to that cable, pull it back and run it to the weapons' power bank."

"I hope you know what you're doing."

"It looks like the cables have disconnects for a situation like ours when the components are jettisoned. We only need one of them."

Tera looked uncertain as she watched Billy go to work on the cables. Twenty minutes later, he connected the cable to the weapons power bank. He stood up and looked proudly upon his handy work. "Are you ready, Tera?"

"The question is 'Are you ready?' Billy." He pulled the lever for the power panel and pressed the button that energized the cable to the weapons bank. The backup power flickered and a loud click echoed from the panel.

"Nice job, Billy," she chided.

Prax voice came over the page, "Should I ask what the two of you are doing?"

"It's okay," answered Billy. "I'm trying to power up the weapons system."

"Remember, Billy, the backup power is all we have left."

"I know. I'll try it one more time."

Billy reset the panel and pressed the button once again. The lights flickered but stayed on. The power bank hummed and several LEDs across the top blinked. "How long does it take for this thing to charge up?" asked Billy.

"Probably a lot longer than we have," replied Tera pessimistically.

"When we enter the portal, we'll fire one shot if we can. That should divert him away from the portal and buy us additional time."

"I hope you're right," Tera remarked, doubtful he could pull this off.

Billy called on the page, "How are we looking, Prax?"

"The portal is in sight."

"How about our friend?"

"He's getting very close. Tell me you have a plan."

"Just tell me when you're about to hit the portal."

"What can I do?" asked Tera.

"Stay here and watch the bank. I need to know when we're close to ten percent."

Billy hustled up to the turret and strapped himself in. "How much has the bank charged?" Billy called down to her.

"Eight percent. Eight and a half," shouted Tera.

"Let me know as soon as it hits ten."

Billy put the headset on. "Talk to me, Prax."

"Ten, nine, eight…"

"Nine and a half, Billy," shouted Tera.

"Seven, six, five…" continued Prax.

"If this works, Billy, I'll…Ten percent!"

"Two, one, now!" hollered Prax.

Billy fired a single pulse at the fighter just before it followed them into the portal. The ship veered away and missed the portal.

Prax raced excitedly down the stairs and crossed the main quarters. "The Council is closing the portal! We made it!"

Billy hopped down from the turret and stepped into Tera's waiting arms.

"I should never have doubted you," she said proudly.

Prax shook Billy's hand repeatedly. "Damn, you're every bit as good as we've heard."

Billy blushed. "When this is over, I want to know everything you've heard about me. It's tearing me up."

"Let's go up to the flight deck and contact Xerxes," suggested Prax.

Tera pulled Billy back and hugged him tightly. "Thank you, Billy." Billy responded with a kiss.

When they entered the flight deck several minutes later, Prax asked sarcastically, "What took you so long? Xerxes is having a fit."

"You mean your dad is having a fit?"

"Well, yeah."

"Xerxes, how are you?" Billy spoke into the speaker.

"I'm doing much better, now. I see you had a close call."

"Actually, several of them. We have a component to replace inside the missile."

"Then you have to physically go into Dark Horizon?" Xerxes responded.

"Yes. We do, I'm afraid."

"Ramador anticipated this. He's getting the second ship. Do you really think that the chase ship was Pendragon?"

"I'm sure of it. He'll have to go back and use his own portal now. That should buy us some time."

"We have ships in position to monitor the Andoran portal. In addition, we have a spy ship near Andora."

"But how can they get word to us if they spot him?" Billy questioned him.

"We set up another portal in that area. They'll be close enough to get a message to us."

"Do we have the ability to shut down the Andoran portal yet?"

"Sam's almost finished with his new invention. We think it'll work."

"How is everyone else?"

"Well, there's some bad news. Perhaps we should wait until you get back."

"What happened, Xerxes?"

"Not now, Billy."

"Tell me, Xerxes! I want to know."

Tera put her arms around Billy for comfort. His face reddened as he waited impatiently.

"I shouldn't have brought this up now. Seneca is dead."

"What? What happened?" he asked, tears streaming down his cheeks.

"A Boromean ambush."

"What about Penny? She was with her."

"She's in critical condition. She may not make it."

"Son of a bitch! They're dead! They're all dead!" he shouted like a mad man.

"Billy, this doesn't change anything. Get control of yourself."

"He'll be okay, Dad," Tera interjected. "We'll see you soon."

"Thanks, Tera."

Prax and Courtney were silent as they felt Billy's grief. Tera tugged at his arm and said, "Come on, Billy. Let's go back to my station."

"We're sorry, Billy," said Prax somberly.

"Pendragon's going to pay. I swear to you, he's going to suffer."

Tera pulled on his arm. "Come on, Sweetie."

When they returned to Tera's workstation, Billy sat on the edge of her bed and covered his face. Tera didn't know what to say so she just hugged him. Billy closed his eyes and wept in her arms. She was content to hold him and provide comfort.

When he looked up at her with teary, red eyes, she felt badly for him. "I'm really sorry, Billy."

Billy cried again before he regained his composure. "I can't believe this could happen. Seneca was special. She changed me and I became the person you see today. Even though my relationship with Penny was over, she still mattered."

"Billy, she's not gone yet. Maybe she'll make it."

"I'll get even with the Boromeans and Pendragon even if it kills me."

"Don't say that. This is a war and you know how that goes. Don't take it personal or it will destroy you."

"That's easy for you to say."

"No, it isn't, because I don't want to lose you. I can imagine how bad I would hurt, so I know how you feel."

Billy hugged Tera like an infant to its mother. He couldn't believe how the nightmare that began with a simple flight to Philadelphia never ended. It only took a break from time to time.

"Billy, we still have a lot to do. Please try to understand how important you are to everyone else. You matter, too."

"I'll be all right."

"I hope so."

Billy broke into tears again. "When will this nightmare ever end? This is cruel. So friggin' cruel."

"It has to end sometime. I promise it will," Tera assured him.

Prax' voice interrupted them, "We're entering the transport bay. Get ready to disembark. Billy, are you okay?"

Billy sniffled as he regained his composure. "Yeah, Prax. Just hurting a bit."

As soon as the *Luna C* was docked, the hatch opened. Billy marched out and met Doc. "Where's Penny?"

"Follow me."

"How is she?"

"Not good."

"I'm going to kick a whole lot of alien ass over this!"

"Look, Billy, Randy had an idea that might save Penny."

"What is it?"

"You and she have the same blood type. She's lost a lot of blood and we've been replacing it with blood from normal donors. The two of you inherited strange healing qualities from Seneca."

"Yes, we did."

"Perhaps if we gave her some of your blood, we could induce enough healing to save her."

"I'll try anything, Doc."

When they reached the infirmary, Billy's friends were gathered outside Penny's door. No one spoke as Billy hurried into her compartment. He broke into tears when he saw her condition. Her head was bandaged on one side where they shaved her smooth, dark hair. She had dressings over her stomach and groin area where the doctors operated. Doc entered the room and prepared Billy for the transfusion.

"Why is she still here, Doc? Bethesda isn't far from here. Maybe they could have helped her."

"It wouldn't have mattered, Billy. We believe that this was the only chance she had. It was just a question of time, if she could hold out long enough until you got back."

Billy lay back on the table and Doc inserted the needle into his arm. "What the hell happened to her?"

"I guess Pendragon wanted his revenge. She suffered a very serious head trauma – a bleeding concussion. She was pregnant before the incident. He apparently struck her in the abdomen with incredible force. Her insides were changing to adapt to a short pregnancy so she was very vulnerable. Most women would have died already from such a blow."

"Pendragon is dead. I'll see to that myself."

"Let's do this first, and then we'll worry about Pendragon."

Billy stared at the blood flowing through the tube into Penny's arm. He tried to communicate with her but her mind was a blanket of darkness.

"Did you find out anything useful from the Archaenians?"

"Yeah. We have a component to swap out on the missile."

"Can you do it?" Doc asked, knowing it would be a suicide mission.
Billy bit his lip in anger and replied, "Oh, yes. I'll do it."
Eventually he closed his eyes and slept.

— X —

Ramador and his troops crossed the barren Dracor wasteland and easily located their ship. He held his hand up for the Andorans to stop. "What is it, Ramador?"

"It wouldn't be like the Boromeans to leave without setting a trap of some sort. Spread out and circle the ship. My guess is that there are a few guests waiting inside the main hatch."

The Andorans followed Ramador's orders and closed in on the ship. They stood on either side of the hatch and prepared to fire their weapons. Ramador pulled the handle for the hatch and waited for the door to come down. He backed away from the door and picked up a stone. He looked carefully at the mist emanating from inside the ship. The Andoran soldiers watched Ramador anxiously, wondering what he was going to do.

"Get ready to fire low," he ordered his men. He tossed the rock onto the bay floor, just inside the hatch. The air was filled with squeals as three grotesque creatures pounced upon the rock, fighting each other as if that rock was the last living thing on earth.

Ramador's men fired at the creatures until there was no further noise. He tossed another rock further into the bay but no more creatures appeared. The Andorans boarded the ship and started its power units. When the lights came on, the ventilation removed the mist from the ship and allowed Ramador to inspect the strange creatures.

They had long thin necks with small heads, big mouths and lots of sharp jagged teeth. The oddity was seeing long strands of hair hanging from the heads. The torsos were long and thin with a leathery skin. There were four legs and two short upper arms, equipped with sharp talons. Ramador ordered two of his troops to remove the carcasses and cleanse the area.

"Don't touch them," he warned. "Anything to do with the Boromeans is likely to be poisonous." The Andorans heeded Ramador's warning. They carefully wrapped the carcasses and disposed of them outside the hatch.

After a careful inspection of the ship, Ramador was confident it was safe to fly. "Take her up," he instructed the pilot.

— X —

Tera waited patiently with Randy, Ronnie and Maggie. The others remained in the waiting area out of respect for their privacy. Randy couldn't stand the silence anymore and asked Tera, "Do you think Billy will be all right?"

"I don't know. He took the news pretty hard."

"He was very close to Seneca in a different sort of way. She's also the mother of his son."

"I know. He knew he'd never see her again," Tera revealed to them.

"That really sucks," uttered Ronnie.

"I know he has struggled over Penny's altered attitude since she inherited Seneca's traits." Tera related.

"Penny was supposed to be his dream-come-true, but it was always an uphill battle. He hurt many times over her," Maggie said somberly.

"I could tell."

"Can you make him happy?" Randy asked, hoping for Billy to find peace.

"I want to. It seems like we're good for each other. I'm happy with him no matter what we do or where we go. I'm happy with his friends and anything he wants to do."

"I'm glad to hear that. He deserves someone special."

"Thank you, Randy."

"Where did the two of you meet?"

"On the rescue mission to the battle star."

"No kidding. You and Billy just fell for each other?"

"Well, it was a strange story. I thought it was going to end when he discovered who my father is."

Randy waited anxiously for a moment. "Well, are you going to tell me?"

"Oh, I'm sorry. He's Xerxes."

"Get out! I never knew he had a daughter."

"For a while, I'm sure he felt like it."

— ✕ —

Doc watched Penny's vital signs, hoping that at some point they would start to improve.

"We should stop the transfusion," suggested Dr. Watts. "We can't take too much from this man."

Doc thought for a moment about what Billy would want. "No, she needs more. Billy would want this."

"But, Dr. Smith, you know what could happen."

"Billy would want this," he repeated.

"No more than another pint or they could both die."

"That's fine." Doc saw the numbers fluctuate a little for Penny's blood pressure. Soon the numbers began to climb.

"That's enough, Dr. Watts. I think it's working."

The two men watched in amazement as Penny's blood pressure nearly reached a normal limit and her heart rate increased. "I can't believe it, Dr. Smith! This story about healing is really true?"

"Yes, it is. We've seen for ourselves. I didn't believe it at first myself."

"I'll be back in an hour to see how they are doing."

"Thanks, Dr. Watts."

— ✕ —

Xerxes entered the waiting room and sat next to Prax. "I know this is awkward, Prax, but I wanted to say that I'm proud of you."

"Thanks. We couldn't have done it without Billy."

"I understand that your flying was exceptional."

"How did you hear already?"

"The Andorans passed the word along. They were concerned about the damage your ship sustained. Unfortunately, they couldn't cover you through the portal," Xerxes explained.

"They did well. We were quite surprised by their support. The whole Boromean fleet was waiting for us. When the battle star appeared, I thought we were dead meat."

"Most of the Andorans have sided with Ramador," Xerxes informed him. "Unfortunately, we can't distinguish between those that haven't yet."

"How did you let it get this bad, dad?" Prax questioned him in a somber tone.

"I was naïve. I believed in the Council and what they stood for. I wasn't aware of their conspiracy until much later. By then, the damage was done."

"But you're one of them, now. Aren't you?"

"Yes, and I'm not proud of it anymore. I thought I'd have a chance to do good things, but it's nothing more than a closed group playing God."

"I'm sorry, dad. I didn't realize…"

"Don't be. It was my mistake. I'd like to start over and be friends. Can we try that?"

"I think it's time to put the past behind," Prax confessed.

Xerxes hugged Prax. "This means a lot to me."

"I know. Me, too."

"What did you find out from the Archaenians?"

"You'll have to ask Tera. She and Billy had a strange encounter with them."

"What do you mean?"

"It was really freaky."

"Did you see them?"

"Oh, yeah. It was it was just freaky."

"What did Tera think?"

"I couldn't really tell."

Xerxes felt deep satisfaction over his reconciliation with Prax. It had been too long and his life was so empty because of it. He approached Tera and stood awkwardly next to her. She looked somberly at him. "What happened with the Archaenians?"

"They gave us a component to swap inside the missile. It has to do with the firing component."

"What were they like?"

"Uh, very different. Very intelligent."

"That's it?"

"It's hard to tell what really happened."

"Did you communicate with them or did Billy?"

"We both did. It was like an out of body experience. It was really weird."

"That's all you know?"

"Maybe Billy could put it in better words."

"I'll talk to him when he's awake."

"Thanks, dad."

"Is Billy alright?"

"I hope so." She put her arms around Xerxes and hugged him. Tears rolled down her cheeks.

"He'll be alright. How about you?" he asked.

Tera regained her composure. "I'll be fine. Thanks, dad."

Xerxes felt like a great weight had been lifted from his back. "Anytime, Tera. Anytime."

Later that evening, Ramador returned to the research center in the second ship. Xerxes joined Doc in the transport bay where they greeted the Andorans. "Well, Ramador, it's good to see you back."

"I see the *Luna C* made it back. How did Billy make out?"

"They received a component that must be installed inside Dark Horizon."

"I'd like to leave as soon as possible," Ramador informed him.

"There's a small problem with that. I think Billy needs at least a day before he's able to travel."

"Was he hurt?"

"No, but he had to give a significant quantity of blood to save a friend's life."

"Did my people help?"

"I heard that a battle star rescued them from a major Boromean assault."

"That must have been the *Promethius*. My friend, Polypheus, is the commander."

"It seems that they did well."

"Let me know when Billy is able to go. We're going to rest until then."

— X —

Billy twitched and opened his eyes. He was exhausted but he was concerned about Penny and tried to sit up.

Maggie jumped up from her chair. "Lay back down, Billy. You need to rest."

"How is Penny?"

"Her signs are improving. It looks like your blood is helping."

Billy tried to communicate with her using telepathy. At first, she didn't respond, but after several tries, she answered back. "Billy, is it you?"

Billy hoped to see her open her eyes and that she'd sit up, but her body still looked weak and pale. "Yes, Penny, it's me."

"I'm so sorry for everything."

"Forget it, Penny. Just get well." Penny's thoughts came very slow to Billy.

He could feel the pain that she experienced. "What happened, Penny?"

"It doesn't matter. You saved me again, didn't you?"

"No, I didn't."

"I know what you did for me. I can feel your blood in my body. How many times have you done this for me?"

"Who cares how many times?"

"Seneca – she's gone."

"I know."

"It's my fault. All of this is my fault."

"No, it isn't. Let it go."

"Billy, you deserve better than me. I hurt you too many times."

"We're still friends, Penny."

"I hope your friend, Tera, makes you happier than I did."

"This isn't about her, Penny."

"No, but I want you to be happy."

"When you've healed, we'll talk more about things."

"There's nothing to talk about. If I make it, I'll be leaving."

"You don't have to leave. We're still friends."

"I can't interfere with your future. If I'm around, we'll both hurt every time we see each other."

"Let's finish this when you're feeling better."

"I've got to rest, Billy. Everything hurts so badly."

"Are you okay, Billy?" Maggie asked, interrupting his thoughts.

"Yes, why?"

"You've been in a daze for a while."

"I was talking to Penny."

"But I didn't hear anything."

"We have telepathy. She's too week to physically speak but I was able to reach her mind."

"How is she?"

"She's in a lot of pain and she's confused."

"What can I do for her?"

"Just be there for her. She's scared. I have to find the others. We have a lot to do."

"Billy, that's not a good idea."

"I can rest on the trip. Where are Doc and Xerxes?"

"I believe they are down the hall in the waiting area."

"I've got to see them."

"Stay here. I'll get them."

Billy refused to heed Maggie's advice. He sat up and pulled himself off of the bed.

Maggie hurried down the hall and interrupted Doc and Xerxes. "Billy's awake and he'd like to see you both."

Billy appeared in the doorway behind her. "Sit down, everyone. I can walk." He crossed the room and sat on a folding chair. Tera knelt beside him and hugged him. "Are you okay?"

"Yes, Honey. I'll be okay."

Ronnie returned from the cafeteria and handed Billy a Styrofoam cup of orange juice. "Here you go, Sport. It'll put hair on your chest."

"Now Ronnie, why would I want to be like you?" Everyone chuckled.

"I see you're doing just fine." She punched him in the arm. "How does that feel, smart ass."?

"Ouch! See that, everyone. She loves me so much; she can't keep her hands off of me."

Billy searched the room for John. He sat in the corner and laughed hysterically. "Can't you control your woman yet?" Billy asked.

"Are you kidding? I'm glad you're here to give me a break." The tension in the room eased and the conversation shifted to the Archaenians and Dark Horizon.

"We have a component that must be installed in the firing train of the missile," explained Billy. "We have to remove the installed component first. This will prevent the weapon from detonating and spreading over a large area."

"Ramador expects that Pendragon is heading to a battle star and will attempt to launch it from an auxiliary bay," mentioned Xerxes.

"Yes, and I'll bet he wants to send it right down the Andoran portal at us."

"Sam and Ginea have developed a new type of bomb that will neutralize the energy which powers the portal," revealed Doc.

"Will it work?"

"We're reasonably sure."

"You're not giving me the warm fuzzy I was looking for," kidded Billy.

"I'd put my money on it that it'll work."

"That'll have to do."

"In theory, it's fairly simple. We've tested it several times."

Billy asked, "Do we know where Pendragon is?"

"Not yet."

"Ask Ramador to help us find the battle star nearest the Andoran portal. That's the one ship that Pendragon is still likely to have control of. I'm sure he knows the other battle stars have already rebelled against him."

"I can check with the Council," said Xerxes. "They may have monitored Pendragon's ship when it veered away from the portal."

"We may need to use the Andoran portal to board the battle star," Billy explained.

Doc looked shocked. "For what?"

"To reach the battle star."

"Can't you use one of our portals?"

"Maybe. But if we use theirs, it should take us right into the bay where they launched their assault from."

"And then what?"

"Then, I suppose we'll have to board it, disarm the weapon, kill Pendragon and return home via another route."

Doc was amused and grinned. "If only it were that easy."

"It's late already. I think we should adjourn until breakfast tomorrow," suggested Xerxes. "If Ramador is ready, we'll coordinate the attack with him and get started. In the meantime, I'll have the Council attempt to locate Pendragon's ship."

"Before everyone leaves, I'd like to say a few words," said Ronnie.

"Don't be a ham," teased Randy.

"Shut up. I have an idea."

"Let her speak," said Billy.

"Thank you." Ronnie cleared her throat and moved to the center of the room. "Since this whole mess started, we've been pretty lucky. Most of us have been fortunate enough to survive some pretty harrowing instances. Tomorrow is a very important event for all humanity. We lost Seneca and nearly lost Penny. In the old world, we almost lost Randy. I think we need to reflect on the fact that some of us may not see the end of the next two days." The room grew strangely quiet. "I've enjoyed knowing all of you, even Billy, and in case tomorrow is my last day, I'd like to propose a party." At first everyone looked surprised but one by one, they warmed up to the idea.

"I like it," said Billy. "I haven't had a chance to have fun since we found the tavern in the ruins of the city way back when."

"And we'll never forget that, will we, Billy?" replied Randy.

Billy blushed as he looked at Tera, expecting a negative reaction, but she smiled and laughed along with everyone else. He was relieved that she had a sense of humor.

Prax and Courtney joined in their assent. "I agree one hundred percent. Let's party," hollered Prax.

Xerxes shook his head in disbelief. "I'll see you tomorrow. I'm too old to party at night."

"Me, too," added Doc.

Maggie laughed at them. "After all we've been through, Doc, can't you unwind for just one night?"

"The next two days are very important days."

"Yes, and it could be our last days if the mission fails."

"Alright, I'll stay."

John and Seamus glanced at each other. "Why not?" said John.

"It's been a few hundred years since I attended a good party," quipped Seamus. "So, I guess I have some catching up to do."

"Come on, everyone. Time is wasting," urged Ronnie.

They proceeded to the cafeteria where they cleared the tables away from the middle area for dancing. Ronnie opened the door to the stereo room and played the part of the DJ for the evening. Randy and Seamus returned with bottles of scotch, rum, vodka and tequila. "Where did you get all that?" Billy asked with delight.

"We were saving up for an occasion," answered Randy.

"What kind of occasion requires that much alcohol?"

"Do you want to tell them or should I?" Ronnie asked John.

"Go ahead, Honey."

"If we get past tomorrow, John and I intend to be married. We were going to wait for a little while but after all we've been through, why wait?"

John continued, "In addition to our news, I think Randy and Seamus have something to share as well."

Randy and Seamus joined them in the middle of the cafeteria. "Seamus and I are also planning to be wed," Randy announced. "If John and Ronnie will allow it, we'd like to have a double wedding."

"We'd be honored," replied John.

"Well, let's have a toast," shouted Billy. "Who's tending bar?"

Tera pulled Billy close to her and kissed his cheek. "Isn't that romantic?"

"Yes it is, Honey." Billy approached Ronnie and whispered something into her ear. She retreated to the stereo room.

"Where'd she go?" asked Tera.

"She's doing me a favor."

Billy and Tera's song 'Closer' played over the speaker system. He took Tera by the hand and led her to the middle of the floor. "Billy, you are so bad," she said.

"And you like me that way."

They danced slowly while the others watched admiringly. Tera and Billy kissed through most of the song.

"That's nice. The two of them are really in love," remarked Randy.

"Are you sure?" asked John.

"Why wouldn't I be?"

"Well, how many women has Billy been through since this whole mess started?"

Ronnie winked at Randy. "I don't know. It doesn't seem like that many."

"It's been enough," kidded John.

"Maybe she is the one for him," suggested Seamus.

"At least they aren't fighting all the time," kidded Ronnie. They laughed heartily.

When the next song played, Ronnie took John by the hand and went to the center of the floor. They danced together.

"Is something wrong with your legs?" Randy chided Seamus.

"No, why?"

"Well, come on, then."

"But I can't dance."

"You'll learn."

Soon everyone was on the floor dancing. They enjoyed themselves until dawn, dancing and laughing, while carrying on like teenagers. They knew it was late when the cafeteria crew showed up for the morning shift.

"What timing. They're just in time for breakfast," commented Billy. He and Prax pushed the tables back in place. Ronnie and Randy put the remaining bottles of alcohol in a box and slid it under the table.

Everyone ate together, including Xerxes who awoke from his sleep and came down for breakfast. Ramador and the remaining thirteen Andorans entered the cafeteria to everyone's surprise. Many of the employees had never seen the Andorans, although they had heard of them. They lined up along the wall and the large room became quiet.

Ramador addressed the room, "On behalf of my fellow Andorans, I'd like to thank Dr. Watts, Dr. Smith and Billy for helping to cure the Andorans of an illness that was destroying our race. My troops have slept soundly for the first time in ages and we'd like to thank you for all your help. At a time when we were at war with you, you chose to be diplomatic and help us to achieve friendship between our races." Everyone in the room stood up and clapped.

Ramador added, "We are proud to fight side by side with the humans to achieve what is right."

Again, everyone clapped and cheered.

"Would you all follow me to the conference room," asked Xerxes. "We need to finalize our plans."

The Andorans followed first, then Billy's friends. The remaining group of people in the cafeteria cheered them as they left.

CHAPTER 12

THE BATTLE UNFOLDS

When everyone was seated in the conference room, Xerxes stood before them and spoke somberly to the group. "Our day of reckoning is upon us. What happens in these next few days will determine whether we survive or disappear into a void. Should we fall into the latter, no one will remember us. There will be no records or history of any kind. We might as well never have existed at all. Should we succeed, we'll have crossed new barriers and created new friendships with the Andorans. When this is over, we will have put to rest the evil that started with Ruger and Diomedes. There will be changes in the Council because of the Council's crimes against the Andorans and other alien races. We will work to correct those flaws that they may never happen again. I place my trust and the trust of the Council in your hands."

Xerxes paused for a moment, then requested, "Ramador, would you please come forward and address the group with our plans?"

Ramador walked proudly to the front of the conference room and spoke in an authoritative tone. "We will overcome the obstacles before us. I have confidence in the Andorans and the humans alike. We will fight as one and stop the madness that threatens both our races." Ramador faced the white board and picked up a black marker with his three-clawed hand.

It seemed a little awkward but he wasn't distracted in the least. He drew several shapes and arrows. "We'll pass through the Andoran portal in the first two ships. The third ship with the humans will arrive slightly later through one of your portals, for health reasons. At the end of the portal, we'll find a battle star waiting. This is Pendragon's launch point. The first thing that must happen is to shut down the portal and prevent him from launching the missile through it. We all know that Dark Horizon is unpredictable. That is the single most important reason we have to stop it. There is no way of controlling it or stopping it once it starts."

Ramador turned to Doc Smith and asked, "Is the weapon ready for the portal?"

"Sam and Ginea will be here any minute with the final results of the tests," answered Doc. "Four bombs have been developed. They are working some final calculations to ensure that the bombs are capable of shutting down the portal completely."

"Your fighters will carry the bombs into the portal where they will be detonated. We'll return by the long way when this is done."

Sam and Ginea entered the room and stood by the door. "I guess you all want to know if our new toys work. Well, that's a big affirmative!" Everyone cheered.

"Our new cluster bombs will disperse enough sodium chloride to neutralize the energy field in the portal." Xerxes breathed a sigh of relief.

Ramador focused his attention back on the white board and sketched a series of hallways simulating the inside of the battle star. "Once we board the battle star, I will take half of my men to search for Pendragon. Dornan will lead Billy's group to the auxiliary bay and Dark Horizon. Once Billy's group has accessed the bay, Dornan will lead his Andorans around the ship to rally support against Pendragon. I expect that we'll have some resistance at first, but I'm sure they can be turned."

"What if Pendragon escapes?" asked Billy.

"We cannot let that happen. His time is up."

Ramador drew a sketch of the docking locations on the battle star. "I will dock my ship in the first location and make sure it does not link up to a power source. It should show about thirty percent power by the time it's docked. The other ships will dock and re-energize as usual. Once the firing circuit for Dark Horizon is disarmed, only the ship will be in danger. It will still explode but the reaction will not ensue. Dornan will lead the Andorans into an orderly evacuation of the battle star. They will use any ships to escape but the first, second and third ships. Those are for the humans and my group. Remember, no one is to use the first ship. I expect that Pendragon will attempt to escape in that one. He won't get far on thirty percent power. That is the plan. Fight well everyone."

Xerxes stepped to the front again and announced, "In two hours, we'll begin the attack. Everyone will meet in the bay."

"Would you mind if I stopped in to see how Penny's doing? Billy asked Tera.

"Sure. I'll be in my compartment."

Billy left the group and went to the medical section. Dr. Watts greeted him at the door. "I was hoping that you'd come back. Dr. Markus gave Penny another checkup and she's slowly improving. She's still in critical condition but we both agree that she has a chance. I don't believe this story about healing qualities in your blood but she is obviously improving."

"Do you mind if I see her for a few minutes?"

"No, not at all. I'll leave you alone."

"Thanks, Dr. Watts."

Billy slid a chair next to Penny's bed. The smell of ether made his head spin. Penny sensed that he was nearby and used her telepathy to communicate with him. "So, you still have a hard time following directions," she commented.

"What makes you say that?" he asked, curious.

"They told you to rest after the transfusion."

"There's too much to do. How are you?"

"I'm feeling stronger, but I still can't move," she told him. "I feel like a punching bag."

"I'll make sure Pendragon pays for what he did to you," Billy vowed.

"No, Billy. Let it go. You have Tera to take care of."

"He's got to be stopped anyway, so it might as well be me."

"Damn you, Billy. Can't you listen for once in your life?"

"I did and it hurt me."

"You're right. I'm sorry."

"What will you do when you are better?" he asked.

"I think I'd like to join the Firenghians on their new world. Someone has to tell little Will about his father. I'd like to help Rena raise him."

"When I get back, I'll take you there."

"No, Billy. I don't think it's a good idea."

"Why not?"

"I have to live with what I did to you and Seneca the rest of my life. I will always have nightmares about that night when Pendragon attacked us. He snapped Tarkus' neck right before my eyes. When he hit me, I felt as though I exploded into a thousand pieces of flesh. That feeling is burned into my brain forever. I'll never be healed."

"You'll see, Penny. When this is over, things will be better."

"No, Billy! When you leave this room, I don't ever want to see you again. When you come to see Will, I won't be there. It has to be this way."

Billy knew she was right. He squeezed her hand and a tear rolled down his cheek. "I'll always love you, Penny. Even if we can't be together, you'll always have a piece of my heart."

"Get out, Billy. Now!"

Billy let go of her hand and walked slowly to the door. Despite everything that happened, part of him would always care for her. He looked back one more time. Penny's words burned in his brain, "Get out!"

Billy returned to Tera's compartment and pressed the buzzer. The doors slid open and he heard her voice, "Come in, Billy."

He entered the room and sat on the couch. Tera saw the sad look on his face and sat next to him. "I know what you're feeling, Billy?"

"Do you?"

"If you care that much for her, then you should go to her."

"Why would you say that?"

"Because you can't love me if you are still in love with her."

Billy weighed her statement carefully. "I'm not in love with her. That died a while ago. I still care about her and seeing her in that condition makes me realize some things."

"Like what?"

"Like what if you were hurt and put in that position. Penny was my past but you are my future."

"Am I really?"

"Yes, you are. Penny and I have come to terms with how we'll deal with the future. There is no 'we' anymore."

"Please tell me that you mean this and that you aren't just trying to make me feel better about this."

Billy pulled Tera to him and kissed her slowly. "Does that answer your question?"

"Maybe. Just promise that you won't get yourself killed chasing after Pendragon."

"I promise I won't get killed. Come on, Tera. After all that's happened to me, I've learned to be a survivor."

"Be careful you don't jinx yourself."

"I can't. I have my good luck charm with me."

The intercom beeped and Xerxes voice filled the room. "Billy and Tera, are you there?"

Billy pressed the button and answered, "We're coming, Xerxes."

"Everyone's waiting for you."

"Chill out, dad. We're only talking," Tera responded, annoyed.

"I'm sure you are. Get down here."

Billy and Tera giggled as they left her compartment. "Do you think your dad is getting worried about us, Tera?"

"Maybe. How well do you get along with my dad?"

"Pretty well. It's good to hear you call him 'dad'."

"You've convinced me to forget the past. Besides, you've melted a little ice off of my heart," said Tera pleasantly.

"Just a little?"

"Okay, maybe a lot of it."

They entered the elevator. When the door closed, Billy pushed Tera against the wall and kissed her. "Try again," teased Billy.

They kissed a little longer until the doors opened and Tera admitted, "Okay, maybe all of it."

"That's better." They held hands as they walked to the transport bay.

When everyone was assembled in the transport bay, Xerxes and Doc wished them well. Xerxes informed Ramador and Billy, "Pendragon's craft has been spotted, docking on the battle star as predicted."

"Good. Now the key components are all in place," answered Ramador.

"Pendragon's as good as dead. I promise," vowed Billy.

"Don't let your emotions affect your decisions," warned Xerxes.

"The decisions have been made. Pendragon's fate is in my hands now."

Tera held on securely to Billy's arm. "As is mine. Don't forget that," she reminded him.

Billy kissed her forehead. "You're stuck with me."

"I hope so."

Billy and Tera boarded their ship. The others were already on board and waited patiently. Billy noticed Randy's smug look.

"I had some things to take care of," he said innocently.

"Guilty conscience?" she teased.

"No, just busy work."

"Oh, please," replied Ronnie cynically.

Tera joined the fun and kidded, "Does Billy have a performance problem I should know about?"

"We'll let him field that question," Randy remarked, winking at Billy.

"Don't worry about me. I'm not the one getting married in a few weeks," declared Billy. Tera enjoyed their ribbing.

"You'll see. John and Seamus will straighten you both out," replied Billy confidently.

John and Seamus entered the main quarters. "Did I hear my name?" asked John.

"I was just telling them how you and Seamus will keep the girls in line after the wedding."

John and Seamus chuckled. "We learned from watching you," John mentioned. "There's no way in hell we're going to change these two."

"See that, Billy," said Randy. The die is cast."

"Oh, that's just great. I counted on you guys to set an example," he chastised John and Seamus.

"Don't worry, Billy. You have me to contend with," Tera reminded him playfully.

"Will you keep Tera in line?" asked Randy.

Billy looked at Tera. She looked back with a somber expression on her face. He looked back at the girls. "That's a big 'no'. I like when she's bad."

"Smart answer, Billy," Tera remarked.

— ⧖ —

Ramador and his troops boarded the first Andoran craft. Their ship roared to life and they were soon on their way through the outer access of the facility.

When they approached the Andoran portal high above the research center, four F-22's circled the area, waiting for their passage.

Billy's group traveled on a new ship, the *Intrepid*. They trailed the two Andoran craft toward the portal.

Billy entered the flight deck. "Hey, Prax, we're changing the plans."

"What do you mean?"

"Stay behind the Andoran ships."

"What? We can't do that?"

"Yes, we can. Just follow my instructions."

"I hope you know what you're doing."

"Have I ever steered you wrong?"

"Not yet."

When they reached to the edge of the portal, the rocky ride became almost unbearable. The walls of the portal took on strange shades and a loud roar like an oncoming train filled the ship.

"What's going on, Prax!" Billy asked, growing concerned.

"We're inside the Andoran portal. That's what you wanted, isn't it?"

They sweated profusely. Tera and Courtney entered the flight deck. Courtney sat in the co-pilot's seat. She immediately noticed the portal's odd-colored sides. "Why are we in this portal? What happened to our portal?"

Tera stared at Billy. "What did you do? I thought we were using our own portal."

"We changed the plans a little bit," Billy replied, sheepishly.

"You didn't tell me about it."

"Uh, I forgot. I got caught up in the excitement and decided that we should follow the Andorans." The shaking subsided.

"You bonehead!" Tera scolded him.

"I think we're okay," announced Prax.

"I certainly hope so," said Tera irately.

As soon as they cleared the gate, the battle star came into view. Ramador's ship entered the transport bay and docked first, followed by Dornan's ship. As soon as Ramador's troops disembarked from their ship, they were met by two dozen Andoran soldiers.

The *Intrepid* glided into the fourth berth and docked. Billy watched from inside the *Intrepid* as Ramador stepped to the forefront to meet the soldiers. "I guess we'll stay on board until Ramador resolves the situation," he suggested. The others glared at him in disbelief.

Ramador stepped to the forefront and faced the troops. "Ramador, we are ordered to take you into custody. You must disarm and come with us," announced the leader of the unit.

"By whose order?" he asked.

"Pendragon's order."

"I have news for all of you. Allow me to explain what has happened."

"Out of respect for you, Ramador, I'll allow you to speak, but be brief."

"The humans have a serum for our illness. We have been cured. We can sleep without threat of dying."

"All of your men have been cured?" the leader asked.

"Yes. You may ask them if you like."

"Why does Pendragon want you in custody?"

"Pendragon is mad from the sickness. He is also insane with a lust for revenge against the humans for the death of the witch, Diomedes."

Another Andoran added, "She deserved to die. She became an aberration."

"Yes, but Pendragon has Dark Horizon with him and is threatening to annihilate all of us."

"What can we do to help?"

"We need to take Pendragon into custody. If he detonates Dark Horizon, we'll need to evacuate the battle star. We can prevent it from destroying part of the universe, but it will still destroy the ship."

"Ramador, if I pledge my allegiance to you, can you assure us that we can be cured as well?"

"Yes, I can."

"Then carry on."

"I suggest, since there are plenty of transports, that you start evacuating everyone."

"Right away, sir."

"You can contact the Earthers and they'll give you instructions."

"Do you need any help from us?"

"No, we'll handle it from here."

Ramador motioned for Billy's friends to exit the *Intrepid* and follow them. When they reached the end of the first hallway, Ramador took his group to the left. Dornan gestured for Billy and his friends to follow him to the right.

When they passed the first hallway, four Andorans fired upon them. Dornan tried to talk them into putting down their arms but they refused. "If you can cover us, we'll pass the hall, one at a time," requested Billy.

"At the end of the next hallway, go right. The third door down the left side leads to the auxiliary bay."

"Thanks, Dornan."

Billy instructed the others where to go and he waited until just he and Tera were left. Billy handed her the bag with the component. "I have to go back for something. You know what to do with this."

"What do you think you're doing?"

"You can do this, Tera. Trust me."

"But you promised me."

"I know. I promised that I wouldn't get myself killed."

"How do I know that you mean it?"

"When we get back, will you marry me?"

"That's not fair. Yes, I will marry you and I'll hold you to it." Billy kissed her and pushed her across the hallway.

"What are you waiting for?" asked Dornan.

"I've got to take care of something. They'll be okay without me." Billy raced back to the transport bay and surveyed the area. Andorans filed into the bay from the other side and entered the transports nearest them.

Billy crept down to the first transport and ducked inside. He stepped down the stairs to the bay and hid between two oxygen cylinders.

— X —

John and Ronnie were the first to reach the auxiliary bay. They attempted to open the door but it was locked electronically. "Now what?" asked John.

"Do I have to show you everything? Watch and learn," Ronnie instructed. She pulled out her pulse pistol and fired at the box. Everyone covered their faces as pieces of the box shattered in every direction. Ronnie inspected the mess. Two wires dangled from a hole in the wall. She instinctively grabbed them and twisted them together. The door slid open instantly.

Ronnie looked back at John and asked sarcastically, "Any more questions?"

"No," he replied humbly. Seamus poked him in the ribs and smiled. John gave him a slightly irritated glare in return.

They entered the auxiliary bay and discovered 'Dark Horizon'. Ronnie stood in front of the red missile with the cryptic markings.

"So, this is Dark Horizon, the doomsday weapon," she mused aloud.

The missile was mounted on skis with small wheels underneath. Tera joined Ronnie and instinctively searched for a panel. Each woman ran her hands along the smooth surface until Tera felt latches on the backside. She circled around the missile and discovered three panels, one which was obviously too small to accommodate the component. Tera struggled with the latches until John stepped in and pried them loose. Finally, they opened the first panel.

Randy and Seamus opened the second panel with as much difficulty. They looked at the two open panels and decided that the second one had to be the firing train. Tera recalled the information the Archaenians gave them and the visions provided to them. She maneuvered the electronic box from the panel without any problem and handed it to John. She then installed the Archaenian replacement box. Just as she closed the first panel, Pendragon entered the room with three Andorans.

"Back away from the missile, now," he ordered.

John instinctively hid the removed electronic box behind his back.

"Back away from the panel, now! I won't say it again."

They reluctantly complied. Tera attempted to reopen the first panel as a decoy but Pendragon bolted across the room and knocked her to the ground. "Who has the Archaenian box? I want it now," Pendragon demanded. No one spoke up.

Pendragon pointed to John. One of the Andoran guards grabbed his arm. The guard shoved him against the wall, sending the box skittering across the floor. The guard fired at the box and blasted it to pieces.

"I hope for your sake that you didn't destroy the wrong box," shouted Pendragon.

The guard looked down at the mess and back away with a puzzled expression.

Ronnie chose that moment to draw her pistol and fire at the guards. Two fell quickly, but the third returned fire, striking Ronnie's shoulder. She groaned and fell to the ground, with her shoulder a bloody, tattered mess. John landed a well-placed shot between the guard's eyes and killed him instantly.

Randy rushed into the hall and managed to get off one shot at Pendragon before he disappeared around the corner. They heard a loud beep and Dark Horizon began clicking.

Seamus popped open the smallest of the panels and saw the display on the clicking device come to life. Strange codes began flashing at regular intervals. "Oh, no! The timer's active."

John helped Ronnie to her feet. "Everyone back to the ship!" ordered John. "Our job is done."

They crept down the hall to the next intersection. Dornan and his troops had been ambushed from behind and killed. Their bodies were scattered across the floor.

Ronnie passed the Andoran corpses and hurried down the corridor to the transport bay. The first craft pulled out, just as they expected. "That SOB is getting away!" yelled Randy.

"Forget about it," replied Seamus. "We've got to get out of here. Besides, Ronnie needs help." They hurried back to the *Intrepid*.

Prax and Courtney hustled to the flight deck. Soon, their ship pulled away from the battle star. "We can't leave without Billy!" cried Tera.

"He's no dummy," replied Randy. "I'm sure he got on another craft."

"But we don't know that."

Tera rushed up to the flight deck and grabbed Prax' arm. "Billy's still back there, Prax!"

"Where did he go?"

"I don't know. He said he had to do something."

"If we go back, we'll all die. He probably got on another ship."

Tera paced the floor and sobbed. "How could he do this to me? He said he would marry me and then he does this."

"He did what?" Randy asked in a surprised tone.

"He asked me to marry him."

"No kidding! Well congratulations, Tera."

"It doesn't do me any good if he gets himself killed."

"Don't worry, he knows what he's doing," Ronnie assured her.

"How do you know?"

Ronnie looked at her straight-faced. "Tera, Billy has done this to us just about every time something came up. He's impulsive but he always pulls it off."

Tera paced back and forth, visibly upset. Randy tried to comfort her with logic. "Billy has a history of doing things like this. We all had at least one encounter where we wanted to smack the daylights out of him. His ideas are sloppy but they usually work."

"Do you really think he's okay?"

"I do."

"Prax, can you check with the other ships to see if Billy's on board?" she hollered into the page.

"Sure, Tera. Give me a minute."

Randy tried to make conversation, but Prax quickly interrupted them. "Sorry to interrupt everyone, but I'm getting a transmission from Pendragon's craft. Anyone care to come up?"

Randy and Tera hurried to the flight deck, followed closely by Seamus. "Are you ready?" asked Prax.

"Take it before we lose him," urged Randy.

Prax pushed the 'receive' button and Pendragon's face appeared on the screen, sending chills down their spines.

"Well, you failed to stop me once again," Pendragon announced indignantly. "You humans have proved to be a worthy opponent but your time is about up."

"What do you want now?" demanded Tera defiantly.

"I want Billy. Where is he?"

"What if we don't tell you?"

"I will detonate Dark Horizon now and we'll all die."

"Does anyone know what to tell him?" whispered Prax.

"He's injured," Tera informed Pendragon. "Give us a few moments to bring him up here. You can talk to him yourself."

"Hurry up," ordered Pendragon. "You don't have much time." Tera stepped out of the flight deck.

Billy crept out from behind the tanks and quietly climbed the stairs to the upper deck. He peered onto the flight deck and was relieved to see Pendragon at the controls. As he listened to Pendragon's transmission, he realized that his nemesis was speaking to his friends. He drew his pulse pistol and stepped behind Pendragon.

Randy watched the monitor and noticed Billy in the background. "Tera, come here quickly!"

Tera rushed back to the flight deck. "What is it, Randy?"

"Look at the screen."

Tera saw Billy standing calmly with his pulse pistol pointed at the back of Pendragon's head. Pendragon was baffled by their actions. "Where's Billy?"

Prax smiled at him. "He's closer than you think."

"What do you mean?"

"I'm right here, Pendragon," Billy startled him. "It's time for retribution."

"I'll kill you."

"No, you won't." Billy fired four shots into Pendragon's arm, legs and shoulder. When Pendragon fell to the floor, writhing in pain, Billy placed his foot against his throat. He shot at four-inch intervals, up and down Pendragon's body. Pendragon hissed and seethed at Billy, but Billy meticulously put shot after shot into Pendragon until the alien was about to lose consciousness from the pain.

"Hey, Pendragon, this one's for Penny." Pendragon opened his mouth to utter something and Billy fired into it, putting a large hole through his head. Pendragon's eyes rolled back and his limbs fell limply to his side. Billy's friends cheered as they watched Pendragon's demise.

"Okay, Prax. Tell me how to fly this thing."

"I don't know, Billy. I've never flown an Andoran craft before."

"Oh, boy. Here we go again."

"Billy, when I get my hands on you, you're in trouble," threatened Tera.

"Hold that thought, Tera." Suddenly Billy's transmission disappeared from their monitor. Ramador's face appeared on Billy's monitor. "So, you want to learn how to fly an Andoran craft."

"Ramador, thank goodness. I only need to fly it long enough to land it."

"We're going to change directions and guide you. We have to keep moving or else we'll be caught in the aftershock."

"What aftershock?"

"The one that happens when the missile explodes."

"Oh, shit! What do I have to do?"

"Don't worry. The craft is easy to control."

Ramador gave Billy explicit instructions and they continued their course away from the battle star. Billy saw on the navigator's screen that the *Intrepid* and Ramador's ship were slowly catching up. He realized, though, that he was heading the opposite direction of home.

"Do you know where we are, Ramador?"

"We're reaching the edges of some uncharted territories. I don't know any of the life forms in the upcoming region."

Billy's craft shuddered. "Ramador, something's wrong. I think I'm losing power."

"Yes, you are. We expected Pendragon would attempt to escape. That's why we didn't allow that craft to recharge."

"What do I do?" Billy asked frantically.

"We're still too far away to help you."

"I think I'm being pulled toward a planet on my left. The ship is steering away from the original direction I was headed."

"If you land on the planet, we'll be there soon. Keep feeding us coordinates through the navigation system. See the two buttons on the top right panel?"

"Yes, I do."

"Toggle them both down." Before Ramador could give the remainder of the instructions, the monitor went blank. Dark Horizon exploded on the battle star and sent a shockwave of unbelievable force toward them.

Billy saw the green wave approaching him on the monitor. It encompassed his friends' ships and was heading toward him. When the shockwave hit, the ship was hurled out of control. The spinning motion rendered Billy unconscious.

The *Intrepid* took off like a shot from a cannon. Its streamlined design kept it from spinning uncontrollably but it was still traveling faster than it was designed for. When the effects of the shockwave finally passed,

Ramador searched the screen for any sign of Billy or his friends. He searched for some time before he decided that it was too late.

Ramador thought long and hard before giving the order to turn the ship back toward Earth. He gazed at the monitor and said to the pilot, "A brave group of people just perished out there. Billy is the reason we have a future."

"Are you sure there's no chance?" asked the pilot.

"It seems so. Besides, if we go any further, we won't have enough power to make it back."

"I understand. We're heading home."

— X —

Prax and Courtney climbed back into their seats. Tera and Randy picked themselves up off the floor. "Is everyone all right back there?" Prax asked on the page.

"We're fine," replied Seamus. "Was that the shockwave?"

"Sure was."

"Where are we?"

"I'll let you know as soon as I figure it out." Prax turned his attention to the monitor.

Tera grew concerned. "What happened to Billy?"

"I don't know. We'll see when the monitor clears." Prax kept an eye on the monitor while he restarted the ship's systems. After checking the diagnostics and the readouts, he informed them, "We're going back."

"What do you mean?" asked Randy.

"We are at the point of no return. We go back now or we don't make it."

"But what about Billy?" asked Tera.

"What about him? We don't even see him on the monitor. Space is a big place."

Tera darted from the cabin to her bunk. She buried her head in the pillow and cried.

CHAPTER 13

DEJA VOUS

Billy opened his eyes and watched in amazement as the ship glided through cloud cover. Two of the engines failed and the other two sputtered. He tried everything to control the craft as the clouds cleared. When he looked at the monitor, he saw the area below him covered with trees and mountains. "Thank God it's not a barren planet. At least I have a chance."

The ship lost altitude quickly. Billy tried in vain to find a spot to land. He cleared a mountain range and followed a long, winding river. When he spotted huge white cliffs ahead, he decided to bring the ship down now before he got too close. He saw a small clearing near a muddy riverbank and landed the ship in thick mud. His head bounced off the control panel and whipped him out of his seat. The craft slid sideways and crashed into the trees.

After what seemed like eternity, Billy staggered to his feet and hobbled to the hatch. He pressed the knob and waited as the hatch opened. When he stepped out of the ship, he was horrified at the sight before him.

He saw the white cliffs in the distance and the large mountains in the opposite direction. The stream had a man-made damn a short distance away. What really bothered Billy was the trench leading from the stream to a primitive fort with a moat surrounding it. This was the area where his nightmare started – his lost world.

Billy's mind was suddenly filled with the thoughts of all the horrible things that happened to him there: the Neanderthals; raptors; crocosaurs; Ruger and his minions.

"This can't be happening!" he uttered frantically. He sat down on a nearby rock and considered his situation. When he realized that no one was coming, he hiked to the old fort that served as their home once upon a time. Several Neanderthals emerged from the forest and approached him.

"You've got to be kidding me," he groaned. He rolled a log into the moat and drifted across. After much effort, he was able to paw away at the soil wall and climb to the top. In a sick sort of way, he felt like he was home again. He lay down on the top of the wall and cried.

— ☒ —

Prax asked John and Seamus to come up to the flight deck. "There's a planet not too far from here. Billy may have landed there," he informed them. "We can do a pass and see if we find any sign of him. We're running the risk that we may not have enough power to make it back, though. We've never been this far away from our quadrants before. What do you think?"

"What are the chances of rescue if we can't return?" asked John. "Is there some way we can be located?"

"Possibly. Except for the portal on Earth, our transmissions won't penetrate other portals and the distance is too great to communicate directly."

"We've always stuck together regardless of the circumstances," reminded Seamus. "I think we should try one pass on this planet you speak of."

"Seamus is right. Let's do it," said John.

"What about the girls? How will they feel about it?"

"I'm sure they'll agree."

"How about Ronnie's shoulder?"

"She's stable."

"Then we're going in for a pass." announced Prax. I'll let you know when we get there."

John and Seamus returned to the main quarters and broke the news to Ronnie and Randy. Prax left the flight deck and went to Tera's compartment.

"Tera, I know he means a lot to you. We're going to take a look at this one planet. It's a long shot but we're going to try. We may not make it back, though."

Tera jumped up and hugged him. "Thank you, Prax. Thank you." She went to the main quarters and sat down with the others.

Randy saw her teary eyes and hugged her. "Don't worry, Tera. We'll find him."

"Thanks everyone. I know you're sacrificing everything for Billy."

"He's done a lot for us," replied Randy. "We've always been a team."

"Do you think he's alive?"

"Billy has cheated death a number of times. I expect that he's alive and well, probably having the time of his life."

"Everyone keeps saying that. What has he done that's so unusual?"

Randy laughed. "I don't know where to start. There's been so many things and places; the spiders, the minions."

Ronnie raised her head and added, "Don't forget the bar, Randy."

"Ah, yes, the bar."

"Do I want to know what happened at the bar?" asked Tera.

"I guess you could say that we learned a lot about Billy. He's not a player, if you know what I mean," Randy revealed, giggling.

Tera cracked a smile. "I can imagine what happened."

"No, I don't think you could," Ronnie said, smiling. "I'll tell you the story some day when we're not saving the world. All I can say is that he's a good guy and I don't say that about too many men."

Prax' voice rang from the intercom and interrupted them. "We're entering the atmosphere. Sensors indicate an oxygen rich environment. If he's there, he can breathe."

Tera hurried up to the flight deck. She opened the door and entered. "Mind if I come in. I'd like to see what's down there."

"No problem, cuz."

"What will we do if we can't go back?"

"Worst case, it looks like we could live down there until help comes."

"We could get close to a portal and hope that help comes along, too," suggested Courtney.

"That might be our best chance. This planet is off the charts."

— ⧗ —

Billy opened his eyes and watched the sunrise with disdain. *Of all the places to get stranded, why here?* he thought despondently.

Billy climbed down from the wall and walked across the compound. The huts were still intact, so he entered the first hut that was designated for him and Penny once upon a time. "Just like old times," he quipped and then sat on the cot to consider his situation.

When he realized that he would never see anyone again, tears welled in his eyes. He already missed Tera. He missed Penny. He missed everyone. Seneca was dead and who knows how many others that he knew. Feeling like he was going to lose his mind, he walked back across the compound and climbed on top of the wall. He surveyed the area and noted the changes. The city wasn't there anymore, nor was the airport.

As he felt pity on himself, he saw Neanderthals emerging from the forest again. He chuckled to himself as they gathered across the moat. They were frustrated that he was beyond their reach. They threw rocks at him, but couldn't reach him. He picked up some of his own and tossed them back. "I hate you!" he screamed. "I'll make you as miserable as I am!" He pulled his pulse pistol and took some pot shots at the creatures.

The first shot struck a Neanderthal in the foot. Another shot struck the arm of a Neanderthal as it poised to toss a rock. Then Billy caught one Neanderthal in the head and killed it. He let loose a crazy laugh. Soon he began to wonder if it would be better to let the Neanderthals kill him.

Finally, the Neanderthals figured out how to cross the moat. They straddled the log that Billy used to cross over and then they tried to climb the walls. It was a slow process, but they progressed. Billy was impressed that they had the intelligence to think of it

As he stood close to the edge of the wall, contemplating his sanity, he saw a bright light in the distance. He watched with curiosity as it descended from the sky and cruised above the treetops.

With his attention focused on the approaching light, one of the Neanderthals fired a rock and caught Billy in the side of the head. He fell from the wall and landed on the ground inside the compound. He got up and picked up a piece of wood.

"All right you bastards. This is war." Billy climbed up on the wall and prepared to do battle.

Billy was surprised how many Neanderthals joined the rush to storm his fort. "This isn't going to work the way I planned," he uttered.

Billy swung at the first Neanderthal and knocked it into the moat. Several others reached the top of the wall. Billy climbed down and ran across the compound. About halfway across the clearing, he felt a rhythmic pulsing in the ground. "No, no, no! This can't be happening!"

A Crocosaurus emerged from the forest and attacked several of the Neanderthals. The Neanderthals hid inside the compound. But then, the Crocosaurus saw Billy and pursued him.

Prax slowed the craft down until it hovered above the trees.

"Look at that," Courtney pointed out. "It's a fort of some kind."

"Maybe he's in there," replied Tera.

Prax searched intently. "I hope he's in there because there are some ghastly creatures on the outside."

"There's the Andoran ship!" shouted Tera. "Billy must be there."

Prax relayed the information to the others downstairs. John rushed up to the cabin and was shocked at the view.

"This is where it started! We built that fortress. The airport was over there and the city was on the other side of the mountains."

Prax couldn't believe what John said. "You mean you've been here before?"

"Yes, we were. I'd just as soon never see this place again. You wouldn't believe the horrors that exist here." John hurried back down to the bay and informed everyone of their location.

"You've got to be kidding," exclaimed Ronnie. "I don't want to see those spiders. Let's find Billy and get the hell out of here."

John tried to comfort her. "We're near the fort. Prax is searching for Billy on the grounds inside. The Neanderthals are parading around outside the fort so something must have drawn them there."

Prax pointed at a Crocosaurus Rex chasing someone. "That could be him!" he shouted. Prax glided the ship over the dinosaur and fired several shots at it. The creature's head exploded and it fell forward.

Billy felt wet pieces of flesh shower him. He looked over his shoulder and saw the dinosaur falling toward him. He dove away from the creature and lay exhausted on the ground. Before he could catch his breath, he was pelted with rocks from the trees.

"Oh, no! Not again!" Billy got up and ran back toward the fort. One of the rocks struck him in the head and knocked him out.

Prax announced on the intercom, "I'm setting the ship down. Billy's going to need help fast."

The ship landed between Billy and the Neanderthals. Tera opened the hatch and rushed out to Billy. She rolled him over and saw the bloody gash on the side of his head.

John and Seamus exited the ship and fired several shots at the Neanderthals. Ronnie and Randy joined Tera and covered her from the Neanderthals.

"Help me get him on board. He's hurt bad," pleaded Tera.

Ronnie and Randy helped Tera carry Billy on board the ship.

"Come on, guys. We've got him," shouted Ronnie.

John and Seamus hurried back on board the ship and Ronnie anxiously closed the hatch.

"We're leaving in a hurry," announced Prax. "The locals are getting a little unruly."

They heard rocks strike the hull of the ship as it lifted off the ground. Seamus gazed out the window and looked disappointed.

"What's wrong?" asked John.

"I didn't think anyone could penetrate those walls. That's how we designed it."

"Just be glad we're not there anymore. At some point, they would have gotten to us."

$$- \mathbf{X} -$$

"Locate the nearest battle star. We're going to dock and recharge," Ramador instructed the pilot.

"What do you plan to do next?"

"I'd like to take one more look for Billy and his friends. Perhaps now that the field is dissipated, we might find them."

"But it is uncharted territory."

"I know. We're going to search one particular quadrant. I'm guessing that the ships would have been forced in that direction. If the sensors can't find their ships, then they had to land someplace. There are only a few places that they could survive landing on. If there's no indication that they are there, we'll return."

"We still have to be concerned about the Boromeans."

"Yes, we do. I think our new alliance with the humans will deter their aggression. We have much to do to restore peace in the galaxies."

"What if it doesn't?"

"Then it's going to be a long war."

— ✗ —

Prax voice came across the intercom, "Well, everyone, we're approaching our moment of truth. We're down to ten percent power and I don't see any place we can go to."

"What do you suggest?" asked John.

"I guess we'll just drift along. I'll set the beacon for an SOS and maybe someone other than the Boromeans will find us."

"We understand."

"Courtney and I will be down shortly."

A short while later, the power flickered and failed. The backup supply took over and dim lighting returned. Prax and Courtney came down to the transport bay and joined the others.

"How is Billy?" asked Prax.

"He hasn't moved. I hope he's okay," said Tera. She nestled Billy against her and held a cloth against the wound on the side of his head.

"We only have enough oxygen to last a short while," he said despondently.

"Well, if this is going to be it, we have nothing to be ashamed of," said John. "I am proud to have fought with all of you. We accomplished some fantastic victories."

"Tell us about the planet we found Billy on," asked Prax.

"What do you want to know?"

"Tell us about your adventures there," asked Tera. "I want to know what everyone did."

"Ronnie killed a giant dinosaur by leaping off of a building with a metal spear," said Randy.

"Randy killed a giant spider in similar fashion using a sword," added Seamus.

"Seamus and John killed a bunch of the smaller spiders and helped rescue us," continued Randy.

"What about Billy?" asked Tera.

"Billy was the spark plug for everything we accomplished" replied Randy. "The dinosaur was about to eat him. The spider was about to kill him. The Neanderthals were about to stone him. Ruger was about to choke him. The list goes on and on."

"So, wherever he goes, everyone and everything wants to kill him," Tera concluded. Everyone laughed.

"It sure seems that way," John responded.

"Now I know why I wanted to kill him. It's contagious," Tera replied. They laughed again.

"He's a good guy. I love him like a brother," said Ronnie.

Billy twitched and opened his eyes. "Did I hear Ronnie say she loved me like a brother?"

Ronnie reached across with her good arm and smacked Billy's arm. "You would do anything to get the attention away from me! You weren't hurt. You were faking."

"No, I wasn't. I heal fast."

"When I get a hold of you, you'll need a lot more than healing."

"But I'm like your brother."

"And I'll kick your ass."

John and Seamus rolled their eyes at each other. "Now children, not again," interjected John.

"Is this a regular thing with them?" asked Tera.

"Oh, yes. They go at it quite regularly," replied Seamus.

The main quarters grew warm. Everyone became fatigued as the oxygen levels dropped.

"What's going on, Tera?" asked Billy.

"We're stranded and we're almost out of oxygen."

"All of you came back for me at the risk of dying out here?"

"Yes, we did," answered John.

"But, why?"

"We're family," Randy responded. "We've been through a lot together and we weren't going to leave you alone to die like that."

"Then maybe we should just lie down and rest," he suggested. "We'll see what happens later."

Everyone agreed and became quiet. They paired off and nestled with their partners.

"If I have to die, I'd rather die like this, with you in my arms," Tera whispered to Billy.

"I'm only sorry we didn't get to do more."

Tera pulled Billy's head against her shoulder and hugged him. "Your head's not bleeding anymore."

"It'll heal soon but I think I'm going to wear a helmet from now on." They chuckled once more and closed their eyes.

CHAPTER 14

GOING HOME

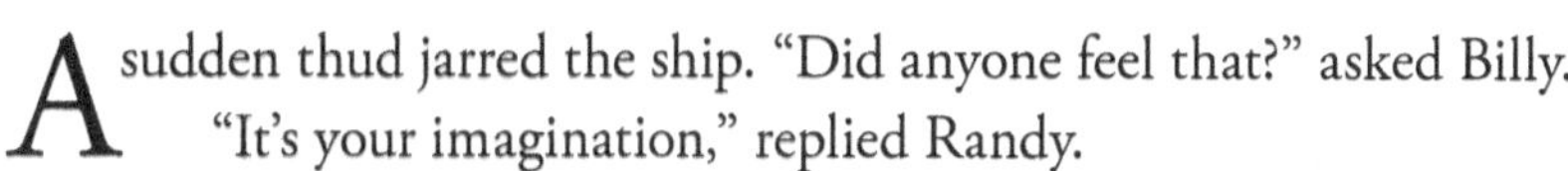

A sudden thud jarred the ship. "Did anyone feel that?" asked Billy.

"It's your imagination," replied Randy.

"No, I felt something."

Suddenly the hatch opened and Ramador entered. "I see that we made it just in time," he announced.

A fresh burst of air entered from the Andoran ship. Billy lifted his head. "Well, it's about time, Ramador."

"Better late than never." Ramador had some of his Andorans help move Billy's friends onboard his craft. "Billy, you look like hell. What happened?" he asked.

"It's a long story. I don't even know where to start."

"Why don't you and your friends pick a berth and lay down? We're taking you all the way back to Earth. It'll take a while but the Council is setting up portals for us to use."

"Gladly. I can't believe that plan went to hell so badly."

Ramador chuckled and then chastised Billy, "The plan was fine. You getting into Pendragon's ship was the error. I told you it wouldn't be recharged beyond thirty percent."

Tera punched Billy in the arm. "See that. You screwed up a perfectly good plan."

"I give up. Shoot me."

Tera wiped the blood off of Billy's head and snuggled next to him. "So, you really do heal fast?"

"Yeah. It still takes time, but my healing is a lot faster than a normal human. Maybe you'll get these traits too."

"No. Seneca told me that it can only be passed from the females to the males. It's not likely that you can pass them to anyone."

"What else did she tell you?"

"Don't worry about it. What I want to know is when you decided to change the plan back there on the battle star. You put me on the spot and bailed out."

"I know, but I had to," confessed Billy.

"Did you mean what you said before about getting married?"

"Yes, I did."

"Then I want you to promise me that you'll never pull that again. Talk to me next time."

"I promise. I've had enough of this hero stuff. Pendragon is gone. Diomedes and Ruger are gone. I think we can finally relax." Billy drifted off to sleep with Tera holding him tightly.

When they reached the research center, a large crowd awaited their arrival. Xerxes and Doc were in the forefront, anxious to greet their friends. The Andorans were the first to disembark, followed by Prax, Courtney, Randy and Seamus. Prax asked for the medical techs to board the craft and assist Ronnie.

Xerxes hugged Prax and said, "I'm proud of you, son."

"Thanks, dad."

"You've done well, too, Courtney. Where's Tera?"

"She's with Billy. They're coming."

Xerxes left them and sought out Tera. She and Billy exited the ship when he spotted them. "Tera! Billy! Congratulations on a job well done."

Tera hugged her father. "Is it over, now?"

"Yes, it is. The war with the other alien races will continue but we are out of danger now."

"What will happen next?" asked Billy.

"We'll forge an alliance with the Andorans through Ramador and find a way to turn back the Boromeans."

"What about the Council?"

"I'm recommending that we disband them. They've failed to live up to their responsibilities and their credibility will always be a blemish. I'd like to institute a new Council with members of each planet and members from Andora and Archaenia."

"That's a smart idea," replied Tera. "We can't let this happen again."

"Xerxes, I'd like to ask you for the hand of your daughter. Can I have your permission to marry her?" Billy asked.

Xerxes looked at Tera, then at Billy. "Of course. I'd be honored to have you marry my daughter."

"Tera, will you marry me?" asked Billy.

"Only if there is no more of this hero stuff."

Billy hugged her and kissed her. "I'm all heroed out," he assured her.

Xerxes hugged them both and said, "Welcome to the family. I'm so glad to say that again after all these years."

"It's an honor to be part of this family," said Billy.

"I'll get you both high positions with the Council if you like," offered Xerxes.

"No, thanks," replied Billy. "I think we'd like to go back to Boston after the wedding and start a new life."

"I understand."

"How is Penny doing?" Billy asked.

"Much better. She regained consciousness and improved quite a bit."

"I should go see her."

"I'm afraid she's not here, Billy. She insisted on leaving for the new Firenghian planet yesterday."

"Did she say anything before she left?"

"No, only that she had to leave. Sam and Ginea left with her."

Billy pondered for a moment and realized that life goes on. Everyone must do what they have to do.

"Thanks, Xerxes. We're going to retire to our compartments and get cleaned up. We'll see you at dinner."

Billy and Tera left the transport bay and entered the elevator. "I'm going to get showered and lie down for a little bit," said Billy.

"I'm sorry about Penny," replied Tera.

"Don't be. She'll be fine. Maybe she'll find happiness with the Firenghians. I sure couldn't give it to her."

"Are you sure about that?"

"Yes, I am. You're my future now, Tera."

"And you are mine."